# Hotel Africa

# Hotel Africa

## NEW SHORT FICTION
## FROM AFRICA

SHORT STORY DAY AFRICA
2019

New Internationalist

**HOTEL AFRICA: New Short Fiction from Africa**

Published in 2020 by
New Internationalist Publications Ltd
The Old Music Hall
106-108 Cowley Road
Oxford
OX4 1JE, UK
**newint.org**

First published in South Africa by Short Story Day Africa in 2019
Registered NPO 123-206
shortstorydayafrica.org

Edited by Helen Moffett, Karen Jennings, Agazit Abate, Ope Adedeji,
and Anne Moraa

Cover collage and design by Megan Ross
Illustration by Candace di Talamo

Typesetting by New Internationalist

Printed and bound in Great Britain by Clays Ltd, Elcograf S.p.A.

British Library Cataloguing-in-Publication Data.
A catalogue record for this book is available from the British Library.

Library of Congress Cataloging-in-Publication Data.
A catalog record for this book is available from the Library of Congress.

Print ISBN:   978-1-78026-505-6
Ebook ISBN: 978-1-78026-506-3

# CONTENTS

# INTRODUCTION

$\mathcal{E}$ ach year, the Short Story Day Africa Board, along with assorted enthusiastic supporters, meets to dream up a theme for the following year's anthology. We know what we don't want: poverty porn, clichés about Aids, Ebola and soldiers hopped up on hash, lush descriptions of the majesty of the (mysteriously unpeopled) African landscape and its wildlife ... we want authentic stories of Africa, from Africa, by Africans. So we try to choose a theme that is broad enough to allow authors room to breathe, to play, to experiment with different genres – but which is specific to our continent, contemporary, timely, which encourages exploration of narratives that are 'African', whatever this means to us.

We will indeed publish stories of refugees fleeing burning villages, hunger stalking the hills, plains full of migrating zebra and rivers dense with lurking crocodiles – but then they need not only to displace that slippery 'single story' into which we are often boxed, but to have that unmistakeable ring of integrity, the voice that whispers, murmurs, shouts and insists: This is our truth. This is how we live, eat, celebrate, play, work, marry and mourn.

At the same time, we want *good* stories. Brilliant stories that tickle and haunt and plague and delight us long after we've read them. We don't mind a few rough spots, as long as we get stories that testify to imaginations running riot, that present characters we recognise, that explore the chosen theme with insight, depth and heart.

So we want the impossible: a theme that attracts the everyday, the ordinary in perfect balance with the extraordinary. And each year, writers across the continent rise to the challenge. Each of our anthologies has offered, in our opinion, an exceptionally fine range of writing by talented authors interpreting the themes in surprising and entertaining ways.

But this year, the contributors who responded to the call for stories on the topic of Hotel Africa ('If these walls could talk, what stories would they tell?') outdid themselves. We asked for 'innovative short fiction set in the rooms, the passages, the bars and the lobbies of hotels across the continent' – and got much more than we could ever have hoped for.

All the judges commented not only on the exceptionally high standard of the stories, but how evenly matched they were. Choosing a winner was almost impossible, not just in the usual sense – how to choose between a crisp apple and a sensually scented orange – but in terms of the democratic voting system adopted by the judges.

It's worth reflecting briefly on the reasons why this was our closest contest to date.

We actively look for potential, raw talent, diamonds in the rough, to give writers starting out the same opportunities as more experienced authors. It's common when selecting stories for anthologies like this one to feel drawn to stories that are 'easy' to read because they've been professionally prepared and polished. We try to correct that unconscious bias. We try especially hard not to exclude stories written by authors for whom English is clearly not a mother-tongue or primary language. We don't discard strong stories that have weak or abrupt endings – because endings can and often should be rewritten.

And this leads to the major reason we think the stories are so evenly matched this year: the in-depth editing process. The editing team gave copious amounts of feedback to enable authors to rewrite and rework where necessary. Notes from the selecting readers were consulted and incorporated into this feedback. This was followed by stringent editing, often characterised by much debate.

The goal of the editing programme and the mentoring process (which encompasses editors and authors) is to develop African writers so that their brilliance can shine on a world stage, alongside writers for whom professional editing is either built into their process, or easily accessed – not often true for writers from and in Africa. Those who read the 'before' and 'after' versions of these stories all commented on how dramatically editing had levelled the playing fields. This is an excellent outcome: but it did make choosing a shortlist and the winners a far more onerous task than usual.

We broke the deadlock by pressganging an additional judge into providing three extra votes, and this is how, by a whisker, Adam El Shalakany's 'Happy City Hotel' took the winner's place, nudging Noel Cheruto's 'Mr Thompson' into second place, while Lester Walbrugh's 'The Space(s) Between Us' was established as holder of the third spot. We congratulate these authors sincerely and enthusiastically while once again noting that this competition was the tightest we've yet seen; if this had been a horse race, we would have had to call for a photo finish.

We are especially delighted to have the length and breadth of the continent represented by the top three stories. Given our commitment to featuring literature from the entire continent, which has to be juggled with practical and financial constraints that enable us to accept only stories in English, we are very pleased that the winning story – which features a small and shabby hotel in Cairo, and a cast of strangely endearing characters – is our first ever winner from Egypt (and North Africa, in fact). Noel Cheruto represents Kenya with her moving story of the dashed dreams of a hotel worker who silently confesses all to a guest. Lester Walbrugh represents South Africa with one of the most unusual and haunting versions of a 'romantic getaway' at a fancy hotel you'll ever read.

The following stories are particularly highly commended: 'Why Don't You Live in the North?' by Wamuwi Mbao, 'Slow Road to the Winburg Hotel' by Paul Morris, 'Outside Riad Dahab' by Chourouq Nasri, and 'The Snore Monitor' by Chido Muchemwa. Mbao's story is a subtle meditation on the landmarks, both inner and outer, that colonial histories leave, while Morris's is a deceptively simple account of a journey to a hotel that has a double twist at the end. 'Outside Riad Dahab', a particularly moving account of contact between outsiders and insiders, describes the interaction between a privileged hotel guest and the homeless man who camps outside the building. And 'The Snore Monitor', in which a young Zimbabwean woman has an unusual job in a South

African hotel, also explores the theme of fleeting contact between wealthy tourists and those who care for them.

In the category of stories that makes readers laugh even as they wince or wipe their eyes is 'An Abundance of Lies', by Faith Oneya, a countrymouse visits town-mouse tale in which the unglamorous side of hotel life is revealed. Likewise, Harriet Anena provides another sparkling story combining humour with horror in 'The Demons Inside My Jimmy', in which a honeymoon night with a prosperity pastor goes very wrong.

Nkiacha Atemnkeng's 'The Jollof Cook-off' makes for a spicy addition, not just because stories from Cameroon rarely make their way to us, but because stories of African food, and especially this iconic dish, aren't often considered worthy of literary consideration. Like Nkiacha's rollicking tale of competition, Fred Nnamdi's 'A Miracle in Valhalla' demonstrates an eye for humour and drama – you'll need to read the story to appreciate the pun here, but it combines a disabling injury, Norse mythology and a larger-than-life cast in a bravura showdown in an urban Nigerian hotel.

There is a fair share of quiet and tender moments as well; Jayne Bauling's elegiac 'The Last Resident', in which an elderly man is made to feel unwelcome in the hotel he considers home, has a thread of connection warming its sombre topic – the loneliness of ageing. Similarly, Bryony Rheam's 'The Fountain of Lethe' tackles the gaps between generations and the pitfalls of revisiting the past as a middle-aged woman takes her daughter and demented father to revisit the hotel of her childhood holidays.

A more chilling treatment of the dangers of nostalgia is given in 'The Tale of Two Sisters' by Tariro Ndoro, in which the search for a sibling at a luxury hotel at Victoria Falls takes a ghostly turn.

Alinafe Malonje, whose first published story this is, gives us a metaphysical account of a hotel in 'Maintenance Check': part-allegory, part-meditation, it provides subtle commentary on what it means to be a woman in Malawi.

Hotels also mean sex: in 'The Layover', Anna Degenaar gives us a sophisticated tale of a hook-up sparked by Ethiopian coffee;

Troy Onyango provides a poignant and unusual Cinderella story of a teenage boy from a traditional Kenyan family caught up in the world of dating apps in 'The Match'; and Davina Kawuma, in her inventive 'Of Birds and Bees' has young Ugandan sophisticates contemplating women's sexuality as they examine the mattress in their hotel room.

In 'Broken English', Adorah Nworah provides a fresh spin on the old tale of the Emperor's new clothes, in which the complex interknotting of language and race is explored. Much of this story is written in one of Nigeria's many colloquial renditions of English, and represents a further shift for this project in embracing the multiple Englishes spoken on the continent.

In 'Shithole' and 'Door of No Return', Michael Yee and Natasha Omokhodion-Kalulu Banda respectively create fabulous fantasy hotels that contain sinister realities. The former provides an impassioned cadenza on racial slurs, while the latter builds a persuasive alternative world – a creation we hope the author will revisit.

It is worth returning to the Editing Mentorship programme, now in its third year. We formally advertised the positions for 2019, and received 57 applications, every single one of them worthy. This meant that we took on three Fellows instead of the usual two, in a year in which the funder for this programme had to withdraw their support. I could not have managed without the help of experienced editor and author (and SSDA alumnus) Karen Jennings, who applied her calm insight and kindness both to the stories and to the editing processes of the Fellows.

It's been enormously satisfying to see this year's Editing Fellows Anne Moraa (Kenya), Ope Adedeji (Nigeria) and Agazit Abate (Ethiopia) develop their editing skills and apply them to their own professional and creative projects. I thank them all for their hard work and the enthusiasm they brought to the stories they tackled.

On the SSDA website, prompted by this year's adventures editing *Hotel Africa*, I wrote:

Editing is not for the faint-hearted. It involves erasing one's own voice to honour the voice of the story (which itself is not always quite the same thing as the author's voice). Yet it also involves the courage to stand one's ground, the diplomacy to negotiate that ground, an ability to see the broader picture, to envisage all the potential ripples spreading out – and in many African countries, this means considering not just literary merits but the political and moral implications of a piece of writing.

In an interaction that by default is hierarchical and 'critical', the editor (especially if she's a white South African, like me) constantly has to reach for the touchstone of decolonial thinking and practice. Working across the continent means holding my own (often embarrassing) ignorance of the context and history shaping an author's story in balance with the specific and specialist editing experience and information I can offer. How do we both honour this process? This can only be done by building a relationship, no matter how fleeting. I have to earn the author's trust, and if I had to boil it down to one principle, it's taking the author's words absolutely seriously. No indifferent editor is a good editor. You have to care about the story almost as much as its creator does.

This may sound serious, but editing – especially the SSDA anthologies – is also huge fun. That fleeting relationship with the author might be brief, but it's often deep and intense. It becomes playful and sincere. There is pushback, and feelings get hurt. It involves coaxing and laughter, trust and mutual respect. The magic is that these interactions are with people you have never met, and may never meet. When that mutual energy crackles across the vastness and multiplicity of the African continent, it's truly special.

We wish you, the reader, a wonderful journey to the hotels in this collection, and hope you enjoy them as much as we did. Check in, put your feet up, and relish the tales on the pages that follow.

Helen Moffett
MENTORING EDITOR

# Happy City Hotel

*Adam El Shalakany*

WINNER OF THE 2018
SHORT STORY DAY AFRICA PRIZE

*T*here lies on Mohamed Farid St, in Abdeen, a formerly upscale district of Cairo now fallen on hard times, a hotel inaptly named the Happy City Hotel. It's squeezed between two dilapidated buildings, one of which houses a butcher on the ground floor, and the other a mechanic's shop. All around the hotel, the stench of the city, its dirt and sweat and blood and semen and shit, rises up with the dry desert heat. The overstimulation in the city turns the constant blare of passing klaxons into a synthetic silence.

The streets are simultaneously dark and over-lit. Busted street lamps hang overhead, but the neon lights of shops, cafés, hotels and bars line the street with a dull, aggressive buzz. The buildings stand up next to one another, without space to breathe or escape between them. Brick building after brick building, interrupted every once in a while by history, now invisible and forgotten. Of all the lights that buzz, there is one that flickers a weak red: 'Happy City Hotel', a home to many a patron and a story.

If you enter the hotel, you must pass through a rusty, non-functioning security door, whose purpose is not to protect, but to remind you of the shallow menace of tyranny. A security guard sleeps peacefully at an old wooden desk to the side, his head resting on his fist. Through the threshold, past a fake garden filled with ceramic turtles, is a small, tight *ascenseur,* that goes up to the rooftop bar, the sole attraction of the Happy City Hotel.

Alcohol is forbidden in Egypt. Haram. And yet it's not. Bars do exist with a special licence, which are expensive to get. A bureaucrat will accept a bribe for most things. A bribe for a liquor licence? Never! Unless you make it double, like the scotch.

Hotels get a liquor licence automatically. And, unlike the rest of the world where bars are attached to hotels, hotels in Egypt are attached to bars. The Happy City Hotel is a shitty hotel, but it's got a bar, and a bar means it's got clientele. So, on the seventh floor of that shitty hotel, there is a rooftop bar, which pays for the whole damn thing. Men and women, foreign and domestic, old, young and in between, sit scattered in their own thoughts, sipping at green glass bottles of Stella beer.

A fat man in the corner of the bar looks down into his bottle of beer. His back is to the railing, behind which downtown Cairo, the City Victorious, extends into the distance. The tops of buildings zig-zag like a wave frozen in time. Beyond the buildings and far in the night is a distant ridge which looms above the rolling wave like the crest of an oncoming tsunami. The tsunami is Mokattam mountain, which Saint Simon the Tanner split, and on which sits Muhammad Ali's mosque. On that mountain once stood Napoleon, Horatio and Suleiman the Magnificent. Many men and women died there for God and glory, with sword and shield, horse and musket.

With his back to history, Hamdi only has eyes for his bottle, for escape. He is round and portly, though not joyfully so, nor does he look weak. There is muscle beneath the fat. Clean-shaven, most likely a government employee, not too tall, not too short and not bald, which is uncommon in Egypt. Aside from his hairline, he resembles most men his age. Hamdi: a common name for a common man. He looks at his drink, the reflection beaming back at him from the bottom of the bottle, a distorted, detracted image of himself. He likes to think that the portly man in the reflection is only fat because of the curvature of the glass. He knows he is wrong, but he prefers the alternative to the truth.

He was once a fit, young man. He was born around the corner, the son of a public notary and a housewife. One of five siblings, he was left to fend for himself. And so, he learned to be a boxer. Strait-laced, sharp body of muscle, square-jawed, with no imagination in style or soul. He shadowboxed in the sixties. Swooping in and out of the light, fighting the shade that loomed larger than life in front of him, and which sparked from the street outside his bedroom window. A pillow hit him in the head. His brothers trying to sleep, kept awake by the sound of imaginary fights. They told him to stop, that he would never amount to anything.

'If you don't shoot for the moon, you'll never end among the stars,' was what he told them. 'I'll box Muhammad Ali one day.'

They laughed. 'You don't know this world,' they told him.

At seventeen, one year before the Rumble in the Jungle, Hamdi broke his jaw. His coach had told him that he wasn't ready, but Hamdi pushed to get in the ring. He shot for the moon, and instead landed head first on the mat, spending a month in hospital, never to box again. Never to be thin and fit again, either.

Still, he had had one solace. The hospital had been full due to the war, so they placed him in one of the private wards. There had been a black-and-white TV in the room, a TV that his family couldn't afford. There he spent the month falling in love with cinema. He left the hospital, dreaming of scriptwriting and directing.

But time makes fools of us all. His dreams were put aside when he fell in love with a beautiful girl and married her. Marriage and children forced him to work, and thoughts of spotlights, whether in the ring or behind the camera, melted away.

Now he finds himself old, sitting on a rooftop reflecting on his reflection in a little green bottle. Waiting to be young and free once more. Waiting for a woman, who is not his wife, whom he has met online. She will wear a rose.

Marie, John and Shady sit at the table next to Hamdi's. Shady has his back to the railing. Marie, if she were to look past him, would see the Cairo Central Bank down the road, but Marie only has eyes for Shady. They are all in their twenties, poor in pocket but not in ambition. They sit hunchbacked and nurse their beers, aiming to make them last as long as possible. Shady is a handsome young Christian man who works as a clerk in a law office. Christians in Egypt are hard pressed, and tend to intermarry to preserve the faith. Marie, being a good Christian, wants Shady as a husband. She is also deeply attracted to him; she would want him even if he were Buddhist. She loses herself in his eyes, in the cologne he wears, mixed with the smell of tobacco bitters, deep and musky.

John is less handsome than Shady, and has eyes for Marie. He doesn't see past her to the plaster cast of Horus placed on the cheap and tacky walls of the Lotus bar. He has a hookah pipe in his hand, but barely smokes. He hates smoking, but if he didn't smoke and he didn't drink, they – Marie the angel and Shady the devil – wouldn't invite him out. John has learned a difficult lesson in life, that good company gets harder to find the older you get, and beggars can't be choosers.

John is an English teacher at a public school. He speaks horrible English, and if he is being honest, knows very little about the language. He became a teacher by accident, not by design. He had done well at training college and went where the State placed him. Then his uncle, who happened to be the nazir of the public school John would end up working at, told him that there was a vacancy for an English teacher, and that John should apply.

'But make sure that you prepare!' his uncle had warned him.

John did. He trusted his uncle's vision blindly. After all, didn't 'nazir' mean both school principal and visionary? John tried to decipher the strange language by reading poetry, and fell upon a snippet that reminded him of Marie, although he understood next to nothing of it. He decided to memorise it:

Had I the heavens' embroidered cloths,
Enwrought with golden and silver light,
The blue and the dim and the dark cloths
Of night and light and the half-light,
I would spread the cloths under your feet:
But I, being poor, have only my dreams;
I have spread my dreams under your feet;
Tread softly because you tread on my dreams.

And when he recited it, poorly, to the interviewer at the Ministry of Education, he was given the job even though, at the time, he had been thinking of Marie. He took this as a sign that his love for her was blessed.

This leaves Shady, whose back is to the world and who only has eyes for John. He will end up marrying Marie, and Marie will spend her days in friendship with John, and her cold nights lonely, in bed with Shady. An almost happy ending where everybody gets what they want, but in the saddest way, like an ifrit's curse. John will finally recite the poem to Marie on his deathbed, long after forgetting about the cool-breeze nights on top of the Happy City Hotel.

'Maître! Beer!' calls a man from another table, and the maître d', Khaled, stands at attention. Because he's the bartender, he can wear whatever he wants. If cleanliness is close to godliness, then he is in hell. But hell pays, and the pious are poor. A man of thirty-plus, Khaled is still unmarried. He has fucked before, so he isn't a virgin, like half the people in the bar. In fact, he had a quickie once in one of the rooms below, in the bowels of the empty hotel. A john had brought a hooker and rented a room for the night, but he had left early. She had come up to get a drink, and had started chatting with Khaled.

'Maître! Beer!' the barfly calls again. But Khaled can't hear him. His mind is flying back to that night four years ago when he was twenty-eight, ignorant of the world. The barfly, who hasn't flown back into the past with Khaled, is still ignorant of the world. One of the holiest shrines in all of Shia-dom, thrumming with spiritual power, lies directly behind him, but he is focusing only on his parched throat. This is a shame, because if the barfly chose instead to descend from the bar of sin, walk through the crowded Cairo night, wind through the ever-tightening alleys until reaching El Hussein, and then prostrate himself before the head of the Prophet's grandson, he would find a ten-pound note dropped on the ground.

'A beer please,' the woman had asked Khaled politely. She was veiled, with a colourful hijab wrapped around a round face. Almond-coloured and shaped eyes looked back at Khaled as she arched forward, not at all demurely. Khaled had fallen for her at that moment, but he hadn't known it yet.

'You've got hair showing,' he said, pulling out a beer for the woman who he later learned was named Mariam. A small black curl wound its way down her face. Instead of placing the hair back beneath her veil, she twirled it.

'So, you're a whore?' He had been raised to hate sex and women, and asked the question honestly, if a little maliciously. The smoke of roasting coals used to grill kebabs had stuck to his shirt. A greasy, heavy scent.

'You're a barkeep?' she asked in return. They both worked in sin, and what of it? The greasy, heavy smell had become a greasy, heavy feeling as he talked to her in between bouts of serving the clientele.

Finally, he didn't know how, they had found themselves in a room two levels down, fucking. He was a virgin, but later that night he was an experienced man. He fucked with his back to the wall. Behind it, and a few buildings down, was the Jewish Temple, one of the last remaining operating temples in Egypt. It had been deserted after the wars, including the war of '67 in which Shady's uncle had died like a dog in the desert. Shady's uncle had also been gay, but he hadn't lived long enough for it to cause him or his family much bother.

When Khaled had finished, he began to cry. He had fallen in love with a whore. Mariam stared back at him with innocent eyes. He slapped and beat her, and she ran out of the room and out of the Happy City Hotel forever.

'Maître! Beer!'

With a heavy heart, Khaled walks over and slams a beer on the table. Fucking sinners. The greasy, fatty scent of roasting kebabs still wafts in the air, but now the smell makes him feel sick.

But not Lamia. She is a student and made of fire. A communist at Cairo University. She has been told not to drink, not to laugh, not to smoke, not to fuck, not to swear, and not to dress the way she does. That is why she does all these things. The guys love Lamia and take her to the top of Happy City Hotel. The guys don't have to pretend around her. They are all in engineering school and they can drink and swear and joke in front of her. She is fun to be around, even if she is crazy. She has short hair, cropped in pain.

She hasn't always been made of fire, but she has always been different. When her girlfriends wrap their heads in fabric, Lamia leaves hers uncovered. When others follow obediently and pray, Lamia does not. Still, she always thinks of herself as a good girl, even if she knows others don't see her the same way. She has always been a string singing without a harmony. Alone in a dark universe where the blind follow the blind.

When she'd first gone to university, there'd been one professor who was young and rash and beautiful. He would stand in front of their class and insult the State and God. People hated him, but Lamia was ensorcelled. His glasses, his chalk-stained hands, even his linen Nehru shirt. His name was Abdelwahab, like the singer. But this Abdelwahab's voice was a far cry from the deep, sonorous sound of his namesake. His voice was nasal and whiny. But Lamia didn't care. She was in love, and she told him so, and he swallowed her up.

They went out for coffee and read treatises and kissed and fumbled beneath one another's shirts. All in secret, until one day Lamia wanted to break the taboo and fornicate. She didn't call it that, but that's what he heard, and it scared him. To the bone. He told her that he couldn't take her hymen. Inside him, instead of fire, was ice – freezing terror. But that night Lamia, terribly practical, took a cucumber to her hymen, removing the professor's obstacle. She rushed to him the next day and told him what she had done. He never spoke to her again.

Lamia, in her fury, shame and guilt, chopped off her hair. Now she hangs out at the top of the Happy City Hotel, her fire lighting up the night.

Stepping out of the white taxi with a meter that doesn't work, is Hamdi's wife. She pays the driver a few guineas over the normal price; she feels like splurging. She is dressed in her Friday finest. A not-too revealing dress, loose and black to hide her growing curves. She walks into the Happy City Hotel, through the broken door and past the sleeping security guard. If the guard had been awake, he would have seen that the black of her dress was seductively broken by a bright red rose.

# Door of No Return

*Natasha Omokhodion-Kalulu Banda*

*S*he hums. The vibrations of her voice reverberate against the walls, giving way to a new sun. The penumbra on the wall reveals familiar furniture pieces as blue light slowly fills the room. Her spirit joins the soul of that in the deep of her being – causing them to float as one – uncertain of their futures after this day.

A thinly skin-gloved hand impresses from inside, against the inner walls of her velvet black belly. Stripes run over the dark mound, each telling a story of whom they belong to. She feels the baby move around violently, causing her to mirror its minute hand with her own.

'Go to sleep, 19!' she says.

'I can't,' it replies.

'You will get us into trouble! You need to be ready and well rested for today.'

'But I don't want to go.'

'I am afraid that you must. It is the order of life.'

'Tell me the story again?'

'Which one?'

'Please, tell me the story, M.'

She looks up at the sterile ceiling. Its chrome coldness returns the stare. Her eyes shut tight, and she groans. Her belly contracts into a tight ball. She breathes in quick, short breaths, until it relaxes again. She does what her first doula said to do. To defeat the pain, she begins to narrate the tale. She speaks the way that she has spoken to all of them who were here before 19. Through her spirit.

'*I*t all started many years ago – when whispers from the West begun. Murmurs of scandal spread like bush fire across the land – tales of Enugu babies being made and sold in factories. The world had changed so much during the information age, that convenience and immediate gratification fed into a live, voluptuary demon that only consumed and destroyed. At the swipe of a screen, people would buy and sell children. Poorer women, with only their fertility to sell, had begun to emigrate.

Up north, my people made long, arduous journeys across forests, mountains and vast thirstlands in order to escape to Europe. Beasts and harsh weather would devour them if hunger did not beat them to it. After the extreme difficulty of the journey across land, they would bob on the big blue sea – twenty people in one tiny, inflatable boat. Vomiting on each other, defecating in full view of the heavens. Fighting and fearful, they had no captain to lead them. Many would be lost to watery, salt-filled graves.

Desperate-eyed people on television screens cried out warnings. Matter-of-fact voices on the radio reported these things, but no one did anything. People were being traded as slaves off the-then Libyan coast, centuries after abolition of the slave trade. In the South, the continent suffered. Doctors, engineers and teachers left for greener pastures until no one remained to tend to home. Our population grew fiercely, but our industries suffered. Our water systems became murky with synthetic waste that would never, ever dissolve. Our governments were corrupt. Some borrowed until they could pay back no longer. All of this continued to plague us until dark clouds began to visit our continent...'

'And then what?'

'But you have heard this story already, 19.'

'Yes, but you never finish it, M.'

'The Chinese had already established strong links in Africa, building us railways, skyscrapers, schools and hospitals. They learned our languages and became like brothers to us. So it was only a matter of time before they came forward and proposed a way to solve our migration and debt problems.'

'What did they promise us, M?'

'They offered to create a massive joint fertility programme on condition we formed a united Pan-African state, what was to become The United Nation of Mbiguli.'

'Mbiguli?'

'Yes. Together, we created a breed of super-soldiers, the Akahn – made through careful genetic selection. Mbiguli's new economic growth and allegiance to China changed the world order. The leaders in the West did not like this. For the first time in modern history, Africans were leading the world. Global trade was affected. Our doctors and teachers returned, and we became increasingly self-sufficient. Having lost access to the resources coming out of Mbiguli, the West decided to declare war on us. However, it did not last long, because…'

'Because of what, M?'

'We…'

'We what, M?'

'In the middle of their coldest night, and during our hottest day, we dropped silent, invisible bombs across their continents. Something vile and irrevocable.'

'Did they die?'

'Not really, 19…'

'Then what happened M?'

'I don't know, 19.'

*C*hristopher looks at his wife, Kate. Her red hair is pasted across her porcelain forehead, her cheeks flushed in the low savannah sun. Pearls of sweat develop along her perfect nose. Tall, golden grass yields to the wind, bending to the left, and then the right, as though in trance. Acacias and jacarandas, burly, thorny but certain, provide camouflage to the few antelope he can see.

She wrings her hands, her knuckles pale. He cups her hands in his own. The canvas flap of the Land Rover's canopy slaps against the sides of the open-air van. The idea of a diesel-run vehicle sounded nostalgic in the glossy accounts given by his virtual agent, but not so much in real life.

A group of super-sized zebra appears from behind the trees, galloping parallel to their car, shaking the earth, dust rising from their hooves. Christopher places a protective arm around his wife's shoulders. The smartly dressed Mbiguli driver smiles with pride as he explains that they are all safe. No animal can come close to them, thanks to the InvisiWall™ infrastructure – 'it is impossible,' he says, emphasising the 'p' with an accent revealing descent from a formerly Portuguese-speaking country.

His voice carries above the wind as he narrates the history of this part of Mbiguli. 'Formerly divided into Zambia, Tanzania and Congo DRC, this strait sits on what was then named Lake Tanganyika. It is the tourism capital of this region. Zambia had a resort on Kasaba Bay, which was built for its president in the 1980s. With beaches so pure, the new nation of Mbiguli decided to extend this wonderful feature by creating a strait that stretches from the Indian Ocean, off the shores of Tanzania.'

They drive on, leaving behind the savannah. Closely cut lawns are the precursor to the verdant, tropical entrance. Luscious sprays of dense green fronds atop striking succulents form impressive leafy fountains. The couple arches their necks backward to see how high these rise, half expecting a Goliath to come through parted palms. Twittering birds fly between trees, aware of the new arrivals. The vehicle passes through the mouth of an open gate made of Mukwa wood, and onto a white-pebbled bridge suspended in mid-air, hung with fuchsia and orange bougainvillea. Tall, wide-chested guardians, the Akahn, flank each side of the bridge, their jet-black hair tied back in flowing pony-tails. They look down, following the moving vehicle with their eyes. Small goose-bumps rise along Christopher's forearm while Kate's damp hand entwines in his.

The bridge runs for hundreds of metres, with white-capped sea lapping beneath. Enormous peacocks with fan-spread wings welcome them at the end of the floral tunnel. Christopher takes a sip of his bottled water, struggling to swallow. He notices Kate's narrow shoulders are still tense.

The hotel is opulent, with lofty chalets suspended against the blue sky. Giant baobab trees boast restaurants at different levels, with lift tubes going up and down their centres, as well as left and right along their branches like a central nervous system.

Inside the main hall on the ground floor, they are greeted by cold, soundless blasts of air and the playful notes of millennial African jazz. Holographic hosts dressed in cobalt togas welcome them, giving knee-deep bows reminiscent of hospitality only found in historical films. Amarula is served on ice, along with an array of eats: roasted pumpkin seeds, chikanda, plantain, smoked impala ribs, watermelon and mango slices. Nitro-cooled cloths are provided by wheeling oval robots. Christopher and Kate enjoy the sensation of the flannels on the back of their necks. Symmetrically lined flower arrangements burst with colour, making the couple breathe in deeply. They smell nothing.

Once they are refreshed, porters arrive to assist them with their luggage.

They mount up to their room through the baobab tubes. The ride is deliberately slow, allowing them to take in the beauty of the strait. The sapphire water below makes the rays from the sun dance, striking against the pure white of the beach. They arrive at the Makumbi floor, and their tunnel takes them left towards their room. Transparent corridors at cloud level startle the couple, but they are reassured by the neon indigo arrows along the floor.

As they approach their room, chambermaids scurry out of sight. Christopher takes out his binoculars, still amazed to think that this was once a land-locked country. Through his lenses, the magnificent islands dotting the bay shift closer. Exotic fauna and flora abound on each, designed to create a unique ecosystem – providing a range for the guests.

A genetically modified giraffe greets them at their balcony. Her right eye peers curiously at the couple, filling most of the window. She chews greenery in large circular motions, breathing heavily in their direction. His wife moves towards the animal as if magnetised, and smiles. For a moment, Christopher feels he finally has her approval.

A virtual fence lights up – giving warning – her cue to step away. A fish eagle sounds three times, and they turn to face the smooth-edged hologram who appears in the middle of their room.

'Mr and Mrs Hanover. Welcome to the *grrreat* land of Mbiguli!' He draws his arms wide apart to display its size. He bows deeply.

'Thank you,' Christopher replies.

'Welcome to the Strait,' he continues in a deep baritone, 'founded in 2030 by the Council of Ministers for Tourism. You have been placed on the most prestigious floor – the Makumbi, named after the magnificent clouds in which it sits. We take you as close to heaven as we believe we can.' He winks, laughing his own joke. Kate remains silent.

'Thank you, sir,' Christopher says on behalf of his wife.

'Call me Mr Bwalya.'

'Thank you ... erhm ... Mr Bwalya. How long do you think it will be until…?'

'Ah, not to worry, Sir. According to our obstetric AI reader, your host is showing all the optimum signs for delivery within the next 24 hours.'

'Will she … rem…?'

'No, Mr Hanover. Our hosts have no internal conflicts or feelings of doubt – or separation. We take careful steps to ensure that they have no memories of the pregnancy either. A series of electromagnetic waves takes care of this as soon as the child is released. In fact, your particular host is one of our best.'

*O*n the other side of the estate, in a white Cape Dutch bungalow, a Soul is making its entrance into this world. Malaika's chest is heaving. The Soul Catcher, a mouthless doctor in red-and-black scrubs, stands at the end of her bed. He places his fingers between her thighs, prompting her to push. Her fists clench. Sharp explosions escape her mouth. Her teeth gnash against each other.

She feels the familiar ring of fire at the base of her anatomy. She is crowning, the top of the baby's head pushing out. She gives one final animal grunt, and it slips out, in a bumpy rush. The silky, warm gush flows. A routine she knows so well. Another push, and with it the last lump of flesh and vessels that connected the baby to her for nine months is expelled. It is done. Her last Soul is released.

Its demeanor is angelic, but its cry torturous. Malaika turns her head and closes her eyes. Exhausted, she tries to ignore the wails of the child. She wonders what it would feel like to have its wet skin against her chest. To feel its heart beating against hers. To smell its white-capped head. Her breasts react to its cry, beginning to swell.

The Soul Catcher checks the child's limbs, fingers and genitals. Sex is the only factor still predetermined by the Souls themselves. Malaika looks for satisfaction in the Soul Catcher's eyes, but they blink back at her. Handed over to the matron, 19 is taken away, as always, through the door of no return. She knows she will never again see the whiteness of the baby's skin against the sharpness of its carrot head.

Emotions drop her into a vortex of memories. Her mind flashes to a day in the market, laughing with her sister, playing hand songs in the red dust of Serenje. She braces for the zap as the Soul Catcher and the matron step out of the small delivery room. Ultraviolet light pulses through her in two flashes, and she blacks out. For the nineteenth time.

*M*alaika comes to life. She is back in her room. Clean, dressed, and even oiled. She prepares not to remember. But for some reason, she does.

Hand-clapping in the market with Elida. A mix of smoke from malasha coals and dried fish on the boil. Melting mirages from snapping tin roofs. The scene looks as though it has a blue smokescreen, like the Instant photo filters on Papa's iPhone.

Papa. Towering, broad-shouldered, the colour of midnight. The smell of the sea always trailing behind him. Fabrics and spices falling out of his plastic bag. Foreign intonations coating his broken, Francophone English. His tales of a land far away, of doors of no return, unfolded every evening after his time on his hand-woven prayer mat. His cracked soles looking towards the sky, his face fervently downward. The reason she was different.

She remembers.

The cacophonic sounds of kalindula and hip-hop music blare from multi-coloured stalls. Women on carved wooden stools braiding thick heads of hair. Their faithful customers on reed mats, with ashy-elbowed babies eating guavas. Battered pans of swirling oil ready to transform the contents of green and white plastic dishes. Fat Hungarian sausages on display, indentations along their casing, covered with black flies, as hungry as humans.

She remembers.

A bicycle with a large television cabinet strapped on with rubber ropes swerves by. A woman on a motorbike dressed extravagantly in traditional clothing for a wedding zooms in the opposite direction. The lady's skin is ashen from talcum powder, and her eyebrows are drawn like upside-down Nike ticks. Her wig sits unnaturally at the centre of her forehead. Malaika remembers – she is laughing with Edina at the spectacle. Papa is on his way to them. He is extraordinarily tall in his white agbada.

Like the locusts in Mama's Bible, a shadow in the sky comes rolling towards them. A mild wind announces its arrival. Everyone freezes, like characters in a picture book. The dark clouds dissipate into tiny drones. The insect machines come to them. One to her, another to Edina. They hover low and steady. A red scan follows. Up and down her body it goes – pausing at her womb. There, it lights up in green. Calculations with foreign characters are done in mid-air. Her face is captured – and so is she.

*A* string of voices emanates from her womb. Questioning, crying, laughing, she can hear them all – the Souls she has released. Questions from past tenants who once claimed abode in her being, for whom she has already collected her fare.

She sits up and brings her feet to the cold floor. Hands on her head, she attempts to block out the voices, but they constellate in her torso, and a brilliant light radiates from her core. She is no longer aware of her environment, because she is one with the force within her.

She moves to the door, and they command it to open. Door after door unlocks in sequence as she strides down the corridor. Dozens of women emerge from their rooms, all in trance. Their uniform of chitenge maternity dresses and white socks make them look like prison inmates. Voices from their bellies join those from Malaika's. At the vault, the Akahn shout at one other – panic in their shrill voices because they have not been trained to take action on the assets. The women, possessed, keep pressing forward.

Malaika bursts into the vault and finds the control board. Mr Bwalya's face, programmed for warm hospitality, appears, giving her a smiling warning. She finds a dial that distorts his pleading image – large, small, stretched – until he spirals downwards like water into a drain and finally to nothingness. She manipulates the control station as though she has known it all her life.

Red lights and siren alarms screech throughout the hotel. The earth shakes, and thunderous sounds follow. In disbelief, the disoriented Akahn glower at the game monitors, which flash colossal animals charging toward secured sites – crushing moving tourist vans and sightseers. Their attention is gripped by the sound of trumpets.

*A* monkey's wedding, rain and sun at the same time, takes place on the estate each time a child is born. The warm orange horizon lets in rays of hope. Christopher looks at Kate, his wife. A birth, the elixir of life. He strokes her red hair.

19 is brought to the room. So perfect. So pale.

Christopher, trembling, receives the baby. His baby. A warm glow fills his body and lights his face. Kate stands across from him, her bare feet planted on the marble floor. Her arms fold into an envelope close to her chest. The fish eagle call turns their attention to the centre of their room.

A hologram appears once more. To their surprise, the image of a tall, astonishingly black woman fills the room. Her energy is so strong, Christopher's child writhes in his arms. His instinct tells him to call for security, but his conscience says not to. The baby begins to scream, its face morphing from chalk paste to scarlet.

The figure hovers, unstable and flickering with static. More silhouettes appear behind her. All shapes and sizes of women, round bellies, dressed in patterned cloth. They stare at the baby in his arms. Malaika lifts her eyes from the squirming bundle, and fixes them on Christopher.

'19, my child. Be quiet.'

# Why Don't You Live in the North?

*Wamuwi Mbao*

*Y*ou took over your route from a man who was half-blind in one eye and had the IQ of a pine table. He had somehow made his name punting Van Wyk & Smith's farming co-operatives in every village from here to the border. Few knew that Van Wyk & Smith were one person, an incongruously named giant of a man who had once been the Vice-Consul in Ghana. Then that country's independence had come, and thirty-four-year-old Van Wyk Smith had quietly resigned his post, amid rumours of an affair with a Gurunsi woman. His desertion was not received well by the Home Country, and Van Wyk Smith had ended up a stateless person. His unwillingness to return home, and his government's unwillingness to have him back, conspired to pitch him into the unknown. He had subsisted for a while, until a benevolent offer had materialised from Harlow Bartesque, the Bechuanaland High Commissioner. Bartesque had suggested that Van Wyk Smith might work with the Bamangwato Tribal Administration. And so Van Wyk Smith had established a co-op in Swaneng, for which the people and the government were grateful, even if they found him difficult to get along with.

Your own encounter with him had been intimidating. Smith was fifty- five, with much success trailing behind him. You were a young graduate unanchored by your education, and feeling that your presence was part of some sort of upheaval. The man clasped your shoulder with his bear-hand and spoke to you bullishly, as though he would soon tire of the politeness, seize you by the ankle and shake you upside-down until your knowledge clattered out.

You had kept your appointment punctually, and when Van Wyk Smith had appeared, he had seemed to belong so completely to this area that he was no more an interloper than the goats that roamed the grounds, worrying the hedges some impertinent early gardener had tried to impose. Van Wyk Smith's shirt was worn shiny, not through cheapness, but because its owner was preoccupied with other things. He lived in a rondavel whose round walls seemed to reverberate his energies. You felt that it was you, and not him, who was the oddity in that place.

He had looked at you serenely as he declared that he wasn't sure if you were suited for this position. 'A bit too young,' he said. You were affronted. 'I can talk,' you said. 'I know every corner of Botswana, and people will be more willing to listen to a black man,' you said. He scrutinised you like a farmer inspecting an unstable fence-post. It was not, he affirmed, that he didn't think you could do it (because he did), but that he thought you might do better in the local community education programme, where the people were friendlier.

You had come back to Botswana like you were breaking into a prison. You blamed yourself daily for giving in to a burst of homesickness, for being unable to stand the cold. Yester-you had left Botswana with the exuberance of any adventurer, glad to be away from 'come tomorrow', glad to be away from the eyes that looked right through you and the ritual of applying and being rejected, and the procession of meetings with worn-out relatives who wanted you to be compliant and dutifully attendant to their perpetual sorrows. Yester-you'd wanted some elsewhere to escape to, and because you were fortunate enough to have stood out among your peers at school, there had been a scholarship, dangled before you like a rope to assist you in climbing out of your pit.

The world had played a dire trick on you, by asking you to surrender to the seductions of travel, by asking you to think of yourself as capable of doing whatever you wanted. Mabele a Bodile Secondary School had doused you in the sour knowledge of your meaning to the country: to improve the collective, to work towards something greater than yourself. These were ideas that soaked your mind while you slept, so that you woke resentful and embittered at having been cast in a play you hadn't read. But the frail old white lady your mother worked for had bequeathed you a sum of money, and her son in the Foreign Office had secured you a passport to smooth the passage. And so, you had travelled overseas – people back home soon spoke about you with the wonder that migrating holds for the stationary.

All this came flooding back to you while Van Wyk Smith

squinted at you and declared that your independence would be equally matched to the territories of Bophuthatswana and Botswana, with an option to extend your area to Zambia after your probation had passed. You agreed, because you were good at doing what you were told, and because unemployment was no alternative, and you left the office clutching a map and a folder and your fists. And now, in the summer of 1977, you were beating a criss-cross path into the Botswana landscape.

You had been equipped with a red Peugeot 404 station wagon, which had languished for a year or two before being transferred to your care with strict instructions about wear and tear, to which you nodded while your mind wondered about all the places this car had been. It smelled of vinyl and of earth ground into the red carpets and never satisfactorily removed. The idea of seeing your country had excited you initially, but as distant names had gained more meaning, the travel had taken on a deadening sameness. You liked the roads best when there was little traffic, on early Saturday mornings and late afternoons. You liked to look not at the limitless bleached sky, but at the vegetation, the gold dry grass that waved on the hot winds, especially between the smaller disregarded villages that dotted the route to the North.

Your journey would usually begin the day before, and you'd drive from Gaborone through to your first client in Shoshong, or to the old farms with their equipment and their old white farmers and their Fords all transplanted from the 1930s, unsure of what to do with the new times in which they found themselves. Your job was to fulfil the strange fantasy Van Wyk Smith insisted on holding onto, a sentimental dream in which the old and new Botswanas were stitched together, and you felt yourself being possessed of the same sentimentality. There was a wilful pleasure in submitting yourself to so massive a task in a still more massive country. Not knowing what it all meant was a consolation.

The strangeness of moving between these constellations of people was less jarring here than it had been during your time in England. You called it 'your time in England' with the seasoned nonchalance of someone putting a bad relationship behind them. The move had filled your world with new and unexpected meanings. That snow could be, not an abstract concept, but a squelching concern, was the first thing. That you could be somewhere so much older than you made it difficult to hold onto any sense of time. Buildings from different eras, some no longer in use, in various states of decay, with tiles that threatened to make your footfall uncertain.

You had arrived in England during an icy winter, clutching your expectations and an old coat: native police issue, heavy and khaki and reminiscent of home. There were accents and smells and train routes that had to be fitted into your mind. You knew the name of the town, and a skeleton of names and places that chimed with the names and places you'd memorised from a dusty library book, until seeing the signs in the real world mechanically called up the page from your mind, and each recollection was accompanied by a list of what the place was known for. The names helped to downplay the horror of being from somewhere else. To create metaphors from these names, however, meant hollowing out your own categories. To think of 'house' as something new was easy. Your walks provided many examples that matched the houses you had known back home. Certainly, your own dwelling here had the same rude closeness of the houses there. But there were other things that required more translation. 'Street' for example, didn't fit quite as well, even though your uneasiness towards those you encountered on it was similar.

The elements joined into ragged and unsteady compounds of meaning, and you learned to configure these meanings by walking. Every journey out was a search for new footholds, day by day forming an alchemy of routes. You kept to yourself, and you learned the different ways the public roads could be combined to get you where you needed to be. One way was cobbled, undulating, with several left turns and a drop beneath an overpass, where men whose fathers had come over from small West Indian islands twenty years before smoked and eyed you with suspicion.

The first afternoon had brought greasy and grey skies, and you'd had to ask the way to the college. A simple enquiry. You never forgot how the person looked at you, a mixture of pity and contempt. You and your question were absurd. You were told to go straight on, past a likely-looking junction, and turn left at some point in the distance, whereupon the road would eventually bring you to where you needed to be.

The directions had been untruthful. You wandered aimlessly down a cobbled street that gradually and deviously gave way to a damp pathway. You walked on because it seemed too soon to assume that you'd been sent on a fool's errand. The wind ravened and you strode, bound by a river to your right, with a short steep bank, punctuated by a wind-break of pines. Through a clearing in these trees, you had glimpsed a solemn collection of rooftops that had turned mossy and green in places, giving the impression of being vacant. But you resolved to head for these rooftops, if you could find passage to the other side.

The way became threadbare, the riverbed grew wider, and the sense of loneliness grew overwhelming. Presently, a bridge suggested an opportunity for crossing. It gave the impression of being unused. You felt like a pioneer. You slithered over thawing clay, and the ooze beneath your feet was also a reminder of home.

The sky was rumbling, and you hastened across the bridge, cudgelled about the ears and neck by an ominous wind. There you were greeted by a truth whose clues you had obviously missed: you were wandering on the far boundary of an archery range. Nearby, beyond the single line of the forest, were people, and buildings, red brick and green copper pipes. Divested of your isolation in that setting, you felt for the first time your separateness from this place.

On the April morning the day after Enoch Powell had made his 'Rivers of Blood' speech, you broke your nose. Or rather, someone broke your nose. You were still taking to England as one walks into a cold sea, hesitantly, with experimental steps. You were strolling past the Mangrove restaurant on All Saints Road.

There was nothing fateful about the day, nor was there anything particularly portentous about the woman with the beehive hairdo whose path crossed yours.

Englishness was not something you had to declare. In fact, declaring any other home seemed enough to place you under immediate suspicion. You had tackled the language well enough at home to pass muster here, and you translated your adverbs and diminutives and foods into their English equivalents, packing away the dusty phrases you learned at school. You were heading down to a sale at a record shop when your favourite scarf fell from your hand and you flung yourself after it, and in doing so, you stumbled over a pile of blankets. The woman walking behind you tripped over you and crashed to the ground in a flurry of insults and flashing teeth.

She rose to her feet and you were surprised at the ease with which the words sprang from her throat. 'Wog!' 'Black bastard!' It took several moments before you realised that she was speaking to you. There was a tautness in her jaw and a set to her knees and her feet with their shoes that had been carefully chosen with no thought for their owner meeting you abruptly, as though interruptions were always for others. You had a memory of a book from your youth, of a woman using some wheel machine to turn hay into gold; you had asked what hay was, and the teacher had smiled indulgently and explained, and you had not understood why you would feed your cows dead grass if you cared for them. And then you had looked at this stranger who had tossed her words at you with rancour rather than indulgence: you'd had time to wonder about her and the teacher and Van Wyk Smith and all the things they presupposed about you.

While you were thinking through the strangeness of it all, the blankets had resolved themselves into a pair of legs, two arms and a head, shambolically clothed, but the same brown colour as your legs, arms and head. A black man whose journey through England had a very different set of meanings than those attached to yours. Those meanings were advertised in the odd sprawling of his body upon the cold pavement. A man from whose eyes there came not the familiarity that your shared project in this country might inspire, but the glazed blankness of intoxication.

It was at this point that a heavy shove interrupted your wonderings, one that had sent you sprawling to a meeting with different meanings, core meanings. Blood. Shame. You, who had never been a good tumbler at school, had fallen to earth and bashed your nose against a drain cover. Hard enough, it turned out, to break it.

You were cruising along faster than you should have been, pushing the Peugeot to make the weekend fuel curfew. The stop in Gaborone the night before had not allowed you the luxury of sleep, and as you sped along the road, you were thankful that you'd arrived just after the bi-monthly ritual in which a felled tree was dragged with superhuman patience along the main road as far as Francistown. A sudden shower meant a very different kind of rain, here. The French car might have been Designed For Africa by the men at Peugeot, but they had evidently left off the wipers, so you were having a hard time seeing where you were going. Then the wheel shuddered in your hand, and something unexpected was happening to you and the Peugeot on this dirt road. A puncture, or worse, the answer confirmed as a black projectile shot past and you saw the tyre and the wheel bouncing off into the bushes as you slewed to a dramatic stop, using the furrowed verge to arrest the car's motion. You got out and surveyed the damage, which, for all of the drama, seemed minor. The fender needed straightening, and one headlight swung from its mountings like the spotlight in a prison yard. The rest of the car seemed fine. You were, however, in the middle of one of those staggeringly quiet parts of the country that hung suspended between the villages that defined the road up to the North.

There was a hotel, or what remained of a hotel, a hundred metres from where you had come to rest. A simple building, with a constellation of things that may have once been offices, or guard buildings, their walls seemingly growing out of the bare earth, with only a sign here or there of roofs nestling in the grass that grew tall and spiky and yellow and through the doors, as if it paid no heed to the idea that people had once made use of these buildings.

The main building itself was a skull of white looking out on grounds of cracked paving and stubborn Thlaresetala. Its eye-socket porticos were ringed with bird-dirt and its forehead bore fading letters that had been rounded by dirt, although there remained, embossed in the plaster, a year. 1932. How recent, you thought, and how strange that it should have been so completely abandoned and forgotten, with nobody even caring to lock the gate. There was the suggestion of a fountain, but a fountain wouldn't work in Botswana, so it must have been a statue of some sort. There were birds, and something that might have been a flagpole.

No doubt it had been allowed a stay of execution because to tear it down would have seemed too crude a metaphor for the migration of power from the old to the new. The oddity of this slowly ruining building among the newness of an independent Botswana brought home to you your own out-of-placeness. Every return to the familiar things you had left when you went overseas was like experiencing the thing anew. It was as though you were upheaving yourself from England once more and resituating yourself in the world you had left behind, returning to a past that was not yours.

But here, at the entrance whose doors sagged on their hinges, there was a pair of shoes, the tongues lolling in the dust. They looked as though they had been discarded recently, by someone for whom the act had been liberating. One bare footprint was faintly visible on the darkening threshold, and you stood staring at the spot for a long time, until the sound of a door closing somewhere in that emptied shell of a building, crisp and purposeful, frightened you out of your natural ease.

Someone's in there, you thought, realising that you might have more options than the one you were choosing. Yet you strode forward, erasing the footprint beneath your own, until you were standing in the cool dark of that place. As your eyes adjusted, your fear of rats and your curiosity coalesced. You stepped forward gingerly, seeing things slowly as they emerged from the darkness, until it began to occur to you that you might not want to startle whoever had shut the door. The person's presence in there was a conscious act, and you were trespassing on this accidental space.

You walked, placing your feet very deliberately, down a corridor where thankfully a skylight admitted the outer world. The doors seemed firmly shut on either side as you walked towards where you thought the noise had come from, daring the doors to open and hoping they wouldn't. Music. A faint tinkle of laughter punched a hole in the dark, and as you pushed open the door, a cluster of young people, none of whom seemed to be older than twenty, solved the mystery. The room was warm. There was a fire, and candles that illuminated the shapes. It was, or had been, a ballroom, with a bar at one end, behind which stood a young woman. Her eyes were kohl-rimmed, her hair a wilderness above her head, and she was all the more beautiful for being in that unlovely place. She was barefoot and wearing denim overalls, and her afro and her demeanour in that room created a sense of height that dispelled the fact that she was not tall. She beckoned you over, as though your being there was an expected part of the day's happenings, and handed you an Ohlsson's that was surprisingly cold.

So you smoked some hash and struck up a conversation, and she told you her family had come up here from a farm called Moedersrekening. You thought at once of the West Indian women who cast currents of anger before them as they walked the English streets. She seemed to be friends with all the people in the room. Her name was Gabisile, and she told you that she had nothing to say about herself. 'I'm twenty-five. What can you say about yourself at twenty-five?' You told her about how you'd just come back from a spell overseas, and how some woman with an attitude had broken your nose, and how you were writing about the whole affair to try to make sense of it all. She told you about the building, how it was called The Old Boma, and how it had belonged to several successive Native administrators, the last of whom had tripped and snapped his neck as he carried his boxes out to the car. Her father had bought the land from the new government, which hadn't really cared about the history of the old place, and they were going to demolish it and build a hotel for travellers passing through. 'But until then,' she said, 'it's ours to do with as we please.' This had brought a whoop from the revellers, and it had taken a while for you to hear her next question.

'Where are you based now?'

'Gaborone,' you'd said.

'Does independence mean what you wanted it to?'

You told her what you did for a living.

'But all the rich farmers are up-country,' she said.

'You're probably right.'

'So,' she said, taking a pull from her joint, 'why don't you live in the North?'

You were on the outskirts of a transit street that was trying to be a town. You hadn't aimed to be hitchhiking to Francistown, but circumstances had found you by the side of the road, hoping to reach it before Saturday night was upon you. Your Peugeot had lost its exhaust, and you'd left it in Molepolole with promises of fetching it on Monday. It had taken you forever to get back to the old North Road, but something had called you back to that place where you'd broken down years before. Now it was getting cold, and you were grinding gravel beneath your feet outside the gutted shell of the Old Boma when you heard a sound, low and sweet. The undulations of the road obscured it from view. A V8.

It was a full minute before a brown Rover with a big white man at the wheel crested the hill. You stepped forward as he blipped down the gears and rolled to a stop. 'Where are you headed?' the man asked.

'Francistown,' you said. It was the thirteenth anniversary of Botswana's independence, and you were heading back to your village to see anyone who cared to be seen.

'You're in luck,' he said with an amiable pat on the Rover's brown velour. 'I'm running up to Palapye. Hop in.' He pointed to the ruined hotel and said, 'Before Boipuso, that used to be the Commissioner's residence. When the capital was in Mafikeng, all the Native Commissioners and their wives would flock here in big Buicks and Fords for weekend dances and dinner parties.' He shook his head solemnly.

The man said everything as though he were a tour guide showing you an amusement park that had shut down. You took a moment to watch the hotel's pale paint flaking into the earth around it, and then you took off towards a hellflame twilight.

You looked at the man and his car, so strange an intervention did they seem. The Rover must've been new half a decade ago; it was just beginning to permit itself a squeak here and there.

'You like my Rover, I can see.'

'It's smooth.'

'They're not the company they once were, but I'm hanging on to mine. You can't get them anymore, now that they've pulled out of South Africa.'

The man had an exceptionally large head, and though you could only see his features in profile, the frosting of grey hair on that head seemed at odds with the vitality of his eyes and a mouth that looked like it was struggling to hold back cruel and amusing things.

'Are you South African?' The last question sneaked up on you.

You rolled your eyes and said no with a half-way grin, and the answer seemed to satisfy him, as he didn't press further. He told you that he'd come from Witbank to head up a road-expansion project. He said that when he'd first visited Botswana in '66 there was barely enough tarred road to bother with. He asked if you were a graduate, and when you said you were, he said some things about that too. He asked what you'd been doing outside the old hotel, and you struggled to find words to explain. He was wearing a jacket which fascinated you. It was conspicuously expensive, and its weave of triangles absorbed you to such an extent that it was some time before you noticed he was speaking to you.

'Go on. Go on,' he said impatiently. He was eager for you to tell him some story about how your foreignness and the hotel and the woman in the hotel had caused something immoral to take place. He leaned towards you, smelling like Old Spice and fried sausages.

'I don't really have that much to say,' you said, and you meant it.

You were crossing an open expanse, and the view back was dismal with dust as the Rover kicked up stones and sand. There were no clear markings to divide the road, and so the man kept to the middle, sawing unnecessarily at the wheel so that the car took up a side-to-side pitching motion.

'I don't believe you,' he said.

'It's the truth.' You sank into your father's jacket and regarded the blazing sky as the sun tracked across the endless sky.

'I've read about those people overseas. They're the ones you hear about making a nuisance of themselves at rugby games and the like. But not in Botswana. This country isn't ready for hippies. How can they grow their hair that long?'

He told you without pause of his two young sons who were doing military service, and of a daughter who lived with her husband at a mission in Nyasaland. That's what he called it, as if time had stood still for him several years before this moment where he and you had found yourselves.

'Am I proud of them? I certainly am. Do I wish they were back home? I certainly do. Am I glad they're not growing their hair and going with black women in Swaziland? I certainly am.' He thought of hippies with the unease of a man for whom the future was like staring out at a clear blue sky from within a cell whose high windows allowed him to see only what he couldn't have.

You felt the laugh come up from your ribs and stopped yourself.

'They weren't hippies,' you said. 'They were a bunch of women who'd gotten tired of carrying on like things were normal, and they'd left their homes and all come together in that one place.'

He skirted what you said, kept talking, filling the car with words and details until you fell into a nodding daze, watching the road appear in the yellow lights of the Rover, or else looking out the window at the distant flash of village fires, while the man recited his old war stories. Until at last, the lights of Palapye swam up at you and you realised you'd been sleeping for the past hour. You thanked the man, and he wished you luck as you got out. You listened as the rumble faded, wondering how you were going to get on from there. Around you, meaning was creaking in the infinite dark, expanding itself in the proximate murmur of people and the myriad awakenings of unfamiliar animals.

# Outside Riad Dahab

*Chourouq Nasri*

*H*e looked for a place to sleep for days. He finally found it: Riad Dahab, a nice traditional hotel situated next to a hammam in one of the narrow alleys of the medina. The riad offered a blind face to the street; the only clue to the identity of the building was its title, and the door made of wood and decorated with exquisite carving. He brought his luggage: a colourless worn blanket and a couple of black plastic bags.

He liked the name. He liked the door. The pavement was wide. There was no security guard around, and the riad's guests were all foreigners, who pretended not to see him and did not bother him. He was not embarrassed; this was now his home, and he had no intention of leaving, unless forced by the police.

The inhabitants of the street, however, did not accept him at first. Children were frightened of him. They pestered him and threw stones at him. Three boys of about ten or eleven used to play football nearby and kick the ball at him. Tired, all he could do was shield his eyes and try to sleep. Once, he was beaten up by a tall boy who didn't even live in the street. But eventually he became invisible, and people stopped bothering him.

This is how he spent his time: sleeping next to the riad's door, wrapped in an old blanket, waking every time a new visitor arrived. His mornings crept by with hazy impressions left by the traffic noise of the waking city. Sometimes he was surprised when he was having his morning piss, right beside the hotel's door. When he was tired of sleeping, he went for walks in the narrow, tortuous alleys of the medina. He got his meals out of garbage cans. Sometimes, especially when he was high from sniffing gasoline, he spent long hours watching columns of ants travelling in opposite directions, to and from their nest.

He became part of the landscape; the inhabitants of the street looked at him, but did not see him. Tourists noticed him when they first arrived, but they quickly managed not to catch sight of him. They were busy taking pictures and visiting the diverse sites of the city. Some of them noticed his smell, wrinkled their noses and moved away. But his smell was meant to keep people at a distance.

He did consider going to the hammam, but he knew he couldn't strip off his coat. His coat was part of him, and he would feel helpless, fragile, without it. He wore it all the time, even on the hot days of July and August.

He didn't like going outside his territory. He envied those foreigners who travelled without fear, coming and going with their luggage. Riad Dahab's door looked different when people came. The door, the air, the noise of the street: everything changed. He could hear children's cheerful voices, street vendors' persistent shouts, and tourists' various accents and languages. During the day, the street was busy with passers-by, children heading to school, old jellaba-clad men going to or coming back from the mosque, visitors to the hammam. At night, it was a haven for Riad Dahab's late visitors or drunkards.

Tourists mainly came in the spring months. It was hard to tell what language they spoke, but he could always tell if they were speaking English. English had been his favourite subject in high school. He still remembered some words, and even talked to an American woman who seemed lost and was having a hard time getting back to Riad Dahab. She was nice and gave him ten dirhams.

Sometimes, especially in winter, when it was cold and dark and the alley smelled of rotten fish, there were no guests, and the street was quiet. The cats came and went. He wondered what tourists did when they were not at Riad Dahab.

When the weather changed, he missed a roof over his head. He watched the clouds gathering and passing by. The rain poured upon his miserable blanket. He didn't move. He thought of his options: the bus station and the park. He scanned the street for shelter from the rain. Huddled in his old coat, he tightened the blanket around him and let himself be soaked while staring at the unstopping rain. He never got sick; he got his immunity from sleeping under the rain for days.

೮ఽ

*O*ne day, he was woken by a knocking at the Riad Dahab door. The knocker was a tall man with a big backpack, accompanied by a much shorter woman. He stared at the newcomers with drowsy eyes.

'David? You're going to love the riad. It might not be the finest riad in Oujda, but it's very convivial,' said the small woman.

David looked familiar, like someone he had once known, but had forgotten. His voice was slow and contemplative, his leisurely, soft talk was full of pauses and silences. His American accent was all over the place. The woman with bright, anxious eyes was talking in a high-pitched voice, her laughter sounding like part of her speech. She was Moroccan: he could tell from her broken English. She did not stay in the hotel, though. Who was she? A friend? A lover? Or maybe a prostitute? No, this was not the kind of hotels for prostitutes. He was an expert on this subject: this was his fourth or fifth hotel. As he thought of the riad's new guest, his eyes closed, his mouth fell open to show decayed teeth, and he began to snore loudly.

He knew why tourists pretended not to see him: they were strangers in a place they did not belong to, and they did not want anyone to remind them of their vulnerability.

What would have become of him if he hadn't found Riad Dahab? It was like a presence that protected him. He didn't remember where he came from. The past was forbidden territory. He had no friends, no family. He felt he was a very old person, although he had no means of gauging the passing of time. He just lived. He had no plans, and he didn't care. His own personal history didn't matter. What he was fierce about was his special connection with this riad: it was the one with significant history enough for both of them.

He didn't know the riad's story, so he invented it. It was a three-hundred-year-old house. The owner, a woman in her mid-forties who was a passionate advocate for the traditional architecture of Oujda, restored it to its original splendour. Mrs Selam: that's the name he chose for her. She belonged to a wealthy family. She bought the house and used her inheritance to restore it. It was a complete wreck and would have collapsed if not for the robust columns that propped it up. Some doors and windows and shutters were replaced, the plumbing repaired, and the place painted.

Riad Dahab was a beautiful hotel; he peeped inside sometimes when a new visitor arrived. He longed and longed to push through the door and feast his eyes on the interior.

One Ramadan day, the security guard, a new employee who probably did not really know the hotel rules, invited him to have iftar with him, as there were no guests in the hotel. Nothing could be better than the harira, laziza and chbakia his host offered him. But he really wanted to explore the riad. While the security guard was busy doing the prayer of almaghrib, he seized the opportunity.

It was strange to leave the smell of his ragged blanket and be inside Riad Dahab. After a small, narrow passageway, another door emerged and let the visitor into a hall with a magnificent white piano. On the right-hand side of the hall were bedrooms with brown cedar doors. A little way down the hall, to the left, after the kitchen, was a library. At the end of the hall was the courtyard doorway, carved in cedar, marble and stucco, and surrounded with arabesques and the traditional tiles known as zellij. Colourful flowerbeds, bordered by tall hibiscus hedges lined each side of the courtyard, which was adorned with blue and red zellij, skillfully laid in the old style. The courtyard was surrounded by four large salons fronted by tiled columns. The first salon was a large room, its ceiling decorated with a radial design of carved and painted cedar. On the white wall at the end of the room was a large painting of Boulevard Derfoufi by Yahya Bassou. On the floor, leaning against the walls, were other paintings bought from different Oujdi artists. Two or three reading lamps stood on the floor so that parts of the room remained in darkness. On one side of the tiled courtyard were stairs which led to a terrace with a breathtaking view over Oujda: mosques, houses, hills and the spires of minarets.

'Drya, you must leave. The manager will be back shortly.' It was the security guard, panting.

℘

*I*t was not hard to imagine living in the riad. Like the numerous guests of the old house, he would feel the morning as it crept through the small windows of his bedroom, and would enjoy the quietness of the rooms. There would be no passers-by, no cats, no dogs, no cockroaches, and no cars. He would be in one of the bedrooms, lying in a big soft bed, and enjoying the enchanting smells of the endless cooking that filled the house.

When he got fed up with lying down, he sat and waited until something interesting happened. Or he would stand on the pavement when the street was empty, when everybody was asleep, and think about the people inside the riad: the tall American man, the French family, the newly married couple. He imagined the conversation between the bride and the groom in one of the bedrooms of the riad. The groom was in his early thirties; the bride in her late twenties. He imagined the groom telling his bride that he loved her and that he was the happiest man on earth.

He felt as if he were watched by the riad's guests. He looked upon them as people separate from the true life of the place, and for this reason not quite real, not as real as the inhabitants of the street. He was nervous of the strange foreigners who showed up regularly at the riad, but he was also anxious to see them arrive. He felt less lonely when he saw a new visitor. When tourists arrived, they were excited and happy; but when they left, they looked like different people.

And he wondered: what would happen if a tourist talked to him or brought a drink? Would he be the same? What would he do? Would he accept this kindness? He didn't know if he could bear to be looked at in the eyes. He would probably just walk away and wait till the person was gone.

People came to Riad Dahab; they disappeared and reappeared. He watched them when they left, and sometimes he wondered if they would remember him; if he'd be part of the souvenirs they carried with them on their journey back home.

ℰ℧

*O*ne day, a taxi came in the middle of the night, its headlights swinging across his grey blanket. A young woman with a stylish haircut got out. She noticed him. She must have seen him while she was still in the red taxi that brought her to Riad Dahab. She did not immediately go into the hotel. Instead, she focused her camera and took a picture of him. He couldn't believe his eyes: a tourist thinking him worth a picture, as if he were a monument!

A tall, beautiful woman smiled at him, unconcerned by how he looked and smelled. She was the first person to smile at him in years. She was in her early twenties, her skin white like milk; her face was long and firmly modelled.

'Hi, my name is Sarah,' she said, smiling all the while. 'Can I take a picture of you? I am working on an artistic project about the people who live in the old Moroccan cities, and I think you have an interesting face.'

He went blank. He sat still in the darkness of the night and looked at the tall, slender girl without blinking. For a while, his eyes held hers. He looked at her face, her smile, her eyes. Her request caught him unprepared, and he had nothing to say. He was amazed by her words, then irritated, then unsettled. He was used to the look of contempt or indifference people gave him. He was not ready for treatment of this kind.

Sarah surged round him to get a closer view. Her kindness had an odd effect on him: it filled him with fresh energy and brought out something of a self he had forgotten. For a few minutes, he didn't feel cast out and alone. The world was no longer drab and without possibilities.

'Do you think I can take pictures of you tomorrow morning? The quality of the photos will be much better in daylight,' she said, without taking her eyes off him.

He uttered a timid 'yes'.

'Would nine tomorrow morning be okay for you?' she asked.

'Yes,' he said.

Sarah disappeared into the riad. Left alone, he felt his eyelids began to droop. A minute later, the door opened again and she reappeared.

'What's your name?' she asked with her rich, fruity voice.

His face brightened: 'Ismail.'

Ismail had an appointment with a gorgeous American woman. Okay, she simply wanted to take pictures. But he remembered that short encounter as one of pure happiness, and he looked forward to an even happier time the following day. He spent the night thinking about Sarah and reinventing her in that posture which bewitched him, standing beside her small red suitcase and smiling at him with her wide mouth and dizzying eyes. Such eyes! Inviting and warm, like the inside of Riad Dahab. Her eyes.

Ismail wanted to be awake at 9.00 am, but he didn't have a watch. And he knew it was no use asking someone in the street for the time. No one would speak to him. But he had an idea. The train station clock! The railway station was one kilometre away. So he lay awake all night, and walked to the station early in the morning to watch the clock. Close to the right time, he headed back to Riad Dahab, to be sure not to miss his appointment with Sarah.

Sarah was punctual, as far as he could tell. She was splendid in her long white dress. And Ismail was happy. No other word could describe how he felt when he saw her, and even after she left. His day was filled with sleep and daydreaming. Riad Dahab seemed small, and his blanket felt immense.

But he was worried when the night fell and there was no further sign of Sarah. Where was she? Had she gone back to America? Did she go to another city in Morocco? He found himself thinking of Sarah, her expression, her gait, her dress, the way she did her hair. This obsession took him by surprise. Ismail was discovering a great, unappeasable hunger in himself. He always clenched his hunger by sniffing gasoline or glue, but not this kind of hunger. Before this encounter, he didn't seem to mind his losses. He was content just to live. But now, he was wild, close to hysteria, wondering where

Sarah was, feeling protective towards her.

The street had begun to empty, and the town to fall silent when Sarah finally got back to Riad Dahab. When he saw her, Ismail felt refreshed, revitalised; even his skin felt new. He smiled at her. His grin was so wide that his rotten teeth showed. She smiled back at him with her beautiful green eyes and gave him something roughly wrapped in newspaper: a sandwich! He waited until she entered Riad Dahab before unfolding his late hot meal. But before he had time to take the first gulp, cats scampered in front of him, maddened by the smell of roasted chicken.

'Sb!' he shouted at them.

The cats moved instantly, but stood silently a few metres away, watching him with their glittering eyes while he finished his sandwich. It was delicious to him, the climax to that tumultuous day and night. He was full of tenderness: for Sarah, for the visitors to Riad Dahab, and even for the street cats.

A car came and parked. A family of five were getting out of a taxi and talking loudly in French accents. New guests of Riad Dahab. Ragged, half-starved old drunks from other neighbourhoods were wandering about, searching in the garbage cans for food. But Ismail didn't notice them. He sat in the darkness, feeling the newness of his skin. He was full of the wonder of what had befallen him. Was this alhoub, or love? That was a word much used in the Arab films he watched at Vox cinema, a colonial movie theatre that lost its public audience since the invention of video recorders; nobody but male adolescents and vagrants like himself went there to watch the same black-and-white Egyptian films over and over and over.

Flowers! He'd give Sarah flowers. Ismail had seen this in many films: the lover gave flowers to his beloved to express his passion for her. But where could he find flowers? He decided to go to Lala Maryam park, not that far from Riad Dahab. He'd been there before; the old city parks provided excellent shelter for people like him. He looked at his grey sneakers, or what remained of them, and headed to the park. He plucked daisies, roses and hibiscus, and prepared a beautiful bouquet. Its fragrance was so strong that it tickled even his drug-damaged nose.

Back to his spot next to Riad Dahab, Ismail was too excited to lie down; he admired the flowers and counted the minutes separating him from the morning. He imagined again and again the moment when Sarah would come out of the riad and he would offer her the flowers.

The door of Riad Dahab opened without warning in the early afternoon of the following day. It was a time of year when it hurt to be in the open on sunny days. Once Ismail had rubbed the sleep from his eyes, shading them from the piercing sun rays with his hand, he found Sarah looking at him with her green smiling eyes. Then she gave him a photo, the one she had taken of him the night she arrived.

Her stare bewildered him. He remained motionless for several seconds, startled by the engine of a red taxi which had just arrived, but then he managed to take the photo from her hands. He was sweating, his mouth dry, his stomach hollow, feeling, wanting to find the courage to give her the flowers: but he couldn't.

The uneasy silence was broken as Sarah started back to the waiting taxi, which was honking its horn. Ismail looked at the photo through half-shut eyes, but could not understand. Was she leaving? He heard the car drive off. As he was wiping away his tears, he had an illumination: Sarah had become part of the past. Like all Riad Dahab's guests, she was just passing through; she was one more person he was not going to see again.

In the photo he now held, a shrunken pale figure wrapped in a worn blanket sat next to a huge wooden carved door.

Ismail hid his body in the folds of his blanket and sniffed glue from a black plastic bag for comfort. Riad Dahab didn't feel like home anymore. His blanket, the people of the street, the trees, the sun, the weather: everything was different.

It was time for him to get away, to search for a new home. There was another hotel in his head, one that was located in the colonial part of the city. Yes! It was time to cut his bond with the medina and try something new.

# The Snore Monitor

*Chido Muchemwa*

' *W*ANTED: Snore Monitor.' The lime-green flyer stood out among the seas of blues and pinks on the Post Office noticeboard. Hamu didn't know what a snore monitor was, but she knew she needed a job, and she knew the hotel, The Chelsea, was the finest in Richards Bay. So, she took down the wanted notice, folded it carefully, and placed it in her handbag. No need to keep advertising the job to competitors.

Hamu sent her résumé the very next day. It was thin, just three months spent as a temporary teacher in Harare right after high school, and nine months as a maid in Richards Bay. She didn't even have a reference from the maid job, from which she had been unceremoniously fired two weeks before. Her employer had informed her that a distant cousin willing to work for less would be arriving the next day from Zimbabwe to take over her duties. Hamu had been upset. She had worked earnestly for that woman. The hardness of her hands would testify to that. Yet all she had to show for it, as she returned to the single room she shared with two other Zimbabweans in eSikhawini, was half a month's pay.

Every morning after that, she had joined the masses on the buses from eSikhawini to the suburbs of Richards Bay. One of her roommates told her to look for jobs in Meerensee because 'that's where all the rich white people live'. For two weeks, Hamu had walked the streets of Meerensee, asking for jobs over intercoms. She soon grew tired of the incorporeal voices hidden behind electric gates that kept telling her to go away. And at the end of every cul-de-sac, she would encounter a gated estate with guards with big guns, who wouldn't even let her explain herself before shooing her away.

One week after sending her résumé to The Chelsea, Hamu was called for an interview. Across a mahogany desk sat the hotel owner, an older woman with cat-eye spectacles who looked like the kind to knock on doors and enter before you answered. She introduced herself as Gerrida Visser, and felt the need to clarify: 'Most people call me Gerrida, but I know you Zimbabweans don't do first names, so you can call me Tannie Visser'.

*A bored trophy wife who bought a hotel as a hobby.* Behind Tannie Visser hung an oil painting of the Verwoerd Tunnels. Was it just ten months ago that she had marvelled at them as the bus from Beitbridge made its way down to Johannesburg? The interview itself was perfunctory, just a handful of cursory questions. Hamu knew that Gerrida wanted to hire her because she was Zimbabwean, and most employers believed Zimbabweans worked harder for less. Then came the critical question.

'Do you need to be paid in cash?'

This would be the only acknowledgment that would pass between the two that Hamu was working illegally in South Africa.

After that, Tannie seemed to assume the job belonged to Hamu. She walked Hamu through the three floors of the hotel, explaining what the job entailed.

'You see, Hamu, your job is to monitor noise levels on our quiet floor,' Tannie said. 'People pay extra for guaranteed quiet and undisturbed sleep. Some of these men, they snore like rhinoceroses, but if they're on the quiet floor, we cannot allow them to disturb the other guests. So you knock on the door, and you ask them to keep it down.'

'And if they start to snore again?' Hamu said.

'Well, the customer is always right. You cannot keep disturbing them. Make a note of the room number, and we'll move them to a different floor the next day. But I'm not worried about you, Hamu. You people always make a plan.'

One signed contract and a uniform fitting later, Hamu was the official snore monitor at The Chelsea. Sitting on the bus back to eSikhawini, she sent a text to her mother telling her she got the job. She got no reply.

*T*hree days later, Hamu moved into her new home. It took her all of twenty minutes to gather her belongings from that little room in eSikhawini, and no time at all to settle into her new accommodations at The Chelsea. Her room was at the very end of the row of staff bedrooms. It was a small room, just a single bed

CHIDO MUCHEMWA

and a tiny desk, but it was the first room Hamu didn't have to share. Growing up, she'd shared a room with her mother and baby sister. Frequently, she'd had to give up her spot in the bed for the latest relative come to Harare from the village in search of a job. And now she had a room to herself where no one would ask her to leave if they needed privacy.

At first, it was hard to sleep while it was light outside. Tannie Visser had been thoughtful enough to put blackout curtains in the room, but knowing that the world outside was awake and buzzing made it hard for Hamu to sleep. She would hear her co-workers chatting and laughing outside her room, and her brain would switch on, struggling to decipher the isiZulu. And as their day ended, hers was just beginning. Back in eSikhawini, she and her exhausted roommates had spent their evenings reminiscing about growing up in Harare. Now, Hamu hardly had the chance to speak to her workmates, except at dinner. At night, she patrolled the third floor. She had a small desk station next to the lifts, where she perched on a wooden stool in silence. Every fifteen minutes, she would pad along the carpeted passages listening for any disturbances. Sometimes, she would knock at a door and a groggy old man, hairy pot-belly hanging out, would emerge and then sheepishly apologise when informed that his snoring could be heard at the end of the corridor. Other times, she would knock on the doors of people who had fallen asleep with the TV on too loud, or who were chatting on the phone in the middle of the night. But most of the time, she just sat and listened.

The days began to look the same. Hamu would sleep in the morning, and in the late afternoon, she would walk down to the beach. By 9pm, she would be sitting at her little station. It was so quiet that sometimes she thought she could here a clock ticking on the next floor. She would sit there straining to hear the sound of time going by, anything to stop her from dwelling on her thoughts.

She started to make up stories about the guests to send to her baby sister. Sitting at her little desk, she would try to imagine where they were coming from, and what secrets they might have.

58

The middle-aged couple apparently on honeymoon? He had another wife in Bloemfontein. The businessman from Joburg? He cried every morning because he hated his job so much. And that stuck-up heifer Hamu had to ask three times to lower her voice on the phone? Frigid.

Hamu happily texted these stories to her sister. And in return, she got stories from home. *I need new shoes for school … Mainini Tendai is staying with us … Baba came to visit and asked how you were.* Baba.

One night, Hamu was summoned by a guest to 'handle' a noisy neighbour. The guest in the corner room was snoring so loudly, the walls should have been shaking. So, Hamu did what she was trained to do. She knocked softly. No response. She knocked again, a little louder this time. Still no response. She knocked some more. She could not stop. Knock. Knock. Knock. The guest who had complained said she should give up. Hamu kept knocking. Other guests began to emerge from their rooms. Hamu kept knocking. One particularly dishevelled man complained that her knocking was more disturbing than the snoring. Hamu kept knocking. Finally, the snoring stopped and a large, contrite man opened the door. *Told his wife that he was on a business trip, but really just stayed in a local hotel to avoid his annoying kids.* Mortified by the sight of the snore monitor at his door, the man apologised. Only then did Hamu turn to see the sea of white faces looking at her as if she were deranged.

When she got back to her room at the end of the shift, Hamu didn't bother going to sleep. She sat on the edge of the bed, still in her uniform, fiddling with the buttons on her jacket, waiting for Tannie Visser. At 8am, the summons came. Hamu entered the office certain she was about to be fired, but the old lady was more baffled than angry.

'But Hamu, my dear,' she said, 'why did you keep knocking?' Hamu wrung her hands. How could she explain herself? How could she explain to this woman the cloud that had descended on her mind, making continuous knocking appear to be the only sensible thing to do? How could she explain the sudden insistence that she be heard? 'I'm sorry, Madam,' Hamu said.

Tannie Visser said she would make an adverse mark in Hamu's record. One more of those, and Tannie would have no choice but to fire her.

'I'm really disappointed in you, Hamu. I really thought you were one of the good ones.'

Hamu listened, but instead of looking at Tannie Visser, she looked at the painting of the Verwoerd Tunnels.

*A*fter that, Hamu walked those corridors in absolute silence. She got flat shoes with soft soles. She stopped using her phone while on duty because she didn't want to make even the subtle noise of tapping the screen. She carried her silence beyond the third floor. Sometimes one of her co-workers would say something to her and she would answer in her head, forgetting to vocalise, as if her brain had temporarily forgotten how speaking worked. She began to eat her dinner in silence, and one of her workmates, a fellow Zimbabwean, rather unfeelingly started calling her chitokwani – a night goblin. She said nothing. She had become chitokwani, haunting the third floor in silence. At the first sign of elevated noise from a guest, she would knock on their door, and ask them in a whisper to keep it down. She hardly sat down at her desk, preferring to keep walking the passages, never making a noise, always listening. And it was because she was so silent, because she was straining so hard to hear any noise, that one night she heard the sound of someone trying desperately to muffle the sounds of their crying.

It was so soft that Hamu almost missed it, so soft that it couldn't possibly be disturbing the other guests, but still, she knocked. She heard slow steps coming towards the door. When it opened, a young white man stood before her in a hotel bathroom robe. *Adrenaline junkie chasing waves to escape his heroin addiction.*

'Am I making too much noise?' he said in an American accent.

'No, sir. I just wanted to make sure you're fine.'

'That's nice of you,' he said. He looked at his feet. They stood in silence.

'So, are you all right?' Hamu said. 'Anything I can do?'

'I'll be fine.'

Silence.

Hamu began to turn away. 'I guess I'll be go——.'

'Don't.' The man grasped at her arm, but quickly let go. 'I mean, please talk to me. I don't… I just…' He frowned.

'Sir, we cannot stand in the doorway disturbing the other guests.' Already Hamu thought she could hear stirring in the room next door.

'Well – maybe you could come in?'

Now, the customer might always be right, but this seemed to Hamu to be taking it a bit too far. But she was afraid he might call after her if she walked away. And he looked so vulnerable. And there was the voice in the back of her head noting how cute he was. So she went in.

There she was in the hotel room of a strange man in the middle of the night. If her mother could see her now! Not to mention Tannie Visser, who would fire her on the spot if she found out. No amount of Zimbabwean work ethic would be enough to save her job. But Tannie Visser was safely tucked away in bed in her Meerensee mansion. And Mama was back in Harare. Right now, it was just Hamu and this weeping white man.

'I'm Ryan, by the way – Hamu,' he said, reading her name badge.

'Nice to meet you, Ryan.' She stood by the door with her arms crossed, even as he walked across the room and sat on the edge of his bed.

'This is a little awkward, isn't it?' he said. 'But I'm glad you came in.'

Hamu nodded.

'I should wash my face,' he said.

Hamu watched him retreat into the bathroom. Her eyes

darted around the room, taking in the tousled sheets, the clothes strewn across the floor, the half-empty bottle of Jack Daniels on the bedside table, the pretty blonde smiling from the iPhone on the desk. Ryan walked back in and noticed Hamu looking at the image.

'That's my girlfriend,' he said. 'At least she used to be. She dumped me.' He picked up the phone. 'She said being with me felt like settling.' A snigger quickly turned into a sigh.

'Did she?' Hamu asked.

'I'm not even sure why I told you that.' Ryan sat down on the bed, then looked up at Hamu as if taking her in for the first time. 'I'm sorry. I shouldn't have asked you in. That was inappropriate.'

Hamu smiled awkwardly. No one knew better than her that she shouldn't have entered the room, yet here she was. 'I don't mind.'

'You're not South African, are you? You don't sound like the others.'

'I'm from Zimbabwe.'

'Sit down.' Ryan must have noticed the apprehension in her eyes because he quickly added, 'Look, I'll even tuck myself into these tight sheets so you'll know I can't just jump you.' He smiled as he took off his dressing-gown and slipped into the bed. He looked at her with an expectant face. She pulled the desk chair to the foot of the bed and sat down.

'So, tell me, Hamu from Zimbabwe,' Ryan said, 'how does a Zimbabwean end up being the sleep police in South Africa?'

'The official title is "snore monitor".'

'That came out wrong. I'm not judging your job. I just – I think it's interesting.'

'I suppose so.' Hamu said. 'It's just a job to me. It pays the bills and leaves a bit to send home.'

'I respect that.' Ryan reached for his bottle of Jack and poured some into the hotel coffee mug. He waved the bottle at Hamu, but she shook her head. He swallowed the whiskey in one gulp, wincing. He replaced the mug on the bedside table and picked up the iPhone again. The blonde girl was still grinning from the screen.

'And you,' Hamu said, 'what are you doing in South Africa?'

'I couldn't spend another day alone in my apartment. So I did that thing where you spin the globe and go where you finger lands.'

Hamu did not know what this spinning the globe thing was, but she nodded as if she did.

'You see, Victoria—' Ryan said, '—that's my girlfriend's name, she said I was too predictable. So I thought I'd try something different.'

'Is it helping?'

'I don't know. It – it just hurts. It all just hurts. Can you imagine someone you love telling you they don't want you?'

'I don't need to imagine. My mother named me Hamundide to make sure I would never forget I wasn't wanted.' *Why did I say that?*

'What?'

'My full name is Hamundide. It means "you don't want me" or "you don't love me". My mother has been my father's mistress for the last twenty-five years. I wasn't planned, and he refused to marry her.'

'That's quite a name to carry,' Ryan said.

'You toughen up really fast with a name like that on the playground.'

'But it works out, right? You learn early how to survive. If you can survive being teased like that, you can survive anything.'

'I suppose so. I used to go home crying from school, and my grandmother would sing me songs to cheer me up. Shona songs are never about romance, having fun, or simple joy. They all just teach you how to survive.'

'You say that like it's a bad thing.'

'Isn't it?'

'Well, maybe if I knew how to survive, one little break-up wouldn't have sent me running all the way to Africa.

'We're all running from something, right?'

'And what would you be running from, Hamu?' Ryan stared at her, and she looked away.

'Do you know the Verwoerd Tunnels?' Hamu said. 'They're a set of tunnels that cut through a mountain on the main road Zimbabweans use to get to Johannesburg. They're the first major landmark you see after crossing the border, and they are spectacular. I looked at them in absolute awe when the bus I came on drove through them. Imagine. In the 1950s, people were cutting roads through rock in Africa! Then the lady next to me told me that Verwoerd was the architect of apartheid. And the owner of this hotel has an oil painting of the tunnels hanging in her office. Henrick Verwoerd written across the top, and 1961 on the sides looking like if you walked through that arch, you'd be right back in Verwoerd's South Africa. Why would she hang that in her office? I think I know why, yet I'm still here.'

'That doesn't answer the question,' Ryan said.

'I guess it doesn't,' Hamu said. She jumped as the air conditioner kicked in. 'All my life, I've watched my mother waiting for a man who will never marry her. Then almost a year ago, she found out that my Baba had decided to take a second wife, and it wouldn't be her. I don't talk much. No one wants my opinion, but this time I had to say something. I told her it was time to accept that Baba would never marry her. Mama was so angry, she told me to leave. And when I went to my Baba to ask him for bus fare to get to South Africa, he didn't try to stop me. He didn't even ask what I was going to do when I got there, not even when I said, 'Truly, hamundide.'

For a moment, the only sound in the room was their breathing. She thought he was going to respond, but instead he poured himself more whiskey, swilling it around the mug before knocking it back. Ryan said, 'Do you think you could sing me one of those songs, the ones your grandmother sang you?'

'Sing?'

'Maybe if I hear it, I'll learn a bit about how to survive.'

Hamu sang 'Hatina musha panyika.' As she did, she thought of her mother. She thought of her baby sister, still living under the roof of a woman who had spent the last quarter-century waiting for a man who would never come home for good. She thought of her father, whose parting words had been, 'When you have to go, you have to go.'

It was a long song. When it ended, Hamu looked over at Ryan and saw that he had fallen asleep. She quietly let herself out. At the end of her shift, she found herself once again sitting on the edge of her bed, fiddling with her uniform, waiting for Tannie Visser to call for her. But the summons never came. Instead, a workmate knocked on her door mid-morning and handed her an envelope that 'the nice American guy on the quiet floor' had left for her at the desk when he checked out. Inside was a slim sheaf of hundred-dollar notes.

# The Fountain of Lethe

*Bryony Rheam*

' *I* notice you've cut down the trees,' Julia said to the receptionist as she filled in the forms. She tried to disguise the accusatory tone in her voice, smiling brightly as she wrote down her details: name, address, telephone number. It had been a disappointment on arrival to find the hotel perched alone on the hill with not a tree near it. The closest plantation was at least a forty-five minute walk away. Only the last fifty metres of the road leading up to the hotel were still lined with massive eucalyptus. Still she had felt a flutter of excitement as she had driven up to the door. They were back.

The receptionist, a young woman of about twenty, who couldn't possibly have been working there long, looked at her.

'The trees,' Julia repeated. 'Pine trees. They used to grow very close to the hotel. I used to come here as a child. With my parents,' she added. 'We used to go walking through the forest.' She weaved her hand through the air in a gentle snaking action.

The receptionist smiled politely and then turned back to her computer. 'Rooms 9 and 14,' she said. 'Do you need someone to help you carry your luggage?'

'9 and 14? I asked for adjoining rooms.'

The receptionist scanned her computer screen. 'You asked for two twin rooms.'

'Yes, adjoining each other.'

'I'm sorry, but we don't have adjoining twin rooms. Our adjoining rooms are double and single.'

'They didn't used to be. They were always twin rooms.'

The receptionist shrugged and drew in her lips in an apologetic smile.

'All right. I'll take a double and a single. My daughter can sleep with me.'

'I'm sorry, but they're booked.'

'All of them?'

'We only have two.'

Julia's heart sank. She leaned closer to the counter and dropped her voice. 'It's my dad, you see.' She motioned over her shoulder to where her father sat on a chair by the wall. 'He...he...well, he wanders off. Sometimes. When he's in a different place.' She watched the receptionist's face, hoping the gravity of what she was saying would sink in without the need for further explanation.

'He'll be on the same floor.'

She pulled herself straight. 'It doesn't matter. I need to be near him.'

She felt the receptionist's eyes flicker over her and onto her father. Rosie, her nine-year-old daughter, slumped in the chair next to him, her head on her backpack and one arm around her teddy.

'Could you bear with us for tonight?' asked the receptionist in a low, monotone that irritated her. *Bear with us*. Julia hated the forced politeness and lack of any initiative on the part of the young woman. If it wasn't on the computer, it couldn't happen. 'Perhaps I can move you tomorrow.'

She thought. Dad was tired; he'd probably just go to sleep. She could lock the door, although she hated doing that sort of thing. He wasn't mad, he just got confused. He clung to familiarity like a shipwrecked sailor hanging onto a piece of floating debris – except that when he got to dry ground, he refused to let go, not realising that the very thing that had kept him afloat was now a dead weight, holding him down.

'All right,' she conceded. 'I'll take those rooms. We need to get changed for dinner.'

'The kitchen closes in half an hour,' said the receptionist, looking up at the clock on the wall.

'Half an hour? It's only eight o'clock.'

'Yes, the dining room closes at nine. Last orders from the kitchen are at half-past eight.'

Julia let out a sigh of frustration and her handbag fell off her shoulder. She pulled the strap up clumsily, ruching the sleeve of her shirt. 'Could you ask them to wait? We've driven a long way today. We're all tired.'

The receptionist shook her head with a weak smile. It was

the perfunctory apology of a schoolgirl who hadn't done her homework.

*T*hey didn't make it to the dining room that night. Julia had taken her father to his room, laid out some clean clothes for him to wear, and run a sink full of warm water so that he could wash his face before dinner. Then she had gone to her own room and done the same for Rosie, who had perked up and was trying the different channels on the television after examining the contents of the mini bar. By the time she went back to check on her father, he was fast asleep on top of the bed, the clean set of clothes pushed into a tangle under his feet. When she attempted to wake him, he raised his shoulder against her petulantly, turning his head into the pillow. She slipped off his shoes and covered him with a blanket from the spare bed.

Back in her room, she found Rosie happily ensconced in bed, watching cartoons and eating the complimentary mint chocolates.

'These were on the pillows.' She held up a chocolatey mess in one hand and, in the other, an untouched sweet wrapped in green-and-white spotted silver paper.

'I think one's for me,' Julia said.

'Oh,' said Rosie, looking from one hand to another. 'I think I ate yours. Sorry.'

'It's OK. You must be hungry.'

Rosie shook her head. 'Nope.'

Julia picked up the room service menu and ran her eyes over the choices. Hamburgers or chicken burgers. Everything with chips.

'Hmm,' she joked. 'Duck with a fresh pomegranate sauce. Sounds good.'

'Sounds yucky to me,' said Rosie, peeling the paper off the second chocolate.

'Rosie, please have something proper to eat.'

'This is proper.'

Julia picked up the phone and began to dial. 'I'll order you a burger.'

'OK.' Rosie settled herself back onto the large, puffy pillows and flicked channels.

But the phone didn't work. Julia tried unplugging it both at the wall and on the handset, but nothing helped. She looked at her watch. The kitchen would be closing soon anyway. She doubted it stayed open for room service orders.

She searched through the large bag in which she had packed a picnic lunch for the journey. Two sandwiches and an apple remained. She offered them to Rosie first.

'Ham, please.'

'There's only cheese.'

'I don't like cheese.'

'Have an apple, then.'

'OK,' Rosie said, taking it and placing it next to her pillow.

'I'm going to have a shower. If you change your mind, take a sandwich.'

When Julia emerged from the bathroom ten minutes later, Rosie was asleep, the remote in her hand and the apple untouched. Julia gently eased her into bed, switched off the main light, leaving only the bedside lamp on, and sat on a chair. A wave of loneliness surprised her. What was it, that particular feel of hotel rooms? That mixture of holiday excitement and disappointment that one wavered between.

She towel-dried her hair and ran a comb through it. A plastic-covered brochure on the desk detailed all the activities available at the hotel: swimming, squash, tennis, bird-watching and horse-riding. The latter had been scratched out with a biro. A separate piece of paper advertised the services of a spa. A sentence in block capitals announced that prices were subject to fluctuation.

It was an automatic reaction to reach for her phone in her bag. She remembered it wasn't there, and withdrew her hand. No phones. No laptops. No computer games. Nothing they wouldn't have had in 1985. *Good old-fashioned fun.* She would have liked to have sent Nicola some photos: the view from the terrace, the path through the trees, the imposing entrance to the hotel. She wanted to say, *Hey, look! I'm back here.*

*You're going there? You're brave.*

Nicola's words.

All those hills.

As it was, the wifi, one of the few additions to the hotel, was useless to her. She fluffed up the pillows on her side of the bed and settled down with the remote, quickly putting the sound on mute in case it woke Rosie. Three grainy channels offered the news, a football match between Juventus and Milan, and a movie she had seen before, but couldn't remember the name of. She watched with little interest as Harrison Ford broke out of jail and jumped over walls with a broken arm. She watched his lips move in American English. God damn you. She heard that much at least.

Tired, but knowing she would find it difficult to sleep, she sank further into the pillows and looked around the room: at the heavy, dull counterpane; the Bible by the side of the bed, courtesy of the Gideons; the curtains which she hadn't bothered to close because of all the white flouncy stuff that blocked out the night. Perhaps she should have brought her phone after all. She could have hidden it in her suitcase to prevent any protest from Rosie, and taken it out at moments like these. She could have messaged Rob to let them know they had arrived safely. *No news is good news.* Isn't that what she had said?

*R*ob said she was foolish to drive to Nyanga that way, but then he had been against the trip from the start.

'Take the road to Zvishivane,' he said. 'Then carry on to Masvingo and Birchenough Bridge. Mutare isn't too far from there.'

'That's easier if you are going to the Vumba. If I went that way, I'd still need to drive through Mutare and on to Nyanga.'

'Still faster than through Harare. All that traffic adds at least another hour and a half onto a journey.'

But she was determined. She avoided Rob's raised eyebrows and that look that said 'heed my words' and talked excitedly about the road trip ahead.

Abba. They had to take Abba. And Bruce Springsteen and Chris de Burgh and Roger Whittaker. Tapes would have been good, but they could no longer be played in the car. Instead, she downloaded five hours of music and dug out a few CD compilations – Hits of the 70s and 80s, and The Complete Leo Sayer.

'Good luck,' Rob had said to Rosie that morning as he disentangled her from the seat belt she had been trying to put round both her and her teddy. 'You're going to need it.'

'Nothing wrong with a bit of 80s music,' Julia retorted.

'No, nothing at all. For the first hundred kilometres. You may want some variation after that.' He ruffled Rosie's hair, gave her a high five and closed the door.

'Nicola always maintains we were psychologically damaged by the amount of Abba we listened to on family holidays.' She laughed, switching the engine on and searching for a particular song on her MP3 player.

'I rest my case.'

'"Dancing Queen". What better way to start. Remember this, Dad?'

Rob glanced over at her father in the passenger seat.

The old man hadn't wanted to go.

'We're off to Nyanga, Dad.'

'Never heard of the place.'

'Yes, you have. You'll see.'

'Rubbish.'

'You used to love it. You and Mom. We used to go every August holidays. We loved the walks through the forest—'

'Don't believe a word of it. Not a word.'

'We'll have a great time. Dad, please Dad.'

*Dad, please Dad.*

She swept up the pieces of green-and-white spotted foil that Rosie had left in a small heap on the bed, remembering the way her mother always had mints in her bag and how, on long car trips, when she and Nicola were getting fractious, she'd dig around and bring them out.

*Let's see what we have in here, girls.*

Another wave of loneliness washed up from inside.

*Mint imperials. That's what they were called. Little rounds of white that smelt of the cool depths of Mom's bag: hand cream and cigarettes and folded letters; an address book and a diary with a dark blue cover and an elastic band wrapped round it. A lipstick – Queen of the Nile – a nail file and an errant curler. School photographs with our fringes cut too short and our hair pulled back so tightly, it made our eyes water.*

You can't make her come back.

Rob's words.

I know that. It's just . . . if I could stir some memory. If I could rekindle the *feeling.*

Perhaps he doesn't want to remember.

More of Rob's words.

He might not remember her, but he might remember being happy.

Who's it for, Jules? You or him?

For him. Everything I do is for him.

What about you? Have you come to terms with your mother's death yet?

*Come to terms.* Come to terms. The words floated above her, but she didn't reach out to them. Instead, she switched channels to what was now a wrestling match. She winced as a man with long silver hair and a red bandana was jumped on from the side of the ring by an equally large man in what looked like a tight black swimming costume.

*After dinner, we run back to the room knowing what awaits. We slip the key in the lock, we twist the door handle, and step inside. The heavy counterpanes have been removed. The top sheet and blanket are pulled down, and there on each pillow is a circle of shiny green. It is as though fairies have come while we were out.*

*We eat them too quickly. The chocolate is sweet. It sticks in our throats and makes us cough.*

*Now the fight.*

*Mom, can we have yours?*

*Please.*

*Please.*

*She smiles. Her hand hovers between us.*

*Why doesn't one of you have it today and one of you tomorrow?*

*That's not fair.*

*Of course it's fair.*

*Dad pops his chocolate in his mouth. He lies on top of the bed wearing only his shorts, reading Time magazine and watching the news on ZBC.*

*Mom searches her bag for a second-place-end-of-the-meal complimentary mint to assuage the feelings of the loser. Usually me.*

*Dad switches off the news. In our adjoining room, Nicola and I lie in our beds deciding who can have the notepaper and envelopes.*

*I take the room service menu and Nicola takes a list of important phone numbers. Tomorrow, Mom will tell us that these are not complimentary and we have to put them back.*

*We decide that we can each have a bar of soap from the bathroom, knowing we'll be given more tomorrow if we make it look like we have used it all up. After more argument, this time in loud, hard whispers, Nicola gets a shower cap and I settle on a bag that says Sanitary Towels Only on it.*

*R*osie was up early, doing handstands on the bed so that she could roll over into the comfort of the pillows. Julia went to check on her father, who was still asleep. In the dining room, Rosie piled a bowl high with cornflakes, Coco Pops and tinned grapefruit pieces. Then she eagerly awaited a full English breakfast while trying out different types of fruit juice. Heartened by her daughter's appetite, Julia approached her own breakfast with more gusto than she felt. A knot of apprehension twisted deep in her stomach.

The dining room hadn't changed that much. A coat of paint, perhaps, and different colour chairbacks, but little else. It was emptier than she remembered, and the buffet not quite as vast in range. She noticed the waiter's eyes following Rosie nervously as she went for her third glass of juice.

*At breakfast, lunch and supper we look for our favourite waiter, Jethro. He knows our names and asks us about school. We ask him about his wife and his children. He is as familiar as a piece of furniture, with a smile like a sunbeam.*

'How long are we staying?' asked Rosie.

'The weekend. Why?'

'Nothing. Just asking.'

'Let's go for a walk,' Julia said. 'While it's still cool. Gumpy won't be up for a while.'

*W̶e start early after breakfast, when our stomachs are full of scrambled egg, bacon, tomato and sausage.*

*'Should keep us going,' says Dad as he pushes his wide-brimmed blue hat on and slings a small satchel over his shoulder. 'Onwards and upwards.'*

*We follow the road through the forest, feeling the pull of our bodies as it winds further down, down, down into the valley.*

She didn't plan to be gone long. Just a short walk down the drive to the road and maybe back up through the scrubby bush at the front of the hotel where the pine forest used to be. The path was bound to still be in use. Then they could get Dad up and give him his breakfast. She changed her mind when they got to the top of the drive. It was unlikely that they would encounter many cars; the hotel was ten kilometres off the main road for a start, at the end of a narrow dusty strip of dirt that dropped into a valley and then rose sharply again. It was situated on a smudge of green on an otherwise grey-blue hill, surrounded by other, larger hills, upon which pine tree after pine tree grew, like soldiers lined up for battle. She had a memory of the trees surrounding the hotel itself, of walking through a densely wooded area, heavy with the smell of crushed pine needles and the warm wet of decay.

She opted to walk through the sparse vegetation made up of straggly pine saplings and occasional thickets of dry bracken. Rosie was subdued as they set off, and clung to her hand, which did not make walking easy. She didn't shake it off though, or encourage the girl to walk on her own. She also had a need to hold someone's hand.

'Smell the air, Rosie,' she said. 'Can you smell it?'

Rosie sniffed in an exaggerated dog-like manner. 'No.'

'Pine. That lovely fresh smell.'

'Oh.'

It was the smell of holidays, of freedom. The smell of walks and woodsmoke and time that unravelled in soft waves behind you as you meandered through the trees.

*Beat you to the road!*

*Last one there is a rotten egg!*

'All this used to be trees,' she said to Rosie, sweeping her hand across the denuded landscape. 'Lots and lots of trees. Aunty Nicola and I used to call it the Enchanted Forest.'

'Why did they cut them down?'

'I'm not sure. There must have been a fire,' she said, noting the blackened stumps. 'Look, this is the original path. Now imagine this is all full of really tall pine trees.'

Rosie looked around and then, with decided resignation, she set off, skipping. Julia felt her heart lift in response.

'We used to imagine we would find fairies here and pixies. Elves, all sorts of magical creatures.'

Without answering, Rosie continued to hop along the path.

'We stopped coming here when I was twelve,' Julia called after her, not really knowing why. 'The road got washed away in the rains and the hotel was closed for months while a bridge was built.'

*Mom says we won't be going there again these holidays. There's been a storm. Nicola and I are aghast, but Mom says we'll have fun at home. We can swim at the club and go horse-riding at Aunty Stella's farm. You'll still have a good time, she says. You'll see.*

Julia glanced at her watch. Another ten minutes, maybe. Dad always slept late. The heat rose. There was no shade to protect them from the rough glare of the sun, and the back of her neck was warm. She wished she had been better prepared and brought more water. Rosie was already most of the way through a bottle. Going downhill was easy. The climb up would almost certainly knock them. She decided not to go as far as the road.

'Can we stop?'

'Just now. I just want to get to the Fairy Circle. It's where we used to stop and have a break.'

Soon they were near the bottom of the hill. Julia remembered a longer walk filled with trees and birds and squirrels. Where they used to stop in a cool copse and rest on the pine needles was now a dull open area bereft of life. An old Coke can glinted in the sun and flies thronged over a steaming pile of human excrement. She was glad neither of her parents was there.

*You're going there. You're brave.*

That was why Nicola did not come. Nicola who lived in Canada, who did not come home, except for funerals.

They moved away and found some tree stumps to sit on. The ground was hard and dry; a brittle shaft of grass poked into Julia's ankle, making her cry out.

Rosie looked around at the scrubby bushes and the withered ferns. 'I don't think there's anything here now,' she said. 'You know, elves and things.'

'No, no. You're right. Not now.'

They sat in silence a little longer.

'Perhaps you can swim when we get back,' suggested Julia.

'The pool's closed. Didn't you see the notice?'

'No, no I didn't.'

Rosie picked up a pebble and threw it at a tree stump. It ricocheted back to her feet.

'I'll show you a nice place where Aunty Nicola and I used to hide by the squash court.'

'Yep?'

'It's lovely. A *huge* fig tree and so easy to climb. We used to hide up there and then jump down and scare people.'

She laughed, but Rosie didn't.

'Shall we go back?'

Rosie looked up the hill, her shoulders slumped forward. Her face was blotched red. 'OK,' she said, her resignation obvious. She picked up a stick.

Julia felt a sudden pang of guilt. 'Tell you what, you can have a milkshake when we get back.'

'Do they do milkshakes? They don't look like a milkshake place.'

'Do they do milkshakes? Do they do milkshakes? Of course they do! The best chocolate milkshakes for miles around. Made with fresh farm milk.'

Rosie wasn't convinced. 'Maybe when you were young.'

'Come on,' said Julia. 'Onwards and upwards, as Gumpy would say.'

Where's Mom?

I look behind me. Mom is always at the back. It's our last day, our last walk.

Mom's not coming, says Dad.

And then, before I can ask why: Mom's tired. She needs a break from you two. Come on! Stop daydreaming. Onwards and...

Upwards, we chorus.

As they trudged up the hill and the hotel came in sight, Julia noticed that there were two distinct parts to it. There was the original low, white one-storey building, characteristic of many of the early hotels, which encompassed the reception, the dining room and the lounge; and a newer block of rooms on two levels, built around the late 1950s. She could see how it had developed out of a lonely stop-over for the first colonials into a moderately well-run establishment, appealing to those of moderate incomes and moderate aspirations.

A lonely stopover. Is that what it had been to them? Two images came to mind: Mom with her hair in curlers sitting on the verandah outside the room, reading *Fair Lady*. The smell of cigarette smoke, Berkley extra mild, spiralling above her mother's head. Dad back from a round of golf, sitting at the hotel bar, drinking a cold Castle, talking to whomever was near. 'Scram,' he said when he saw them at the window, looking in. 'Go and play.'

One, two, three! Coming ready or not!

I climb further into the thick green of the tree. The sunlight flickers through the cool shadows.

The nearer they got to the hotel, the more she felt a dark wisp of fear rise up from somewhere inside of her. She began to walk faster, trying not to look worried or afraid. Dad. She looked at her watch. Was that how long they had been away? Theirs had been a long journey. Surely he would still be asleep? She felt guilty, negligent. He wouldn't know where he was. He would come and look for her.

*The smell of the tree. The feel of the large, shiny leaves against my face. Sweet and cold. If I could just draw them back; if I could just part them. But I don't want to be seen. I can't be seen.*

She grabbed Rosie's hand. The girl glanced at her, surprised by the quick jerk of her mother's arm. They walked faster.

Why had they stopped coming?

He wouldn't have gone anywhere, would he? He wasn't interested in anything. He just wanted to be left alone.

What else? What else does she remember?

The path seemed to disappear. A clearing that opened between two bushes led nowhere. A strip of white sand meandered through stunted trees, but ended soon after. Why had they changed everything? Why hadn't it stayed the same?

*There were voices. Dad's voice and that of another man. Could I look now? Would the branch creak? What if I drew my foot up? What if I turned just a little to the right?*

They began to run. The sun was high in the sky now, and she wished she hadn't worn a long-sleeved top. Black-jacks stuck to the bottoms of her trousers, but she didn't want to stop. The hill seemed to grow steeper and steeper in front of them. If he had wandered off, would anyone try to stop him? There were the stream and the waterfall at the back of the hotel on the other side of the hill. What if he slipped?

They stopped running. They had reached the hotel garden and stood with their hands on their hips, trying to regain their breath. Julia struggled to calm herself, her throat contracting in a pain that extended into her chest, her ribs. It reminded her of another time, another pain.

Rosie started crying, but Julia pulled her along. Up the stairs, along the passage.

*You're going back. You're brave.*

*There is a fumbling sound, like someone undoing a belt. Then another sound. Soft, like mumbling, but getting louder. A deep moan, like someone in pain.*

Unlock. The door wouldn't budge, wouldn't open.

'Dad! She pounded her fists on the door. 'Dad can you hear me?'

*The leaves part. The world below shivers in shadows of green.*

'Dad!'

*Dad!*

*I smell cigarettes. Madison, for which there is no extra mild. He takes me by the collar and slams me against the wall. What did you see? For God's sake, tell me what you saw. Nothing. Nothing, I promise. A light flickers somewhere in his eyes. He lets go and I slump against the wall, holding my throat. I am sorry, he says. I am sorry.*

'Dad, I'm sorry. I left you too long.'

Dad sat on a chair looking out of the window. He turned his milky eyes towards her, and then back at a spot in front of him.

All that could be heard was Rosie's soft sobbing.

'I'm sorry. We'll get a milkshake.'

She shook her head, wiping her tears with the back of her hand. 'I want to go home. I don't like it here.'

*J*ulia knelt by the little girl and took her hands in hers. 'I'm sorry, Rosie. I'm sorry. It's my fault. I just panicked. Everything is okay.'

Rosie nodded.

'Dad?'

He was crying, too. Soft, slow tears made their way down his cheeks. She took out a handkerchief and wiped his face.

*That night, Mom puts on too much make-up. Her cheeks are red with lashes of blush, and her eyes purple and blue like two swollen bruises. They twitch nervously.*

*She drinks too much, and talks too loud in a bright, sad way. Jethro avoids us, but she keeps calling him over. He is tired. Unhappy. She sends the fish back three times for being in various states of cooked, none of which suits her. She lights a cigarette. Nicola waves the smoke away with her hand, but there is no stopping her.*

*Later, Dad closes the interconnecting doors between the two rooms, and Nicola and I lie in silence.*

*I hope we never come here again, says Nicola.*

*I think of the pool, the pink soap in the ladies' bathroom, the soft glade of trees at the back of the kitchen, the walk through the pine forest, how the trees reach out to touch you. An enchanted forest. I think of the dark warmth of the tree at the back of the squash courts. I think if I can climb higher, higher, higher...*

*I hope so, too, I say. But in the dark I cross my fingers.*

Eventually, she got through.

'Hello?' It was Rob's voice. 'Ah, the landline. How are the 1980s?'

'We're coming home. It's not the same...a bit run-down, if the truth be told.'

'I see.'

'And Dad – he needs familiarity. He...well, he likes what he has chosen to remember.'

It's an apology of sorts.

She puts the phone down.

It will do for now.

# The Match

*Troy Onyango*

*I*n the beginning, when he swipes right, he does not think much of it. He is new to the application, and he imagines that the workings are different from dating in the real world. And for the most part, it is different, but he is seventeen, fresh out of high school, and he is at home waiting for university admission, so he installs the app on his phone to while away time.

The match happens quickly, and when he receives the notification, he realises he has been fooled, or rather, he is a fool. There is no way the person in the photos could be the same person on the other end of the phone. Someone else must be using the photos to trick him. Regardless, with a bit of urging from the app ('what are you waiting for?'), he sends a message.

'Hi.'

Two days pass without a response. He checks daily, every few hours, to see if the message has been delivered, but there is no way of knowing. He thinks of sending a second message, a follow-up to the first (perhaps the person has an obvious disdain for people who send one-word messages), but he does not want to seem overly eager or to betray his inexperience.

And then, a message on the third day.

'Hi there.'

He is getting ready to go into town to help at the kitenge and kanga fabric shop his father runs, and he does not respond to the message. He thinks about it in the tuk-tuk on his way to the shop, but the large woman seated next to him has her prying eyes glued to his phone screen, and the scowl on her face tells him that she would pass judgement if he were to open the app. He ignores her, puts his palm over his screen, and reads the message again. If this is truly her, then he is the luckiest man alive.

It is a busy day at the shop, and he does not have much time to think about the message. He measures and cuts fabric while his father collects money and tells customers to come again. He listens to the slow Taarab music that seeps out of the small radio, and imagines listening to it with his newfound match, sprawled on the beach, the warm sand beneath their bodies, the blue sky above them, and the sound of the ocean slapping the shore lulling them.

The day drags its feet slowly; noon stretches out into a period that feels as if the sun is intent on burning everything on earth, leaving behind only ash and dust. He takes a torn piece of fabric from the floor and wipes sweat off his face and neck. His father tells him, 'The customers will think that is what we do with our fabric, Ismail.'

He drops it back on the floor and asks his father for fifty shillings to buy a bottle of water.

His father hands him thirty shillings and jokes, 'Only a camel needs that much water.'

On his way to the shop to get the water, he checks his phone. There is another message from her, but he is too terrified to open it. He wonders if out here in the open, in the wide streets with the sky above, Allah watches his actions. He knows Allah watches regardless, but he imagines that the safety of his room is different somehow. He waits.

His father closes the shop fifteen minutes early, saying business has been bad for the day. They walk home together. They pass the other fabric shops all in one line, then the row of Italian shops that sell better-quality fabric, and take business away from his father. It is quite a distance from the shop to the house, but Ismail enjoys the walk home. They don't say much to each other on the way, and he looks at the makuti-thatched houses and the small children playing in the sand. The silence between them is satisfying to both of them. That is how it has always been. In fact, he is still surprised that his father bought him a phone from his trip back from Dubai, but he knows that is his father's way of loving: of expressing the love he has stored in the crevices of the silence. He had shown his father his own way of loving by passing his exams. The dynamics, to someone watching them walk in silence, might seem strange, but father and son have their way, and it works.

His mother has prepared chicken biryani and he eats greedily, gulping every spoon of rice until his mother, who has been watching him, says, 'Don't eat with such greed, Ismail. You will choke.' She laughs and disappears into the kitchen.

He helps her wash the dishes, and his brother wipes them with a cloth. The evening is unusually quiet, except for the muezzin calling people to prayers. The crickets have not yet started chirping, and the bullfrogs are just finding their voices. They all sit on the verandah and watch the night, the breeze from the ocean blowing cool towards them. His mother tells them a story.

He tells his mother that he has a stomach ache and he wants to get some rest. She prays to Allah to keep him well, and he goes to his bedroom. He hears his father say, 'He has been distracted lately. I think it's that phone.'

His mother sighs, and goes on with her story for his younger brother.

Inside his room, he opens the application and sees the message.

'Are you there?'

'Yes. Sorry I was busy all day,' he responds. He wonders if he should ask how her day was. He is uncertain if this is even her. He closes the app and opens Google. He types her name and reads about her. He makes mental notes of the most important stuff.

She was born in England to a British father and an Italian mother.

Her family moved to New Jersey when she was still a baby.

She is either 32 or 35. (Media speculation about her age has revealed nothing.)

She sings blues, pop and hip-hop, and has won two Grammy awards.

She has been married twice and has two children with her current husband, a famous actor from the Caribbean.

He watches one of her songs, and realises that it was a popular song about five years ago. He wonders if he liked it.

The notification comes, and he opens it eagerly. She asks him what he is doing, and he responds by saying he is doing nothing, and then she goes quiet. Just like that. He thinks: *She is fake. Someone is using her photos to lie to me.*

On Google, he learns about catfishing. He reads every definition on Urban Dictionary. He is left more confused than he was before, but now he has learnt that there are people who use celebrities' photos to lie on dating apps. He is convinced that this is one of those cases.

*Forget about it, Ismail. There is no way one of the biggest celebrities in the world is chatting with you on a dating app. I mean, how is she even in Malindi?*

He types her name into Google again and adds the word 'Malindi'. Apart from a gossip blog tied to a former porn star, which mentions that her mother's side of the family owns a group of hotels in Africa, there is nothing. But this is Malindi, *not* Africa. He checks again, adding the word 'Kenya'. Now he sees that she has been to Nairobi before, in 2006. He clicks on the other pages until it asks if he wants to 'repeat the search with the omitted results included'.

He closes the tab.

*You are a fool, Ismail.*

He is drifting off to sleep when he opens the app and sees three dots that show she is typing. He wants to block her, but he decides to see what she has written.

'Are you feeling better? Do you want me to make you some tea?' His mother's voice, shrill but steady, startles him. Her small figure is leaning against the frame where there is no door, and he wishes at such moments that there was one so he could lock it and have some privacy. She walks in, sits on his bed and touches his forehead with her slender, henna-painted hands, as if a stomach ache would show itself in that way. She asks him if he is okay and tells him, in a whisper, that his father thinks his new phone is distracting him. He wants to admit that this is true, but he knows it will mean something else to his parents – a go-ahead to take the phone from him – and he is not ready for that yet.

Once his mother leaves, he checks the app. There is a message from her.

'Come to my hotel.'

He looks at the message and switches off his phone.

*I*n the morning, he tells his father that he is too sick to go to the shop. His father tells him to stay at home and get some rest. His brother has left for school, and he is left at home with his mother. He goes to the sitting room and watches her clean the house while she hums along to the Bongo songs on the television. Occasionally, she asks if he is feeling better and if she can bring him tea. Feeling guilty, he declines her offers of kindness, and she goes on with her chores.

'Hey. You went silent.'

'Sorry. I fell asleep,' he lies. His parents would never allow him to leave the house at night. The government has been cracking down on terrorists and radicals, and any Muslim boy his age found out and about at night is picked up the next morning with bullets in his body. Also, he doesn't really know if she is the person in the profile. He decides to ask her.

'Is that you in the photos?'

'Yes. That's me.'

He realises that if anyone was going to catfish him, they wouldn't admit this if questioned.

'Prove it.'

'Well, it's me. I'm on vacation at our family hotel here. Just taking a small break,' she responds.

He wonders how to proceed with the conversation, if there is a way of verifying her identity, without seeming like an amateur, without annoying her in case it turns out that it truly is her.

'Um, okay. I just didn't think someone as big as you would be on this app.'

'Big?'

'Yes, a big celeb.'

'Ah well, things are far more complex than you think. Plus this town is dead anyway, and the few people around don't imagine that it's actually me.'

He spends the rest of the afternoon on the sofa trying to verify her identity, asking her questions about herself and typing her responses into Google to check if they are true. Family. Songs.

Awards. Everything matches. If he is being catfished, this person must have done a proper background check on her.

In the late afternoon, his mother goes to the market to get the ingredients for the evening meal. Before she leaves, she announces that she plans to make coconut rice with fried catfish, and heads off with a big basket under her arm. It will be at least two hours before she comes back.

He sends her a message asking if she wants to meet. She does not respond.

*T*he following day, he is at his father's shop snipping fabric and sweating in the sweltering heat when a message comes in. He stops everything, and the white-and-yellow fabric falls on the dusty floor, getting soiled in the process. His father sees this and walks over to him, hand raised as if about to slap him – but he takes his phone away instead.

'Akh! Ismail, this phone is making you act like a fool. I should never have given it to you.'

He feels a hole inside, for if his father giving him this phone was his way of showing his love, then taking it away is the equivalent of taking back that love. He watches as his visibly annoyed father, who is grumbling about the loss of the soiled fabric, locks the phone in the drawer where he keeps his money. Then he takes his cap off, wipes the sweat off the bald patch on his head and smiles at the queue of customers, while apologising profusely for Ismail's incompetence.

'These children of nowadays…'

The rest of the afternoon, he wonders if she has tried to reach him. He worries that she might be upset with him, and block him or never talk to him again. *What if she leaves to go back to her country thinking that I didn't want to meet her?*

In the evening, after his father has handed back the phone to him, he tells him that he is going to meet his friend Abu so that they can go and watch the match between Man City and Chelsea at the video shop. He remembers too late that his father, who is also a Chelsea fan, knows that the match is not until tomorrow. But his father only says, 'Make sure you come back home early. Your mother will be worried.'

'Sawa, Baba.' He runs in the opposite direction to Abu's home, leaving his father shaking his head. On the way, he remembers overhearing his father once saying to his mother, 'Mama Ismail, when children reach a certain age, they no longer belong to you. You can only pray to Allah and trust that the upbringing you gave them will serve them well.'

*H*e gets back home earlier than expected and heads straight to his bedroom. His mother follows, asking him through the door, 'Is it that stomach again, Ismail?'

He grunts, and his mother promises him that he will be better in the morning, and if not, they will go into town and see the doctor. In truth, his stomach is fine. Everything in his body is okay. The emptiness in his stomach comes from the feeling that he has wasted his time talking to her. He vows to uninstall the application and move on with his life. He will wait for his university admission, go and study to become the engineer he has always dreamed of becoming. He will come back home and marry the good girl, from a good family, with a good upbringing, chosen specifically for him. His hand lingers over his phone screen as he thinks about all this. He opens the app.

'Sorry, I didn't mean to ghost on you. I spotted some paparazzi a few minutes before you showed up. I have to be careful. I'm sorry if you were upset.'

'Are you there?'

'Hey, I suppose you don't want to talk.'

'Hi Ismail. Please, I'm sorry.'

She sends more messages, but he ignores them.

*E*ventually, unable to bring himself to uninstall the app and go on ignoring her, he responds. He tells her it is fine and agrees that she has to be careful. He is now convinced that she is a celebrity. She tells him she is relieved that he understands. What she does not know is he has spent the past three days sulking, barely eating and not talking to anyone, his mother always asking, 'Ha Ismail, what is wrong?' and his father saying, 'Let him be. The boy is becoming a man.'

His heartbreak heals when she suggests meeting him. They agree on a Thursday evening.

Right after his father closes the shop, he makes up another lie, and goes to the hotel to meet her. At the gate, the watchman lets him in without the usual harassment Ismail has seen accorded to beach boys and young guys looking for work.

He notices her on the balcony, a figure so beautiful and unhuman-like that he stands there at the gate and wonders if she is an angel. He is dazed until she signals for him to come up to where she is. He takes the stairs instead of the lift, and when he gets to the fourth floor, he is panting and sweating. He takes a moment to cool off before knocking, and she opens the door.

It is her, without a single doubt, standing in front of him.

*T*hey have sex in which he struggles to stay on top of her because of his lean frame and the fact that he has only done it once before – with a girl with catlike eyes named Khadija. (She cried all through the act, and he wondered if he was doing it correctly, but she had nodded to urge him on. He never heard nor saw her again.) His breathing is loud, and he is embarrassed when he is unable to finish, but she pats his head in a reassuring yet unsettling manner, and tells him he was perfect.

She gives him a blowjob. Nothing. Afterwards, they have nothing to talk about. They lie on the bed and listen to the sounds of the street below. A tuk-tuk roars. Someone calls the name of a child, and he has no idea if it is a boy or a girl. The gate opens and closes. He tilts his head towards her and scans her body. He marvels at how smooth and flawless her skin is, and the only spots on her body are her two darkened nipples and pubic hair that looks like fur. And yet, as she lies here next to him, she seems like any other woman. He watches her chest rise and fall.

'My family owns this hotel,' she declares, breaking the silence inside the room.

He does not know what to do with this information. He fidgets and stares at the whitewashed walls and the badly done paintings of the Big Five animals under acacia trees in the sunset. The painter's name is signed at the bottom, and he wonders if that is a sign of pride in the work.

'My grandfather – my mother's father – came here in the 1980s and built three hotels. This is the smallest and most private. My family has been coming here since I was a child.' Her voice is thin, like she is not used to talking. It sounds different when she sings in her music videos.

He leaves the hotel at dusk with the promise to see her again. Before he goes, she kisses him on the mouth and asks, 'How old are you, Ismail?'

'Nineteen,' he says, hoping his voice doesn't betray him.

She smiles. 'Perfect.'

*F*riday is for prayers and he does not go to see her. Right after the Jum'ah, he watches all her songs on YouTube and masturbates to one of her earlier videos, made when she was around his age. She has blonde hair in the video, and is wearing a spaghetti-string top and a skirt that shows her legs and thighs. Afterwards, he kneels on his mat and asks Allah to forgive him.

Before he sleeps, he messages her to tell her he misses her.

She does not respond.

They see each other again on Saturday evening. They have sex again, and it is better this time. He fucks her slowly – in chunks, with controlled thrusts – and cups her breasts in his hands like he saw in a porn clip Abu once showed him. His breathing is the hum of a generator, and he ignores her loud moans and trains his mind to listen to something else. A bird cooing lazily but noisily. He thrusts faster. The gate creaking open. Steady. The droning dragged-out call of the muezzin. She is shaking, her thighs clasped around his waist. Allahu akbar! He comes inside her.

The world is silent in his head.

They are quiet for a while as they catch their breath. Soon, they talk about her music, and she tells him she is releasing an album. He is glad to hear this, having learnt to like her music. They talk about her husband, and she tells him they have been having marital problems, and are to divorce; that is why she is here. They talk about her children, and she says she is going to give full custody to her husband so that she can focus on her music.

They do not talk about him.

They have sex again, and he leaves at dusk.

At home, his mother asks why he is in such a good mood. He does not respond and eats his pilau, devouring it slowly as if he wants to feel the taste as it travels through his gut. His mother looks at him and smiles.

'Is it a girl?' she asks.

He drinks from his cup of water while his father's piercing eyes watch.

He goes to bed early and watches more of her music videos. He types her name into Google yet again, and checks the news. He finds out that she has indeed filed for divorce. He reads the blog, but it offers no concrete information apart from speculation about possible infidelity by her husband with an Australian who won Best Supporting Actress at the Academy Awards three years ago. He tries to find more information, but all the other websites have copied from the blog, simply adding different images of her husband and her.

He wonders if he is part of her plan to get back at her husband.

He searches for the hotel name and checks TripAdvisor, where the hotel has a rating of three stars and has been praised for the privacy it offers to its clientele. Below these comments are accusations of racism. One man whose avatar has no photo has written: 'Fuck this hotel! I came here for honeymoon with my wife and they would not let me in, saying that I was a beach boy. Shame on establishments in Kenya that treat Kenyans like second-rate citizens.' He tries to imagine what the man looks like, he tries to imagine what must have transpired between the man and the watchman at the gate, he tries to imagine the man's new bride, but he fails.

He falls asleep still looking at the page.

The next morning, he receives a message from her saying that she has to fly back to New York. He asks if they can meet one last time, and she says it is not safe. He types a long message saying he understands, thanking her for the wonderful time he has spent with her, and wishing her well. He adds that he looks forward to listening to her new album when it is released. When he hits 'send', he realises that she has blocked him.

He deletes his final message and uninstalls the app from his phone.

He listens to her music every night.

$\mathcal{T}$he new album, titled 'Fire in Malindi' is a success, and Ismail reads that the critics have praised her for the ability to make music with such raw honesty and passion. He downloads it illegally off some site where he is required to skip several ads. He listens to it every morning on his way to class at the university where he is studying mechatronic engineering. He is happy for her, and soon learns to forget how her body felt when he was with her. He knows he will never see her again.

He goes back home for the holidays. That same period, he learns from a gossip blog that she has reconciled with her husband and given birth to a baby boy, whose name is some Swahili word he has never heard before. She does a photoshoot and the photos get more than five million likes on Instagram. He adds his likes too, and comments with a love symbol, but his is lost in the sea of responses. Some media house buys the photos of her baby for two million dollars. He follows every news update, gulping every detail he finds.

He reads the latest gossip blog. He goes down on his knees and prays to Allah. He gets up from the mat and checks again. The blog says the paternity test is not conclusive, but her husband has released a statement saying he doubts very much that he is the father of the child. Ismail wonders if the child could be his. Filled with a sense of dread, he lets out a prolonged wail.

His mother calls out from the kitchen: 'Ismail, is it that stomach again?'

# Mr Thompson

*Noel Cheruto*

$\mathcal{A}$ fool who is yet to come to terms with the breadth of his foolishness. That's who you are, Mr Thompson. A giant loophole pretending to be a person. It is the only reason I can trick you. That, and the fact that you think me foolish. The wine you sip – tilting your angular chin and sticking your slender nose up in the air – that wine is not a Chablis. You believe it is, though, so does it matter that I decanted a three- hundred-shilling bottle into an old Chablis one? I served it yesterday, as the crisp Chardonnay that went perfectly with your grilled tilapia. I will serve it tomorrow as the woody Elgin I will recommend for your dinner. It doesn't matter what you do, Mr Thompson. You are here. I will eat off you. I am only doing what I must.

We can spend all day, Mr Thompson, going back and forth through history, trying to catch the exact moment that made me this way. We can comb through the days, sort them and stack them in piles, looking closely at each one, wondering whether that was the one that changed me. The truth is, everything did. Every event, good and bad, chipped away at my goodness. I ignored them in the beginning: a rude guest here, late salary there, long hours everywhere. Little things that did not seem to matter in the moment, but collectively, silently, they spun a web around me. One day, I woke up, and there was no me. Just a cold pile of meat hidden behind a backlog of disillusionment. I woke and drew the curtain, then closed it again when it hit me; whether the sun rose or stayed under my feet, it made no difference to me. It was the morning after I fired Nancy, the chambermaid.

There was only one word to describe Nancy – practical. Her skirts, wide, circular and falling just below her knees, were practical. Her fingers, chubby with clean square nails, were practical. Even her nose was practical; just enough nose to breathe in a practical amount of air. She was the only chambermaid then, working through the morning to turn out all twenty rooms before the midday check-in rush. Our whole operation depended on her, which was unfortunate because she was a regular no-show.

This would mean pulling on a pair of yellow rubber gloves and cleaning the rooms myself. I was young, Mr Thompson. Youth is a terrible curse, especially because it comes wrapped in naivety. I would spend the first hour of my work days dialling her number continuously. If I was lucky, she would answer irritably and let me know she was on her way. Most days, though, her phone would go unanswered. Back then, my heart was warm and crippled with feeling. I could not bring myself to fire Nancy, not even after finding out that her absence was because she moonlighted at the Regency. Her whole clan depended on her sole income.

One time, she did not come to work for three miserable days. When she finally did, I followed her around, staring at her practical canvas shoes while summoning the courage to scold her. Sometimes, especially after having had to clean up behind a particularly hairy person, I fantasised about the things I would do to Nancy. They mostly involved shouting wildly at her, then dismissing her and laughing at her tears. In reality, I could not even bring myself to look her in the eye.

I sat on the entertainment stand in Room 8, resting my feet against the back of an armchair. I watched her make the bed, spreading white linen over it by holding one edge and flinging the opposite up in the air, then waiting as it fell back over the mattress with a gentle sigh. She walked around the bed, stopping at intervals to bend over and tuck in the loose edges. She worked as though she was automated – taking the exact same number of steps in every direction. When she was done, she took a steam iron from the cupboard, sliding the door shut slowly, repeating it a little more sharply when the cupboard light failed to turn off. She winced at the clap of plywood against plywood, uneven teeth gritting, eyes sinking deep into a cluster of wrinkles.

I sat, tipping the armchair, using my toes against the back edge to play a game of balance. Nancy plugged the iron in, and it hissed into life. She flattened one half of the bedspread, then turned off the iron, walked around the bed, plugged it in on the other side and flattened the next half. Each wrinkle disappeared under a puff of steam. When she was finished, the bed stood proudly in the middle of the room, an altar of perfection.

'Do you love your job?' I asked, following her to the bathroom where she picked up dirty towels off the floor, gathering them into a large ball which she threw into a cart parked outside the door. My voice was high and squeaky. I cleared my throat and leaned against the bathroom door. I was afraid, Mr Thompson, that she would see that I was afraid.

'It pays the bills,' she said, squirting blue liquid soap into the bathtub. The white tub turned into a child's piece of art. She crouched and used a stiff brush to scrub. I watched as white suds slowly found their way up her hands. She did not wear gloves, just bare hands, dark against clouds of foam.

'Why, then, did you not come yesterday? You didn't call in sick, nothing, just did not come at all. Why, Nancy?' I shifted my weight from one foot to the next. I was terribly uncomfortable, Mr Thompson. I could see her scalp through her cropped hair. It is a terrible thing to stand over someone whom you resent and pity in equal measure. She was older than my own mother.

'I was sick, my family was sick, we were all sick,' she said, not looking at me, rinsing off the porcelain, cupping her hands under the tap and aiming water at particularly soapy parts.

'That can't be true, Nancy. Next time, pick one person and label them sick. Assigning disease to your whole family is too dramatic.' I was trying to help her along. I was a new manager; she was a new chambermaid. Nobody knew what they were doing. We all just wanted to get by.

'Okay, okay, only my son was sick, that's the truth,' she lied. I sighed, and let her off with a sharp look and a disapproving shake of the head. I could not bring myself to fire her. I found out later that she moonlighted at The Regency, and whenever the morning crew failed to turn up, she was compelled to pull double shifts. I resorted to praying hard that she would show up.

I had to let her go a few months later when I caught her going home with a packet of stolen salt hidden underneath her blouse. I was deeply shaken, Mr Thompson. I felt the cold settle deep within my bones. Here was a woman who worked seventeen hours a day every day, yet was too poor to afford salt? The system was obviously flawed. I saw it clearly in that moment. There is no justice, only tricks to keep you going. We only have one of two choices: do, or get done.

Don't look at me like that, Mr Thompson. Our differences make us exactly alike. Should I have sought work at The Regency? Well, I did not. Probably for the same reason you chose not to stay there. I was once invited for an interview there. Right after my training, back when I foolishly believed that everyone had in them the power to make a change. I laugh at the thought now: how naïve was I? The truth is, most of us are simply pawns, moving up and down some other person's chessboard. We live in a tragedy, Mr Thompson, but tragedies, too, can be beautiful.

Years earlier, I walked into The Regency through the back, into a long laundry room, lined on either side by silver washing machines. Ladies wearing stiff blue frocks with hairnets over their hair bent over large buckets, sorting through bed linens and stuffing them into coloured bins. They laughed and gossiped loudly, pointing me through to the exit without taking their eyes off their hands. I took a wrong turn and found myself in a large kitchen. The heat made my shirt cling to my back. Chefs in white jackets served food out of steaming pots onto plates that lined a counter against which several waiters leaned, notebooks in hand. I moved quickly, cowering at insults from a tall chef in a tall hat who screamed at me to 'get out of my bloody kitchen now, fool!'

Nothing in my life had prepared me for the sight that met my eyes when I burst through the restaurant and into the lobby through a side door. From where I stood, the marble rolled out through the vastness of the room. The walls were made of spotless glass so that it looked as though the outside was inside. The air smelt of mint, from the drinks in short glasses on silver trays that beautiful ladies in little white dresses walked around offering to guests. It amazed me how the staff, dressed in different uniforms to symbolise their variety of roles, moved. They floated soundlessly from guest to guest, so that they looked invisible but available, as in a dream. It was obvious that I did not belong there. I walked back out, careful to avoid the kitchen on my way. No one ever called to ask me why I did not show up. My spot was probably filled before I even crossed the street.

I thought it through recently while I hid in Room 3, sipping real Chablis from a three-hundred-shilling wine bottle. I burrowed down between the crisp, white sheets and really thought about it. Why did I walk away? Would I do the same if I got that opportunity now? I really don't know, Mr Thompson. Obviously, The Regency does not have silly problems like the accountant running off with our pay or me having to work as the manager, waiter, receptionist and everything in between. I am sure their staff doesn't get told to 'just put on anything black and white' as uniforms. I also know that they have good medical cover and transport arrangements. Everything works at The Regency. The system is orderly. But you must show up every day. And work. Not walk up and down the stairs, pretending to work. That sounds like too much trouble to me. I know my way around here. I know how to get the most out of doing the least.

Do you feel the same, Mr Thompson? At three in the morning when you come in with girls a third your age hanging off your elbow? I saw you on Thursday, Mr Thompson. I did. I was there to check in the newlyweds arriving from Dubai. I told the driver to wake me when they were five minutes away, then slumped over my desk trying to catch the last of my sleep. That was when I heard giggles from across the lobby. I looked up to see four girls with big behinds stuffed into undersized pants. You were outside pulling at your cigarette before throwing it on the ground and stomping on it. The yellow taxis parked across the street blinked their lights at you, hopeful for one last fare before daybreak. One of the girls had her arm draped around your shoulder, using you as a walking stick. She was a good head taller than you, although that could have been as a result of the hideously high heels she had on.

What do you do with them, Mr Thompson? What *can* you do

with them? You are old and hairless. Your skin has given up on your muscles and decided to gather around your elbows and knees in protest. Your back does not stay upright for more than a breath. What use do you have for a swan of giggling girls in your room? Is that why you choose to stay here and not at The Regency? So that no one asks you these questions?

I could be wrong, Mr Thompson. It could be this location that made you choose to stay here. Right in the middle of everything that you might need. Or it could be the sunshine that washes in through the tall windows as you have your morning coffee; the exact right temperature most of the year. It could also be the silence we all work hard to keep.

We do treasure the silence that rings through the corridors. That is why we choose not to have music in the lift. Yes, Mr Thompson, that is intentional. Our guests, too, are admitted by what we judge is their ability to contain their noise within their room. I made a mistake once, when my cloak of naivety was still over me. I checked in a mother with four children to Room 16.

She wore her hair in large brown ringlets that framed her face, falling just below her ears. Her hips were the width of the twin pram she pushed in front of her. Twin boys, judging from how they were clad, slept peacefully next to each other in the pram, little fingers curled affectionately around each other. A little girl hid behind her mother's skirt, peeking up at me once every few minutes, her round eyes full of fear. Her hair was gathered into bunches that were held in place by a rainbow of rubber bands. A fourth child, a boy, the eldest, ran around the reception area, annoying and charming other guests in equal measure. He took off his shoes and started to skid from one end of the room to the other.

I gathered them into the elevator and up to their room. The mother walked beside me, chatting, at first shyly, then quickly gathering momentum every time I nodded in agreement. Within ten minutes, I knew what she was in town to do – wait for her husband, who was on his way back home from working in Somalia

– and how long they would stay: three days. I settled them into their room, then went down to the basement to find spare baby cots and bassinets for her children.

It only took me eight minutes, Mr Thompson, to get back into the room. I know because when I opened the door, I was so shocked that I looked down at my watch to see how long I had been gone. The screaming reverberated off the walls so that I could not exactly tell where it came from. The mother was waiting by the dressing mirror, applying lipstick and removing it with a baby wipe. Again, and again, without thinking. Her eyes were glazed over. She must have lived through this too many times to care.

There was a splash of green on the ceiling. It looked like someone had flung a cup of green soup and smashed it against the plaster, just missing the overhead light. Bits of glass and green chunks were spread across the bed. The girl, who had stripped off her shyness like a jacket on a hot day, dangled upside down from the curtain rod shouting, 'Call me Mowgli!' Her little ankles, trapped in the space between curtain rod and wall, supported the entire weight of her body. She twisted her arms about, fingers wiggling in excitement.

Yet her voice was not the loudest in the room. The boy was everywhere I looked: under the wooden desk, yanking cables and squealing as they came off the wall with a sharp click, on top of the mini fridge, fingers reaching in and fishing out miniature bottles and flinging them across the room, sending the sharp whiff of good whisky up my nostrils, in the bathroom, washing his hands with shampoo and splashing it all over the mirror. The twins, who I could now see were toddlers, were on the floor, wailing.

I stood transfixed as I watched their mother calmly detangling her curls. She turned to me with a defeated look, not really asking for help. There was one poison apple in the lot, I noticed. The boy. His energy was infectious, rubbing off on the rest. All I needed to do was silence him. I tried to bribe him, catching him in the stillness between his movements and offering money, fruit, water. Nothing seemed to work. In the end, I took him firmly by the head and pulled him out of the room. This made him screech even louder. I led him out into the lobby and sat him sternly down by the window. Behind me, the rest fell into an unsure silence. The whole place was back in the quiet. We treasure quiet out here. We will do anything for it.

That is why, Mr Thompson, this is a conversation I will have with myself in my head as I watch you sip wine. I, too, am a fool. A fool who chooses to stay foolish. And when you call for me, I will ask simply, 'How was your day, Mr Thompson?'

# A Miracle in Valhalla

*Fred Nnamdi*

*J*ude always had a way with people. He and I were co-tenants in a compound at the start of Chinda Street. We'd become friends shortly after he moved into the self-contained room adjacent to the two-bedroomed flat I shared with my wife. He had intervened on the compound's behalf the day PHCN officials embarked on their monthly exercise of disconnecting defaulters. All the other tenants had been out at work at the time, and, but for Jude's assistance in paying off the outstanding debts, the compound would have been disconnected from the main grid. As the caretaker, I'd ensured his complete reimbursement the following day, and, in an additional show of gratitude, had taken him out for a few drinks afterwards. We became more than just acquaintances thereafter.

He had a charming personality, which explained the numerous visitors at his apartment. There were the young men with their raucous laughter and fancy haircuts who smoked and drank and hung out late into the nights, and there were the pretty ladies with their throaty moans and chuckles, who swept his verandah each morning dressed in his shirts, their long legs bare. I envied him; his exuberance, his bold carelessness.

Jude was largely unemployed for the better part of the four years I knew him. I'd read from his tenancy agreement forms that he was a polytechnic graduate who engaged in regular skilled jobs, as well as the odd business deal to meet his needs. I'd also often heard him say that, save for the desperation that a regular monthly income helped to abate, he wasn't sure he'd ever need a job. He believed salaries were no adequate recompense for the modern-day slavery people had come to accept as employment.

I would soon begin to visit his apartment or hang out on his verandah during idle moments, mostly in the evenings after returning from my civil service work at the State Secretariat. Sometimes we'd play a game of draughts and share a drink; other times I'd go simply for the company, after which I'd return home and quarrel with Celine through most of the night because she had peeped through the windows and seen me flirting with one or another of Jude's girlfriends. It didn't take too long after that for his apartment to begin to feel like a second home, a respite from the many disagreements that characterised the union of two people who had no business engaging in cohabitation.

It was on one such occasion that he introduced me to Valhalla Hotel and Suites at the tail end of Chinda Street, a five-minute walk from our compound, beyond a row of zinc shacks. The hotel had been completed two years before Jude's arrival in the neighbourhood, but until that evening I had neither visited, nor expected to visit its premises. I remember returning from work that day, tired and itching to freshen up, only to find that the door to our apartment was locked and the drapes drawn. Celine, who worked shifts at a shopping mall, was supposed to be off that day, which was the reason I hadn't taken my personal bunch of keys to work with me. I rang her mobile.

She picked up on the fifth ring. 'Eh hen?'

'Where are you?'

'I went out.'

'The door is locked.'

'Eh hen?'

'What do you mean "Eh hen"?'

No answer.

'Am I not talking to you?'

Still nothing.

'Celine…'

She snapped, 'Don't you have key again?'

'You didn't know I left it when I went out this morning?'

A pause, then, 'I went to see Mama Victory. I'm not done. You will have to wait.'

'What do you mean wait? I should stand outside and wait for you to finish your women's gossip? You're testing me Celine, you're—'

She'd already hung up.

I lashed out. At the door. I kicked and punched and scratched and tore. The metal was unperturbed. We had argued the previous night; she about my mother's interference in our marriage's childlessness, myself about her unceasing bickering, which I blamed on her barrenness. I'd enjoyed the hurt in her eyes when I'd used the word. It meant I'd won. Now locking me out was her means of exacting revenge.

I found a loose brick somewhere in the compound and was about to smash in the lock when Jude's door opened and he peered out.

'Bros welcome, o,' he greeted.

The shame that tempered my rage caused me to mope at the floor. 'Thank you, Jude.'

'How far na?' He was looking at the brick in my grip. At the edge of his features was the mischievous glint with which he often taunted me whenever he succeeded in making me feel silly for lashing out at Celine.

I was still puffing. 'I dey.'

He chuckled, shook his head. 'Come make we comot. There's a place I want to show you.'

'I'm just coming from work, I haven't even—'

'Madam went out. She may not come back soon. If you break the door, you will still pay someone to repair it.'

He had me. I dropped the brick.


$T$he premises of Valhalla Hotels belied the environment in which it was situated. The mowed lawns and paved walkways lined with trimmed hedges were in stark contrast to the potholed undulating dust of Chinda Street and beyond. From outside, the edifice was a replica of an Olympian temple, complete with massive pillars. Walls of marble and high windows reflected the evening lights that were just starting to come on. Inside, the lobby was a vast space with antique-style furniture arranged as though in expectation of some great assembly. A gold-plated sign in Old Norse hung from the ceiling just beyond the main entrance. A bracketed translation beneath it read: Odin's Great Hall. Reception was in a decorated cave at the end of the hall. I had never before seen anything like it.

That first night we had a few drinks, and Jude introduced me to the owner, Chief Bruno Mbuh, popularly known as Exec. In the weeks and months that followed, we became regular patrons of the establishment.

Then the motorcycle accident occurred, the one that lodged shards of shattered glass in my cornea and made it impossible for me to see any more. I was still in hospital when Jude brought the news that Celine had moved her things out of our apartment. I wasn't surprised: she'd barely tolerated me when I was in good shape. She'd come to see me in the hospital only once, four days after the crash, two days before she moved out. My old mother, perched by my bedside when Jude brought the news, broke into songs of celebration, relieved that I was now unhindered from finding a better woman, one who could bear children. A few weeks later, once I was able to manage without much assistance, I sent my mother back to the village.

I also lost my job. The procurement department where I worked had no facilities to cater for the needs of the disabled, stated the compulsory retirement letter that Jude read aloud to me. I received my benefits in full, as well as sympathy contributions from colleagues. With these, I was able to pay for my surgery and settle other bills accrued in the course of treatment.

The oculists thought I was lucky. They said the splinters had stayed away from my iris and therefore hadn't caused any serious damage, and they were almost certain that within six months, as soon as the wounds had healed, I would regain partial, if not complete, use of my eyes. Three months after the accident, I was discharged from the hospital, with weekly appointments to monitor my progress. Six months arrived, passed, and became a year. By the eighteenth month, the veil of darkness still persisted.

I learned to adapt, my senses of smell and hearing becoming sufficient in meeting my basic needs. I even started to learn to read braille, so that I could become employable once more. It kept my mind occupied against those occasional feelings of helplessness that overwhelmed me whenever pessimistic thoughts about my predicament emerged.

Jude was supportive. He got me a stick, the foldable kind, and huge Raybans. He visited often with his friends, who asked me questions.

'What's it like?'

'Is it painful?'

'Are you seeing black, or white? Or just a collage of colours like when you normally close your eyes?'

He made me guess who was who. They wouldn't talk, I'd feel their faces and arms, sometimes sniff.

'No dey tap current, my guy!'

He made boring jokes. All the time. When he cut my hair, he turned me to face the mirror. 'What do you think?' he'd ask. 'Look and tell me.'

We once played a game: things you don't need eyes for.

'Eating,' I offered.

'Bathing.'

'Sleeping.'

A dubious pause.

'What?' I asked.

'I see in my dreams.'

'Idiot. How about fucking?'

'What?'

'Fucking.'

He burst out laughing.

He taunted me when we went on daytime walks. 'Mehn see that chick, see nyash … see hips.' Or, 'Blind Bart, come let's go sit at the junction and sing. People will give us money. You can't be broke when God has blessed you this much.'

In the evenings, we still went to Valhalla together. Chief Mbuh was nice. He gave me money, and ensured I received as much comfort as was possible. We sat in the Great Hall, but often, especially on Sunday evenings when patrons moved to the bush bar to watch local artists perform, Jude left with them. He'd attempt a weak joke: 'Come make we go look woman.'

And it was while I sat in the lobby on one of those Sundays that I picked up the words of a televangelist. His teachings weren't so much religious or spiritual as inspirational. They were what I needed.

'Who was the guy talking?' I asked Jude as he led me back home later that night.

'Which one? The guy in a black shirt?'

It was too dark to make my it's-not-funny face. 'On the television. The one with the melodious voice.'

'Oh, that guy. They call him Daddy GO. I don't know his real name.' He paused, then, 'Oboy, you don desperate o. When did you start believing in miracles?'

'Well, if you were in my shoes, you'd be grasping for something to hold on to.'

'But surely not fake pastors with their unrealistic promises?'

'How do you know which pastor is fake, or which miracles are real? I think you're judging this the wrong way. Real or fake, I know I felt the touch of the supernatural just from listening to him, something got involved … something huge. God, hope, freakish coincidence, whatever. And that was enough.'

It became routine thereafter: Sunday evenings at eight. Daddy G. O. and I, with Jude leading me to the appointments. A few times he plugged in his mobile and thumbed at it, or chatted with the hotel workers. But most evenings, he left while I watched. Or listened, rather.

*T*hings continued in this way. Most nights by 8pm, patrons of the Valhalla Great Hall had either left for their homes or retired to their lodgings, and I was left alone. But on this evening, Sade and Gloria's voices kept carrying across the length of the empty space of the reception cave to where I sat in front of the television. I'd been considering turning to ask them to keep it down, but knowing Sade the receptionist, she was likely to take offence, retort with some nasty remark, and even increase the volume of their conversation. She's a hornet's nest that one, best left unstirred.

Jude had already gone. It would have been easier if he had been the one appealing to the women on my behalf, as he was better acquainted with them. Also, he'd been putting the moves on Gloria, the recently hired laundry lady who, he'd whispered to me, had one of the most well-endowed chest regions he had encountered. In my frustration, I kept wishing he'd had his wooing game on that night.

Just then the swing doors were thrown open and the air that pushed in carried smells of stale sweat and smoke, mixed with too much perfume and some other thing I couldn't quite place. I heard two pairs of footfalls, heavy, not refined like the usual guests; boots I was guessing, probably Timberlands. They headed away from me towards reception.

The sound of chitchat from the ladies died quickly, the way it often would whenever guests or would-be lodgers came in, leaving only the television speakers to continue in Daddy G. O's voice. It was sweet relief, albeit temporary, and I reclined further into the armchair, a purring selfish cat.

Still, the rough voices managed to penetrate my concentration so that I was now half-listening in.

'We want to see Exec.'

'You have an appoint...?' Sade's voice.

'What?'

'Is he expecting...?'

'No. Is he around?' A local accent, irritated.

'Where are you from and what is the nature of your visit?' Sade's nonchalance delivered questions that people like myself, who hung around all evening, had grown accustomed to, might even have committed to memory.

'...Plenty plenty question be this ones?' The spokesman was getting impatient. 'I say we want to see Exec ... inside or not?'

Now this was interesting. Whoever this was, he'd just worsened the situation. Sade's sauciness preceded her for miles, to the extent that patrons advised one another not to engage the fair lady at reception, no matter the provocation. I'd also witnessed others who, upon checking out, had sworn never to visit the Valhalla premises again so long as Sade was still in its employ. Her temper was attached to a very short fuse. Any perceived hostilities, and she'd assume her 'bitch-this-is-my-territory-behave-or-fuck-off' mien, after which an ignorant yet persistent opponent might be given a taste of the caustic contents of her mouth, as well as the artistic skill of her well-sharpened talons and teeth, should the quarrel assume a more physical nature. She could never get the sack as it was rumoured that she was closely related to the proprietor. The busybody inside me ached for the Nollywood-type drama that was likely to unfold soon.

'Okay, go and find your Exec na.'

There was a drawn-out hiss and a slight pause before she resumed her chat with Gloria. 'So my sister, that is what he said to me o, that he may be married but still wants to taste out of the honey...'

Gloria's screech of laughter, louder now than before, reverberated through the wide hall, complete with the claps that usually accentuate a gossip session. I wondered what kind of hell was about to be let loose.

'See this BST....' Yes, he was furious now. '...Ordinary secretary ... na play we come play?' I wondered who he was asking.

His companion, quiet the whole time, started, 'Dis na Vikings o, na Vikings be dis o, na Vikings dey here, dis na Vikings...'

'I say we want to see Exec and you dey jonze us. Dey use us do guy. In fact, everybody come outside here now.'

'Jeezuz!.' Gloria sounded startled.

'Na Vikings be dis o...'

'Hay God!' Sade exclaimed.

'Come out, come out here and lie down!'

'Dis na Vikings...'

The hushed alertness from both ladies, as well as their hastened footsteps, gave me an idea of the happenings. These weren't lodgers wanting to stay the night. They were trouble, the wrong kind of trouble. And now Sade had succeeded in getting their attention with her big mouth. Things might soon get out of hand. I heard some pushing and scraping and grunting.

'If you move, I'll blow ya head…'

From where I sat, I wondered if I was supposed to be afraid, but dismissed the thought. In learning to cope with my visual impairment, I'd become used to being easily forgotten whenever I was in a gathering. Once people got over the early expressions of sympathy and the awkward silences that usually followed, they were quick to turn their attentions to other subjects. Then I became hardly a bother, much less a threat. I was more or less a pet someone brought to a sitout. Whatever could these fellows want with me?

'You know who I be? You dey talk to me anyhow. For dis our Potacult. You will see today. Where your phone? Give me your phone.'

'You started it. I asked you simple—'

'Shut up dia. You dey maaaad? Bring your phone.'

'Vikings dey here o…' The companion wouldn't stop his chant.

I had to give it to Sade, she did have some guts, talking back to an armed fellow.

'So fine boy like you, you came here to steal—'

'Your mama. I look like thief to you? I am ingrate. Two of us … ingrate. I go UNIBEN. This my man, him go LASU, in Ibadan.'

'Seme border,' his friend stopped his Viking announcement to interject. 'Seme border…'

Were they really serious? Or was this a prank for an audience's benefit? An ingrate from LASU in Seme border. I couldn't help myself; I chuckled. I caught myself in a moment, hoping my foolishness hadn't been loud enough to be heard, but my sixth sense told me I was wrong.

'Who be that bastard? Wetin? Who be…?'

Vikings' footsteps began a menacing approach.

'He's blind. Him no fit see,' Sade called out. 'Leave…'

'Shut up dia,' the master of ceremonies barked.

Vikings reached me, snatched off my Raybans. There was a pause during which I wondered how hard he was going to strike me.

From the television, Daddy GO bellowed, 'The kingdom of heaven suffereth violence...' Talk about imperfect timing.

I felt Vikings lean over me. His breath, an uncanny mix of smells, fanned my face. That's right, Einstein, I thought, blindness is best detected via sniffing. Go on!

He straightened, called out to his friend, 'Na true, him blind.'

'Bring am here,' the MC ordered.

I was roughly pulled up by my collar and dragged over to the scene of the commotion. Through my disorientation, I heard Daddy GO continue, '...taketh by force. Say again...'

MC pulled me up to himself and spoke into my face. 'Na we you dey laugh, abi?'

And then it hit me. The smell I'd been unable to place when these two entered the Great Hall. Maybe it was my sensitive nose, but the MC's breath carried an odour like waste pits from the bowels of hell. It would have hurt less to have been shot. I impulsively pulled away from him.

He gripped my shirt tighter. 'Wetin be dat?' he asked. Into my face. Again.

I shook my head. I couldn't speak. Doing so meant gulping down his strangling breath.

'You won't talk? I say wetin be dat?'

I shook my head again.

'Wetin?' He shook me violently.

I held my breath. Daddy GO continued, this time louder, 'Say again ... taketh by force ... again...'

What remained of my senses were being horribly assaulted: the noise from the telecast, the odour from MC's pit. My sanity was being taken by force.

'Wetin? Talk now ... I say wetin be dat?'

Unable to stand it any longer, I cried out, 'I can't breathe ... abeg ... I don die ... your mouth.... E don do ... please ... abeg...'

I felt his grip loosen for a moment before a searing pain coursed through me. He hit me again in the face with the heavy metal in his other hand, and I fell. Then he lashed out at my body with his heels. His friend joined in. I cowered, trying to protect whatever part of my body I could. The more I cowered, the harder they kicked. Soon the pain became distant, and the sounds from the television and from the two ladies who had begun screaming at my assailants to stop, began to fade. MC and Vikings were panting heavily by the time they were done with me.

It was then that I noticed the tingling sensations at the corners of my eyes, the way a cramp slowly eases away from a taut muscle. I blinked repeatedly to stop the discomfort and began to rub at my eyelids even as the pain started to return to other parts of my body. When I withdrew my hands, I was able to make out blurred images of the two men standing a few feet away, both with their backs turned to me, their concentration now diverted to Sade and Gloria, whom they were shushing menacingly.

The events that followed happened so quickly that I'm still hardly able to keep track of them. I leapt up.

'I can see, I can see! A miracle, I can see!'

Daddy GO bellowed at the same time, 'Praaaiiiise da Lorrrd!'

'Halleluiah, I can see!'

I jumped on Vikings, embraced him, lifted and swirled him around. At first he didn't appear to mind, even hugged back for a moment, but then recalling his purpose, he pushed at me, struggled to get free. Then his gun went off with a loud bang and we ducked clumsily.

MC lay immobile on the tiles, a red swamp spreading slowly from his upper region. There was a large hole where his left eye once was, and a mash of brains leaked away with the blood. His body gave a long loud fart.

Vikings ran over to his friend. 'Sunny, Sunny, Sunny…' he called. Then he wailed and dashed through the swing doors and out into the night. A wave of silence echoed through the Great Hall. And it smelled really foul.

Meanwhile the blurriness in my eyes cleared further. I looked over at Sade and Gloria. They were visibly shaken and stared at me like I'd lost my mind, their faces a mixture of fear, delight and disgust. Jude had been right; Gloria did have a massive rack.

Then Daddy GO yelled again, 'Praise da living God…'

*J*ude wasn't home when I returned later that night. The police came to ransack his apartment the following day. Chief Mbuh was with them.

While the officers tore the room apart, he told me how he had gone to the Ada George police station the previous night to make a formal report of the incident at Valhalla, and had seen Jude being led out of the cells to a nearby hospital for treatment of a gunshot wound. The officers on duty informed him that Jude had been apprehended by a patrol unit as he and an accomplice tried to commandeer a vehicle at gunpoint. Jude had fired into the air several times to scare the lady driver into slowing, but had only succeeded in alerting the unit parked less than a block away. The ensuing gun battle had left him with a slug in his shoulder. His accomplice had surrendered voluntarily. Sade, who had gone with the chief to render an eye-witness account, recognised Jude's accomplice as the companion of the corpse lying in the Great Hall.

I saw Jude three days later, one day after he was discharged from the hospital and one day before he was to be transferred to the state criminal investigation department. He sat across a table from me in a room that smelled of pain. His right arm was in a sling made from a bandage that had forgotten how to be clean. He still had the mischievous glint at the edge of his features. He grinned after the officer I'd bribed to let me see him for two minutes retreated to the entrance.

'I see you got your miracle.'

I managed a wry smile. 'At what costs?'

A pause. 'How you dey?' I asked him.

With his head he motioned to his arm in the sling, and in the same movement, he motioned all around him.

I watched him and he watched me. There was nothing to say and we both knew it. I wondered if it was possible to hate him, or to judge him even. I wondered if I could ever see him as a criminal, as anything else but the guide, the friend, the ally and by some weird happenstance, the restorer of my sight. I knew I couldn't. I wouldn't be able to.

# The Demons Inside My Jimmy

*Harriet Anena*

*T*he calamity of my manlessness raised the weight of my head two-fold as my thirty-fifth birthday drew near. The elaborate poverty at home hadn't allowed me to join university, and so my A-grade transcript stayed locked in the cupboard like a family photo with a secret story.

If Mama had gotten over her dislike for Loum, my tuition would have been paid – for the little price of marrying the forty-year-old rich man. Instead, Mama helped me open a salon, saying I would do better than the job-hunting graduates wetting the streets with their sweat.

The business picked up all right, but the men didn't pick me up. The ones who came behaved like customers who made appointments, but never showed up. The next time I saw them, they had new hairstyles done elsewhere. That's what Lubangakene did. He dangled yields from his farm, cash from his teaching job, and promises of a blissful life together. The next thing I knew, he had married a girl from across the hill.

Mama said she always saw insincerity in Lubangakene's laughing eyes. Still, I asked her to pray with me so that God would send a loving man my way.

'Stop itching about marriage, Ruth,' Mama said.

'I'm your only child, Mama. Do you want my womb to expire before you get grandchildren?'

'There are children roaming the village, their buttocks peeping out from shredded shorts. Why don't you pick one, clean them up and raise?'

'Mama, you know it's not the same.'

'A child is a child. Unless you want something else…'

'I want a man too. Someone who can take care of me.'

'Ruth, how many years have I been alone since your father died?'

'At least you had time together.'

'What matters is that I have not died because I don't have a man. That man will come.'

'That has been your song for the past many years, Mama.'

☙

*H*ellen had been telling me to leave Kilak village for Kampala. Her salon, she said, was doing well because city women loved *spoiling* their hair, and they had the money to spend.

'That village life has clogged your head, Ruth. Take a risk,' she had said.

'Hellen, you know Mama will be alone.'

'My mum is there. They will take care of each other.'

'Okay, let me think about it.'

'Think quickly, my friend. By the way, your Jimmy is here. He's now a rich pastor.'

She whispered the last sentence like we did in high school whenever we were gossiping about Jimmy.

Two weeks after that phone call, I closed my salon and left for Kampala. On the first day at work, it was clear why Hellen needed another pair of hands. Unlike my one-roomed salon, which had had two chairs, a single dryer and five towels, Hellen's three-roomed hair clinic had five hair driers, dozens of towels, and huge mirrors covering two opposite walls. Two long sofas were placed in the main room where customers waited for their turn to be worked on as they watched TV. Different types of hair tools and accessories were kept in two small sideboards.

That first day, when we left for Hellen's two-roomed apartment in Buziga two kilometres away, my fingers ached from plaiting so many hairstyles, my feet throbbed from standing all day. But my pocket was happy for the first time in a long time.

*M*onday was our day off. We spent it house-cleaning, doing laundry, or taking walks on Buziga Hill. On one such slow day, we sat to watch TV. Hellen flipped through channels until something caught her attention on NTV. Pastor J, glittering in all white, was standing on a podium before a mass of people whose faces were painted with anticipation for a breakthrough, and eyes that said *Father, forgive our sins.*

Pastor J held onto the wooden rostrum and spewed messages of hope and condemnation, laced with aaiimmeennss and hhaalllleelluujjaahhss, in ear-soothing English.

My eyes stayed fixed on the TV. My chin took a seat on my palms.

'How fast is your heart beating?' Hellen asked, and winked.

'Normally. Why?'

'Come on! That is your Jimmy, in case you can't recognise him anymore. The one you had a mega crush on at Bright High School.'

'Of course.'

'What happened between you two, by the way?'

'Nothing. We lost touch after school.'

'Eh! But that guy, he used to look at girls the way a dog looks at stones. Except you of course...'

'Leave me alone.'

'I'm sure that has changed, though. Do you see how those girls in the front pew are piercing his chest with their eyes?'

We laughed. Hellen's laughter was long and hard, like it was well fed before it came out of her mouth, but mine was shaky.

Seeing Pastor J on that screen, after years of not knowing where he was, of forgetting him even, had subjected me to a second crush. I knew where I had to be come Sunday.

*I* wore a long black dress with yellow flowers to the service at Holy Ghost Ministries. The neck was low-cut and the sleeves lacy. Hellen said it pumped my figure without making me look slutty.

At the start, when Pastor J called out for first-timers to raise their hands for recognition, mine went up. When he called out for those who wanted to accept Jesus as their Lord and Saviour, I stood up, hands clasped together, and walked to the podium.

Pastor J mumbled *glory glory glory* when he saw me. He held out his hand to help me up the podium. My hand trembled in his.

'Welcome into the arms of the Lord,' he said, as he laid hands on my head. I got born again a second time.

For the next six months, I went to church every Sunday. Every time I did, I returned home with remnants of the firmness of Pastor J's handshake and the lingering echo of his *hello Ruth, praise Him, how are you, it's great to see you again, how is home, and your good life? Great! Always good seeing you. See you soon? Great! Bless you!*

It became a song whose lyrics I wanted to change so that I could get to know him beyond the shine of his Kiwi-ed shoes, his A+ performance, countable words, and the awkward hug we had shared on the last day of high school.

When the date for the Marrieds' Retreat was announced, I volunteered as an usher. At Haven Resort in Entebbe, I got a proper chance to talk with Pastor J. He took off his man-of-God robes when he found me standing on the hotel's sandy beach.

The years had given J more words, louder laughter, and the boldness to look women in the eye. I loved it. I scooped words from his mouth, and he let me. I held his gaze for as long as I could, and he did the same. At my feet he laid bare what I needed to know – that he was still one rib less, that he hadn't joined university because there was a bigger purpose in life – pursuing the devil, whom he had floored many times with fire, water and light.

I ignored the tremble of his hands when he talked about the devil. Instead, I fixed my gaze on his toenails that competed in whiteness with shells, his dimples that had become deeper, and I listened to the echo of his laughter spreading across Lake Victoria.

The distance that had stood between us all those years was no more by the time we left Haven Resort. Pastor J gave me his phone number, but said he preferred writing letters. I was not surprised when a week after the retreat, he called me to his office one Sunday.

'I have been hearing really good things about you, Sister Ruth,' he said.

*Sister Ruth?* Well, that's how he referred to every woman at church, but I thought we had left 'Sister' and 'Pastor' on the shores of Lake Victoria.

'Thank you, Pastor,' I said, playing his game.

'My heart dances when I see my flock grow in the Lord,' he said, eyes closed.

'Amen.'

'When I see young people flee the claws of the world and choose the goodness of the Word, I rejoice.'

'Amen.'

'When I see a young, focused lady like you touch lives with voluntary work, with humility, Gaaad I sing Hhoossaannnnaa!'

Hellen had told me to shoot the man of God with the I-love-you magic words, and he would eat from my palms. I'd told her I wanted a man, but I wasn't desperate. She insisted that times had changed. 'If you like a man, tell him,' she'd said.

Sitting across the table from Pastor J that day, the temptation to let it all out grew by the minute.

'Jimmy…' I said, rising to my feet.

At the mention of his name, Pastor J's eyes shot open.

'Yes, Sister Ruth. Tell me, daughter of Gaaad.'

I took a deep breath and fixed my gaze on the portraits above his chair – one of Jesus holding a lamb, another of Pastor J with a bottle of holy oil.

'Jimmy, I know this may shock you, but the first time I came to your church, God spoke to me. He said, "Ruth, blessed are you, for you have found a companion." Then he showed you to me – you, seated on that very chair, floating on the clouds and smiling at me.'

'Oh Ruth.'

Pastor J removed his hands from his desk top and placed them on his thighs. From where I was standing, I could tell that his hands were trembling again. The smile on his face had no character. He was back to Senior Five, when his words were countable, because all he could say was 'Oh Ruth', over and over, like my name had become the Lord's Prayer.

'Sit,' he said, leaning forward and taking my hands in his.

My face broke into a smile that wasn't in a hurry to fade.

'I'm very excited that the Lord has revealed His goodness again,' Pastor J said, rubbing the back of my hands.

I inched closer, waiting for him to say he felt the same way. Just then, Anna, a fierce rival for J's affection, knocked on the door and pushed it open. Our hands were still locked, eyes probing each other's. Pastor J turned to look at Anna, and instead of rubbing the back of my hand, he tightened his grip.

'I see it. He is here. The big fat devil has invaded this place again,' he said, his eyes widening.

My jaw dropped in surprise. 'What do you mean?'

'I can see it, right there. Do you see it?'

'No, I don't.' My voice went up, not from the confusion of the moment, but the pain his grip was inflicting on my knuckles.

I pulled my hands away.

'Do you see what you've done?' Anna said, teeth clenched. She stayed at the door.

'What did I do?'

'Leave, and take your wayward spirits along,' she said.

I got up and headed for the door. Pastor J was now shaking his head and muttering, 'I see you. I know you are here. I will defeat you.' Anna didn't step out of my way. We stood there for a minute, her eyes roaming my body from toenails to hair. I fixed my gaze on the door frame behind her. By the time she let me pass, I could still see the smile on her face dying from when she walked in on us. She had been silently pursuing the man of God for five years. The Church Council said she had the true anointing. All this while the Women's Group said Sister Abigail had the humility of Christ, and *she* didn't take herself like a pastor's wife-in-waiting.

I wondered if Pastor J would wash my linen in church like he did with other members of his flock – telling Sister Eva to pray against the spirit of selfishness (without saying she needed to open her doors to fellow worshippers like the rest), how Brother Emma must pray harder to overcome the bondage of poverty (without saying he needed to tithe more).

❧

'*W*hat if dude tells the church that I hit on him?' I told Hellen as we waited for customers at the salon.

'He wouldn't waste your offer, fwaaa. Plus, you are edible, just like him.'

'You are stupid.'

'Thank you.'

We laughed.

'But you know there is a third candidate to the throne, right?'

'Your profile still reads better than Anna's or Abigail's. A well-groomed village girl who is potentially a virgin?'

'Don't be silly, Hellen. I'm not waiting for Jesus to break my virginity.'

'Aren't you supposed to be the born-again good girl?'

'I am.'

'Anyway, the only roadblock is that those two are more spiritually elderly than you.'

'Lol! Who wants to be spiritually elderly?'

'Pastor J might.'

I smiled, but deep down, thoughts of Pastor's J's devil-sighting incident at his office clouded my mind. I postponed telling Hellen about it when two customers walked into the salon.

Pastor J's office stayed locked for a week. His brother, Apostle Samuel, led the Sunday service, explaining that Pastor J was busy holding a special personal prayer. Jimmy didn't call me, and I resisted the temptation of sending him a message to ask if he was okay.

The following Sunday, Pastor J stood at the church door, greeting people. When I stepped up to him, he took my hand in his without a word. His eyes were set on the person behind me. He was smiling. He pressed a small folded note in my hand. My heart thudded.

*Beloved,*

*Let's for a moment forget that I'm the man of God, and you, my loyal follower. Let's for a moment imagine that we are in Senior Five, sharing the desk that made a crick-crick sound whenever we moved, even a little.*

*I knew you were God's chosen, when you stuck by me, even when others called me a zombie. They didn't know it was the devil that set all my words on fire.*

*I couldn't tell you anything, even when God told me, 'Son, that's your rib.' And when school ended before I could defeat the devil's conspiracy, I had to pursue him. And God in His wonderful mercies, God with His never-ending greatness, brought us together again. Oh how my heart sings hosanna!*

*You are my angel.*

*Yours,*

*J.*

*T*he next Sunday, it was me pressing a tiny note in Pastor J's hand, telling him *I'm yours too.* He smiled when our eyes met. When he got to the podium and declared that God had given him a special message the previous night, I knew the hour had come.

'The Lord said, "Servant of God, your wife is beautiful. Her heart is pure and her body purer",' he said.

There were lengthy claps, followed by aaiimmeenns and hhaalllleelluujjaahhss as though the church was saying, finally! Everyone poured their eyes towards the front pew, where Anna and Abigail sat. I saw a katogo of anxiety and excitement on their faces.

'And the chosen one is…' Pastor J said as if he was announcing the winner of a beauty pageant. Then, he paused for five long minutes during which the choir started singing praise songs. I focused on the lines:

*You waited for me*
*even when the wait seemed eternal.*
*You waited just for me*
*even when the devil stood in the way.*

*You waited for me*
*coz you knew we were blessed.*

Abigail and Anna were not taking the suspense very well; their smiles had started drying up.

And then Pastor J called me to the front. Me, Ruth, whose spiritual weight couldn't even make a mini-devil stagger. It's not like I was a committer of hell-shattering sins. I just hadn't reached the level of spiritual ripeness where people could start coming to me for counselling or dream interpretations, as expected of the second in command of the church.

Looks were exchanged, lips pulled, eyes rolled, and jaws hardened. There was uneasy shifting to the edge of their seats by the two other contenders. But who was I to defy the Lord's choice? I walked to the podium. The claps found me there, but they carried a wonders-shall-never-cease tone. I concentrated on Sinach's 'I Know Who I Am' lyrics to which the choir was dancing vigorously, like the devil had scored an own goal in the last minute of a match.

Wedding meetings started in earnest. My pleas to Pastor J that we should have a small, intimate wedding with what we had, were ignored. His response was the same: 'Our big day is the Lord's big day, we can't keep His people away.' The words forced their way out of his mouth like his teeth had become street humps, hindering smooth movement.

I didn't relent. I reminded him weekly until he lost it one day. He poured his eyes on me, his breathing quickened, and his hands started trembling. His nostrils throbbed, and his body shook like he was being besieged by the devil. He looked like the people he called to the podium so that their demons could be cast out.

From that day on, I shut my mouth. I watched as the wedding committee chairman unleashed one trick after another at the begging meetings.

'Brothers and Sisters in Christ,' he would start, 'the Lord said, those who give, shall receive more.'

While many had to be coerced into giving, there were those who dropped wads of cash into the basket, and cleared the most expensive items on the budget – decorations, cake, food, venue. Sister Anna was one of them. Two weeks before the wedding, she offered to pay for my wedding gown. I had to break my silence. 'The gown has already been bought, Sister Anna. But thank you so much. Bless you.'

*W*e went back to Haven Resort for our wedding and reception. Five tents, erected in the vast gardens that overlooked the beach, were decorated with white and purple drapes. A thin white carpet trailed the distance between our guests and the two-seater tent where Pastor J and I sat. It was there that we had chatted during the Marrieds' Retreat. Flower stands, six on either side of the white carpet, held bouquets of white roses and a stem of purple daisies, reiterating the day's colour theme.

All guests were in white with a dash of purple, except for Mama, who wore a purple-and-black striped kikoyi with a red sash. Guests walked into the reception area to music that I had selected, except for Mama – who walked to a tune that seemed to be coming from her head. She had asked me on the eve of the wedding if I was sure about *it*, and if I knew enough about *him*.

'He's a man of God, Mama. How bad can it be?'

'We all know they are just vendors of selected parts of the Bible.'

'Mama, at least be happy for me.'

'If you know him enough, go ahead. Just don't forget that some of those men of God carry spirits underneath those well-ironed suits of theirs.'

I didn't respond. Doing so meant the conversation would never end, but my mind kept going back to the time Pastor J saw the devil in his office.

At the reception, Mama kept shaking her head and pulling her mouth at the sermon, the speeches and the music. She tapped her thighs when the gifts were delivered – a Toyota Wish from Prophet Peter of Hymn Ministries, a TV, sofa, suitcases, kitchenware. She held her chin with both hands as the gift basket filled up with envelopes, especially after Pastor J made a last-minute decision to recognise all the money givers.

We danced. The guests cheered, except for Mama.

෴

*W*e left the wedding reception for our honeymoon at midnight. By the time we checked into Nairobi Hotel, I was exhausted, and sleep was killing me. But Pastor J insisted that we should take a shower before bed.

'I'll go first,' I said, even though he'd said he would give me a shower on our wedding night.

I had a quick shower as he unpacked our bags. When I stepped out of the shower, he towelled me up and told me to wait for him. But we both knew by the time he got done showering, I would be summarising my second dream. He had already warned me that he had a thing for water.

The bed swallowed me when I fell on it. The mattress was thick, but it must have housed a lot of bodies, or maybe it was the cheap kind that lied to you on the first day, promising firmness but a few weeks later, shrinking at the touch of any weight.

I steered my mind onto something more pleasant, like the well-lit exterior of the hotel I had seen on arrival. The tall Christmas trees were trimmed, each a neat cone sheltering the brick wall around the building. In the compound, white-petal daisies with yellow buds lined the concrete walkways. A night rose perfumed the air.

I flung the two pillows across the floor and pulled the bed sheet over my body. The once-white sheet had assumed an off-white shade. Strands of thread dangled from one of its edges, and it smelt of Sunlight washing powder. I wondered how many people had covered their bodies with these sheets, how many had slept on this same bed. My skin goose-bumped at the thought. I wondered what made Pastor J choose this hotel; had he wanted a low-budget hotel? But where did all the money from the begging meetings go?

My eyelids were heavier now. I said a prayer.

*Father in the mighty name of Jesus, thank You for putting my enemies to shame. Thank You for showing them that You ... alone ... are...*

I woke up with a start. The windows were open, and wind nudged the curtains. A cold breeze poured into the dark room. Lightning lit the sky, a sign of impending rain. Other than the shouting from Room 33, the hotel was quiet – like the walls were straining their ears to understand what was going on.

'I command you to leave. Burn! Fire!'

'Leave who?'

'You don't belong here. Flee. Disappear. Scatter.'

'Jimmy, it's just a nightmare. Wake up.'

I whispered, as if doing so would lower the noise levels of Pastor J's condemnations. I shook him so that he could snap out of the thing that had taken refuge in his head, but the man of God had the strength of two Satans. He lifted me up and tossed me back on the mattress like a rag doll.

'Get out now! Out! Down! That's where you belong.'

'Jimmy, please.'

He sat astride my legs before I could escape, placed his hands around my neck, and growled. Our eyes met, and the security lights outside flickered back on, partially swallowing the darkness. He was breathing fast, his eyes popping, red veins prominent. His neck was a tree stump.

'Stop ... please,' I said in between his choking hands.

'I have caught you today. I warned you. Didn't I?

'J ... please.'

'It's done. It's over. Thank you, Father! Aaiimmeenn! Hhaalllelluujjaahh!' he mumbled and slumped on top of me, eyes closed. I pulled my body from beneath him, limped to the two-seater sofa at the corner of the room, and listened to him snore.

'Is everything okay, ma'am?' asked the guard from the open window.

'Yes. Everything is okay,' I said as I got up to close the windows.

The guard looked at me for a while, then walked away from the window. I knew he wouldn't go far, just in case Room 33 burst out in holy screams again.

I kneeled to complete the prayer I had left half-way earlier.

ço

*W*aking the next morning, I wondered if what had transpired the previous night was a nightmare, or if Pastor J had transformed into a *thing* that had tried to kill me.

'Good morning baby,' he said, when he noticed I was awake.

It was the first time he was calling me *baby*.

'Good morning!'

'How did you sleep?'

'I didn't sleep well.'

'Is it because we didn't…?'

He drew me against his chest.

'Jimmy, we need to talk about last night,' I said, pulling away.

'What about last night?'

'You almost killed me.'

'What are you talking about?' he asked, scrambling out of bed.

'Don't tell me you don't remember.'

'Remember what?'

I took deep breaths, sat up and narrated everything as I remembered it. His face betrayed nothing. He didn't utter a word. He stood by the bedside and we stared at each other, the room adjusting its size – smaller, smaller – around us.

'I'll go shower, okay? Join me…' he said, and dashed to the bathroom. I got out of bed, walked to the landline to tell the restaurant that we were ready for breakfast, even though I didn't feel hungry. Fifteen minutes later, Pastor J was still in the shower. I got out my cellphone to WhatsApp Hellen.

'Why are you on the phone?'

'Babe, something happened last night.'

'What did you expect?'

'Silly. Do you even know what I'm talking about?'

'How was it?'

'Hellen! We haven't had sex. Yet.'

'What are you waiting for?'

'We were tired last night.'

'Oh yeah ... that's understandable. Kati, go back to your man before he catches you using the phone.'

'He's in the shower. Not about to come out.'

'Go join him there.'

'I'm here for serious stuff, Hellen. Pastor J turned into the devil last night.'

'Whaat?'

'I woke up and he was screaming and commanding me or whoever to get out.'

'Aha?'

'I tried shaking him out of it in vain. Instead, he started strangling me.'

'Whaat?'

'Yeah!'

'Babe, you should pray about it.'

'Pray? You are supposed to tell me to leave?'

'Leave? For where?'

'Hellen, I don't know the man I married.'

'You can never know anyone completely, you know that.'

Ahead of the wedding, Pastor J had recited Bible verses on fornication whenever I asked if I could sleep over at his house. It's not like I wanted to dive into his pants or anything. Well, at some point, of course. I just needed to know the man I was going to marry in more detail.

'Ruth, maybe you are just scared. Marriage is scary, I hear. Maybe you just had a nightmare,' Ruth said.

'So you think I have lost my head.'

'That's not what I mean...'

'Wait ... brb.'

I threw the phone back into my handbag when I heard repeated thuds on the bathroom wall. Then there was a thump, followed by silence. When Pastor J didn't come out of the bathroom, I walked to the door and called his name. Nothing. I tried opening the door, but there was something blocking it from inside. I pushed harder until I saw Jimmy's legs on the bathroom floor.

There was a knock on the door. I took a long breath, thanking God for sending help when I needed it most. With hands shaking, I turned the key and pulled the door open. It was room service. I grabbed the man by the sleeve of his shirt without a word, and pulled him towards the bathroom. The tray holding our breakfast fell on the floor.

'Madam, what is the problem?' he asked, voice shaking.

'My husband, my husband is dead,' was all I could say.

At the bathroom door, I sank on my knees. The breakfast man, instead of entering the bathroom to help my J, dashed to the phone and spoke on it, his voice urgent and low.

'What is going on here?' a voice called from the open door, as the breakfast man tried to lift me up.

It was the hotel manager. He had come with a butler, a man so tall he had to bend to enter the bathroom door. He pushed Pastor J's legs towards the centre of the room, which gave him space to enter.

There was blood on the wall. Pastor J's knuckles were red and wet. The butler lifted him off the floor like he was a feather, and carried him to the bed. They felt his pulse, the butler at his neck, the manager at his wrist. I couldn't read anything on their faces. The manager dialled the hospital for an ambulance. By the time we heard the siren in the distance, Pastor J was awake.

'The devil is a liar!' he screamed.

The butler, the breakfast man and the manager looked at each other.

'He thought I wouldn't manage him. I did. I struck the hell out of the devil. Did you find his body?' he continued.

He attempted to get out of bed but stopped and groaned, his

face contorted. I held him as he grated his teeth.

'Let me go see his corpse. Let me go dance on the grave of the devil.'

When the ambulance arrived, the butler lifted Pastor J and carried him to the waiting vehicle as he kicked and cursed. They held him down throughout the fifteen-minute journey to Nairobi Medical Centre.

I picked the phone from my bag to inform Apostle Samuel, and Mama about what was happening, but the phone screen flickered with a message from Hellen.

'Ruth darling, someone from your church was here to do their hair and we got talking about Pastor J. Of course I didn't tell her that you and I are close. But apparently, the Pastor *sees things*.'

I leaned against the side of the ambulance, once again at Haven Resort, reciting my vows, only this time, the words were different: *I, Ruth Laker, take you Pastor Jimmy P'Lubanga, to be my wedded husband, to enjoy and to endure, in sanity and during demon-possessed moments; to carefully love and to cautiously hold, until we can't stand each other's demons anymore.*

# An Abundance of Lies

*Faith Oneya*

*A*fter 4.30 Hotel was two storeys high with yellowish-brown walls that had more dust than paint on them. Green plastic plants, also choking in dust, lined the entrance. That should have been my first red light. A reluctant curtain was draped over the door, and my eyes darted to the dusty, wooden staircase with a careless carpet.

Where were the shiny glass walls that needed cleaning all day long? Where were the lifts Domi had said one had to be trained to use? Where was the lush green lawn that she had described in such detail? Where were the red roses that infused the air with their beautiful scent as guests entered?

My heart was still stewing in disappointment when I asked for Domitilla at reception.

'Nobody by that name works here,' said the woman, who rolled and unrolled her plastic hair in her hands as if I was bothering her. Or maybe it was the hair that was bothering her.

'Are you sure of what you are saying?' I asked. She needed to be sure. I was not going back home to Mother.

The woman looked up at me as if addressing someone who had escaped from a mental hospital.

I insisted. I spelt Domitilla's name out to her. I took a piece of paper and wrote it out. Flavia Domitilla Nekesa.

'Do you think I am lying to you?' she finally asked loud enough for the Asian man passing by the reception area to hear. He walked to us briskly. A hairy man. I mean, he had hair peeping out from underneath his shirt and stumbling from his wide nostrils. And when he spoke, one felt the urge to keep telling him to clear his throat. Was hair clogged there too?

'My name is Rajan, I am the manager. Iko nini? What is the problem, my dear?'

'I am looking for my friend Domitilla, she is a cook here,' I told him, my voice sharpening and rising in panic. Had she lied to me?

'Eh ... eh!' He held up his index finger to slow me down. 'My dear, what is your name?'

'Lady Liza.'

He looked at me like I had made the name up. Was that why he kept calling me 'my dear?'

'There is no cook with that name here. Where did you say you are from?' he asked while looking me up and down as if trying to decide how to send me back to where I came from.

'Kisumu.'

He thought about it for a few minutes, shifting on his feet like someone who needed to go to the toilet. I began to think I had the wrong hotel.

Where was Domitilla?

'There is no waitress by that name either. Maybe we can check the cleaning department. They are very many, you know, so I can't remember all their names.'

He summoned the cleaning supervisor.

The cleaning supervisor saved me. He said he knew a Domitilla from her ID card.

A brown girl. Very quiet. That's how they described her.

He took me to meet her at her work station, and that is how I came to learn that the only food Domitilla came close to was the shit produced by those rich folks who came to After 4.30 for late lunches and dinners.

'Why did you come here?' Domi hissed through her teeth, eyeing me like one would a house rat. Her face had changed. Much like the exterior walls of the hotel, it was now yellow with brown patches that glistened and looked like they wanted to break free.

'Domi ... you told me to come. You invited me here. Don't you remember?'

'Tilla,' she responded.

'What?'

'Tilla. My name is Tilla here. Don't call me Domi again ... that is what a village pumpkin would do. Hiyo ni ushamba.'

'Domi, you told me I could come here. That you could find me a job. What has changed?'

Well, I could see that the colour of her face had changed, but her hands remained the colour that I remembered. Dark and flawless.

'I have just told you not to call me Domi. What's wrong with you? And I told you that you could come because that is what you village people like to hear. I did not mean that you should actually pack your bags and come here! I could lose my job! *Sheesh!*'

Domi bit her lower lip and breathed heavily, then held her forehead with her forefingers and rubbed her eyes with her palms.

'My house is too small. My bed is too small. Liza, why have you done this to me?'

I apologised because it seemed like it was something *she* might want to hear. I searched her face for the warmth of the friendship I once knew, but her eyes met mine hard ... and I dropped my gaze. I bit back the greetings I carried from Mother, and held my bag a little tighter.

Anyway, her anger made no difference to me, as I knew I was not going back home. I was a city girl now.

But still, I couldn't believe that she had lied to me. She had lied to me about many things, but it was the thick crust of paint with which she had coated her life in Nairobi that nearly choked me. That lie was what had me taking a bus to Nairobi, after lying to my mother about why I wanted to go to the city.

*I*f you ever met my mother, then you would know why I was sweating when I spoke to her about coming to this Nairobi that you people praise so much. One wrong word to Mother, and a slap could easily land on your face! Or worse, she would ignore you for the rest of the day, saying, 'When you find my daughter, tell her I am looking for her. There is a stranger in my house.'

She purses her lips when you are talking to her, and says many 'Eheeee, Eheeee, Eheees', squinting after every sentence so that you never know whether you are convincing her or enraging her. Wueh, I did not want to take any chances this time.

And I had missed many chances with Mother.

I think I was cursed because I missed qualifying for a position at a teachers' training college after Form Four by two points a year back. Mother blamed Domi for this. She said Domi distracted me and made me start knowing boys before my time. Never mind that I was eighteen and itching with desires that not even Mother's prayers could quench. I wanted to tell her that I dreamed about boys at night all on my own.

Anyway, Domi was a delicate topic that needed careful handling when talking to Mother. So I painted her in a better light than my mother had ever seen her in, and it blinded her enough for her to give me bus fare. I told her about the Quaker church that Domi attended. About her big job at a big hotel.

'Domi found me a job too, Mami, and she said she could host me while I am there!' The words stumbled out of my mouth. They came out so fast, so smoothly that even I had trouble remembering they were untrue.

'Nyathina ... my child, are you sure? A girl like you. An apuotho, a village pumpkin like you, that city will eat you alive,' Mother said.

'Domi will protect me, Mami. She has a good job and lives in a big house. I prayed to God about it, and I know He will make a way for me,' I added.

Mother pursed her lips further, twisting them right and left. Right and left. As if considering which weighed more: her disdain for Domi or her love of God.

I remembered how she once told me of the dream she had about Domi and me. She said that in her dream, I was crossing the road, but there were snakes between us. Whenever I moved close to Domi, the snakes would hiss at me, but I kept going back. My mother often repeated this to me as if it was a dream she had every night. And every repetition was punctuated by her fervent prayers for God's protection.

Domi and I had been best friends ever since we were nine years old. I remember how we used to compare the progress of the hard knots on our chests every month. The knots rose into little mounds and finally blossomed into breasts that deserved bras. Our periods came at the same time, and we danced around like we were little girls again to celebrate becoming women. Our hearts grew restless about living in a small place like Kisumu. We both wanted a bigger life in a bigger city. Houses next to each other. The same jobs.

Domi was the first to lose her virginity to a fast-talking bus conductor, and we giggled and giggled when she used a piece of firewood to explain to me what an erect penis looked like.

'Does it hurt when it's going in?' I asked, and she laughed and laughed.

'One day you will find out,' she said when she had caught her breath. Then laughed again. I did not really think I wanted to find out what a piece of firewood would feel like inside me – Domi had always been the more adventurous of the two of us – so I just nodded.

She said she would introduce me to someone too; someone who would make me feel like a woman. I told her that I would tell her when I was ready, but the truth was I was afraid of what I needed to give up. I knew the efforts Mother was putting into praying for a good husband for me, and I did not want to taint her prayers.

'Liza, this thing is never lost. That is not what they mean when they say losing your virginity. It's more like giving it away temporarily. It's not as if it is soap that washes away. It remains with you once the man is done with it,' she said.

I was confused.

And then she went to the city to work at a hotel. After 4.30 Hotel. She told me she had found a job as the head cook. I did not know what head cooks did, but it sounded very important. And everybody spoke about how soft Domi's chapattis were, so I was very happy that she had found someone who could pay for them. On her last visit, she told me that perhaps I could join her one day. That perhaps she could teach me the ropes.

I knew I could learn to make soft chapattis like hers.

Now, I did not like my mother calling me a village pumpkin.

I did not like her calling me any kind of pumpkin, actually. I also knew that she never liked Domi. She said Domi wore her skirts too short and tops too low.

'Disrespectful!' Mother said, twisting her mouth as she always did when disapproving.

I asked her how many metres of cloth were enough to be respectful, but she said my smart mouth would land me in trouble one day.

But thoughts of a prestigious job in the city had mellowed her, and she called church members to pray for me and my journey. They laid their hands on me and beseeched God to walk before me. They cursed the devil for even imagining he could cause an accident along the way, and told God that they were now putting me in His hands.

'You are her Father and the Shepherd of her life,' they shouted, invoking the name of Jesus and saying enough amens to last me the whole journey to Nairobi.

Now, I don't know whose life God was busy shepherding that day, because I spent a whole night in a Mbukinya Express bus from Kisumu to Nairobi swatting the hands of a randy bus conductor who told me he could 'show me a good time in Nairobi'. I had gone to sit at the back of the bus to stretch my feet on the empty seat, and he followed me there. Was it the length of my skirt?

But later, the shock of seeing the After 4.30 Hotel made me regret not exploring the good time the sweaty conductor had offered.

*D*omi took me to her house in Majengo that night, fuming all the way in the matatu. I rambled on and on about my mother, her church, the boy who wanted to date me and everything else that she responded to with little grunts and grimaces.

We shared the boiled maize I had carried from home and a threadbare mattress, but the silence was harder to bear than the hard floor.

I did not ask her where she was going when the door creaked

open at midnight, but I caught the whiff of Bint El Sudan perfume as she left. It was the same perfume she wore on the day she lost – eh, gave – her virginity.

We went back to After 4.30 Hotel the next day. Domi told me she did not cook in her house. Not breakfast. Not lunch. Not dinner. The hotel gave all workers lunch. The rest of the day, she survived on God's air.

Domi organised a job for me in the cleaning department. Rajan agreed that I looked strong and capable.

If I knew I was coming to clean rich people's refuse, then I would have stayed back home in Kisumu with Mother's rules and nagging and her endless prayers to God to save me.

But perhaps toilet cleaning would have been easier were it not for the cheap, pungent smell of the detergent that Rajan insisted on buying. It nauseated me. It made me want to go back home to confess my sins to Mother. I imagined how she would twist her mouth to the side and then say, 'I have never liked that Domi. There was always something sinister about her. It's ironic that she was named after a saint.'

I confronted Rajan about the toilet detergent. I told him it was too rough on the skin of my hands.

Rajan sniffed the air as if trying to detect the smell, turned to me and asked, 'Are the toilets complaining?'

Then he walked away.

The nerve of that man! But when I heard that the only reason he had become a manager was because his father was the owner's cousin, I understood why he asked such stupid questions.

My mother had always told me that my big mouth would land me in trouble one day. I just did not know that trouble meant cleaning rich people's shit. I thought trouble meant falling pregnant or something.

Domi told me my mouth was too big for the job, but I told her it was my hands that were too delicate for the job.

But perhaps the work would have been easier if the hotel guests did not have constant amnesia about where their shit should land.

I cleaned enough shit off the sides of toilet bowls to make me wonder why they were called hotel guests. They should have been baptised hotel pests. Well, at least some of them. They used too much tissue, and often stuffed the whole roll in their handbags. I'm telling you things I have seen with my own eyes.

And when they peed, you would hear the loud sounds: 'Kuuurrrruuu, Kuuuruuu! Shwarraaa! Shwarraaa!' – a clear sign that their buttocks were hanging above the bowl, as if they were too precious to sit on the toilets we worked so hard to clean.

I asked Domi if I should tell Rajan about the guests misusing the toilets, but she reminded me how lucky I should feel to have this job so soon after arriving in Nairobi. 'That big mouth of yours will not take you anywhere,' she said.

My big mouth never took me anywhere with the hotel pests either. I thought I would start with a hello, but they never replied. Even if I was standing next to the door as they slapped it open, they just swung past me while talking loudly on their mobile phones as I stood there in my invisible dark-blue uniform, as they messed up the toilet, splashed water all over the floor, washed their hands and ran them through their weaves, and removed food from their teeth with their long nails.

I was fed up with the job after the first week. I asked Domi how she had survived there for a whole year.

'You are not as special as you think you are, Liza,' she responded and kept mopping the floor. We had to mop the public bathroom floors on an hourly basis and sign our names against the work done on the supervisor's form hung at the back of the door. I had already signed it three times without cleaning the toilets. I was afraid of signing it without working a day, so I took a mop and joined Domi.

I stared at the tight skin around her eyes and mouth and her black knuckles. Her eyes were as dull as the mop she was using to dry the floor. What had happened to her?

'Domi, where do you go in the middle of the night?'

'Where do you think? That is what will get me out of this life.

And I told you to stop calling me Domi! Nkkkkt!'

But her 'Nkkkkt' was the softest one I had heard since the day I came, so I just nodded and smiled. She smiled back. Her first one since I had arrived.

'I mean well, you know. It's just that you surprised me,' she said.

I was tired of cleaning toilets.

That night, before she snuck out, I asked her to take me with her.

'Are you sure?' she asked.

I was.

'You will need Bint El Sudan.'

# The Layover

*Anna Degenaar*

*S*kin heavy from the eight-hour flight, Mia steps out of Addis Ababa Bole International Airport and into the early morning haze. The transit slip handed to her has the name of the hotel written on it in a rushed scrawl. The shuttle marked 'Top Ten Hotel' is the last in the row of vehicles. Although there are a few people already on board, no one speaks. Mia pushes aside the thick curtains, rests her forehead against the greasy pane, and waits.

Eventually, the city starts moving past the small window. They pass cars piled high with goods and the beginnings of roadside markets. Earthy pumpkins in neat lines next to rows of onions and green tomatoes. A group of men seated around a small table. A backyard full of dyed goats. Every second high-rise is paused somewhere along the path to restoration. Plastic-wrapped buildings flap in the wind and apartment blocks wear suits of wooden scaffolding. Children play between the rubble and dust. The city hangs suspended in a state of change.

The shuttle stops in the shadow of a tall building. Perched on the roof like a spindly crown, the 'Top Ten Hotel' sign sways in the wind. Mia lifts her suitcase out of the shuttle's paint-chipped trailer and walks past the fake palm trees towards the reception desk. A light touch on the shoulder from the security guard stops her. He guides her through the free-standing metal detector. The machine shouts its warning into the quiet lobby, and she unloads her offending items into the tray. She hands her passport to the receptionist. Above her head, clocks from the world's major cities tick out of sync. Paris, London, New York, Tokyo. A porter helps her into a lift just big enough for two. His sharp features gather around colossal eyebrows. Mia follows one strand that disappears into his hairline. She imagines his entire head of hair growing from that single strand.

The floor numbers glow a dull red. He pushes number six and the lift jerks into motion.

'Are you from here?' Mia asks to fill the space.

'I've lived here all my life,' the man replies. 'How long will you stay?'

'Just today. I'm waiting for my next flight.'

The porter nods and turns to watch the floors tick upwards. Mia suddenly wishes she were staying longer. The doors open with a ping.

The room is large, and the linen is a crisp white against the speckled walls. The art above the bed could be worse. The bathroom is clean. Mia puts her suitcase down in a corner and opens the heavy, red curtains. The city sprawls away from her into the cool morning. The expanding flatness calms the buzz in her chest. The airport is not far from the hotel, and the planes appear and disappear into the city, while the sun shakes itself free from the bumpy horizon. She finds the wifi password and watches her phone as it connects. She opens her email and slides her thumb down the screen to refresh. No new messages. She puts the phone face down on the bedside table and pulls clean clothes from her bag.

The bathroom is tiled in shiny charcoal. Mia places her toiletry bag beside the sink. She undoes the clasp of her thin gold chain, twists the wedding ring off her swollen finger, and removes her earrings. She looks at her reflection in the mirror, squares her shoulders and moves her lips into a smile, but her cheeks feel like plastic. She unbuttons her shirt, and turns the shower taps as far as they'll go. The hot water washes the lack of sleep from her skin.

Towel-drying her hair, she steps out the shower. She secures the towel under her armpits and tries to open the bathroom door. It doesn't move. She tries it again, and then again with both hands. She wraps the towel tighter around her, and puts the whole force of her body into the door. Nothing. She looks around the small room and her breath becomes solid in her throat. It'll be hours before anyone knows to look for her. Desperate, she pushes her shoulder into the middle of the door, and the swollen wood finally pulls away from the frame. Mia spills into the room. She looks around, embarrassed, and readjusts the towel around her chest.

*T*hree waiters stand with their hands behind their backs at the entrance of the hotel's dining room. They welcome Mia in quiet voices as she walks past. The tables are surrounded by sturdy wooden chairs and covered in bright orange cloth. Dark-green stems hold plastic blooms high above too-short vases. Mia chooses a table in the corner, near a man who is sitting alone. He is reading from an iPad, and she takes advantage of his lack of attention, studying his profile.

His beard is flecked with grey, and his shirt is creased like it's been pulled from a badly-packed bag, but his skin is smooth and his eyes are soft. He looks up and nods with a half-smile as she gets up to fetch breakfast.

Mia imagines his eyes on her as she spoons food onto her plate from the buffet. Everything is yellow from spice. The pieces of meat have taken on a waxy sheen, and the sauce has turned to jelly. She takes her time choosing from the different stainless-steel containers, careful to stand up straight and keep her movements light. She pours herself a cup of coffee and decides against the milk before heading back to her table. She looks out the window and takes a large sip. The bitterness stings the back of her throat and her face contorts. When she looks up, the man is laughing.

'Strong?' he asks.

She looks at him over the rim of her cup. 'Apparently.'

She resists the urge to trade her coffee for a glass of orange juice, and focuses instead on spreading a tiny square of butter on a dry bread roll.

'Where are you from?'

Mia anticipates this question. It's the first one people ask. As if understanding where you're from will have a bearing on where you're going. 'Cape Town.' She is about to ask him the same, but hesitates, and decides on a different direction. 'What brings you to Addis Ababa?'

Amused that she doesn't care to know his origin, he pauses before responding. 'Business, mostly. My next stop is Bangkok. And you?' He adds the question with mock emphasis.

'It's just a layover.' She waits and then adds, sitting up straighter, 'I'm on my way to India.'

'Ah.'

She stops to study his expression. 'What?' she asks. She wonders if she should mention the conference. She decides against it.

'Nothing.' He smiles, and there's a challenge in it that she feels just below her belly button.

*T*hey carry their conversation over to the hotel lounge. The wallpaper mimics dark wood, and the fake velvet couches are the same shade as the curtains in Mia's room. Bottles of amber liquid glow in the pale light, side by side above the barman like a false library. The blinds in the lounge are closed, making it easier to forget it's still morning.

'Shall we have a drink?' he asks.

Mia raises an eyebrow.

'It helps with the jetlag.'

She finds herself nodding, and he gets up to fetch two beers from the bar. They are the only two people in the lounge.

'How long will you travel for?' he asks.

'I haven't decided yet,' Mia lies.

'So is this usually how you spend your time?'

'How?'

'Picking up men in hotel bars.'

'No. Sometimes I pick up women too.' Mia rolls the words over in her mind. They fizz on the tip of her tongue.

'And there's no one waiting for you at home?'

She tilts her glass back. 'What's it like where you're from?' she asks, resisting the urge to rest her hand on his thigh.

'Hot. Busy. Chaotic. You'd love it.'

'Would I?'

'Yup.'

'How do you know?'

'Because I know.'

Mia has missed this dance, the easy rhythm of vying for the lead. She melts into the synthetic fabric. The man is older than she originally guessed. His smooth skin and sarcasm had thrown her off initially. She imagines his life, taking care to indulge in the banal and unimportant details. Whether he worries about which fabric softener to buy. Or complains when his partner leaves the cap off the toothpaste. How his diary is filled with dentist appointments and reminders to take his car in for a service. She conjures up his office parties with not-too-many whiskeys. Bored women with bobs and ill-fitting blazers. She pictures them talking about sport and property prices. Their assumed agreement in matters of politics and the snack platters covered in cling wrap at the end of the evening. She imagines everyone mid-conversation. All suspended in the moment before beginning to speak.

He drives the same way to work every day, she decides. His socks all match, and he only eats tuna sandwiches from the office canteen. His weekends are made up of christenings and family lunches. He daydreams of meeting someone like her. It all makes sense. She is here to save him.

*H*e stands naked now at the foot of the bed, taking off his socks. His limbs are long and slender, bending into clean angles when he moves. Mia is abruptly aware of her own body. She looks down at the folds of skin as they disappear beneath one another. The ghost of her bra burns angry red on her skin. This margarine body is foreign to her. She doesn't remember when her skin grew lumpy and coarse. When dark blotches started to surface, and the fleshy expanse moved in. She tries to sit up straighter and stretch out her torso. The rolls separate from each other, exposing the crease marks between them.

The man crawls onto the bed and kisses the crinkle of skin near her ankle. She watches the top of his head as it moves up her body, planting wet lips at intervals along the way. His hands travel over the stubble on her legs. His arms are strong, and she focuses on the way the muscles dip and rise. He traces a finger along her eyebrow, down her nose, across her lips and up her cheek.

Mia presses a condom into his palm. He hesitates, but doesn't protest. She is relieved at how different his body feels. He is much lighter than her husband, his movements less fluid, but more intense. Soon, they are lying side by side beneath the water-stained ceiling. Mia feels goose-bumps rising on her skin as the fan cools their sweat. She runs her hand along the outside of his thigh. The man rolls onto his side, turning his back to her. She's sure he has fallen asleep when his shoulders begin to shake. Quiet whimpers give way to sobs when she reaches out to touch him.

'Are you okay?'

He curls further into himself. Bewildered, Mia holds him. She wraps herself around him, speaking comfort into the back of his head. After some time, his breathing slows, and he starts to snore. She stays like that for a while, stroking his hair. As she listens to his breathing, she notices the carpet for the first time. It's the same red as the curtains, but with a faint yellow overlay that changes depending on how you look at it. The oscillating lines cross over one another and loop back on themselves in a way that is impossible to follow. It makes her think of the optical illusions she saw in the centrefold of her mother's dog-eared *YOU* magazines. Jetlag tickles her eyelids as she leans into the body sleeping beside her.

$\mathcal{M}$ia feels the panic before she's opened her eyes. Scrambling for her phone, she checks the time. It's still three hours until the shuttle will be there to pick her up. The man is still asleep beside her. She gets up, quietly, and goes into the bathroom. She turns on both bath taps and watches the water fill the tub as steam crowds the room. It billows away from the porcelain and makes a second roof above her head. Tiny beads condense on the charcoal tiles. The droplets grow bigger and bigger until the weight is too much and they slide down the wall, taking smaller drops with them.

Mia steps into the warm water and sinks until her whole body is submerged. The miniature soap is still in its packet, and she unwraps it like a chocolate bar. It fits in the palm of her hand. She lowers her fist into the water and waits as the soap disintegrates. The surface of the water takes on an iridescent sheen. She lets her knees make little islands in the middle of the soapy sea. The suds cling to the exposed skin. She waits until a thick, bubbly halo gathers around each knee and then dunks her legs into the water, leaving the frothy mass without its anchor.

Climbing out of the bath and wrapping a towel around her body, Mia eases through the sticky door, and lies back down on the bed. The sun is lower in the sky, throwing a gentle light over the body stretched out next to her. Her eyes trace his outline. The square shoulders, the dip of his waist, the constellation of freckles along his collarbone. His eyelids are paper-thin, each eyelash doing its best to stand alone. She studies the mole under his left ear. She takes note of all the details that a partner would remember; the aspects of a person that take years to learn by heart.

She stops at his hands. Perfect ovals mark the tips of each finger. Unlike her own gnawed fingernails, his are whole and untouched. Office hands. She lets herself imagine the ordered comfort of his home. One of those neat hands resting on the small of her back, guiding her from one air- conditioned room to the next.

The man takes a sharp breath in and stretches his body out to span the length of the bed. He rubs the sleep from his face, and leans over to check his phone.

'How are you feeling?' Mia asks.

'Fine, why?'

The words fall in the space between them until the silence prickles with awkwardness. For a moment, she has the sense of being very wrong.

*T*he sun falls into the city haze, growing bigger and redder the closer it gets to the horizon. Mia hugs her backpack to her chest as the shuttle jerks its way to the airport. She puts in her earphones and turns up the music to drown out the sound of the people around her. The dusk pulls a cloak of gold over the city that passes by her window. The day is ending, and the buildings sag with the weight of their own shadows.

# The Space(s) Between Us

*Lester Walbrugh*

2ND RUNNER-UP OF THE 2018
SHORT STORY DAY AFRICA PRIZE

*E*arly spring, a Monday morning, and she had died in the night. Just like that. No goodbye. No see you later.

He recalled a friend who one day coughed up blood as he was about to leave for school. The boy struggled to breathe, they said. He left red streaks on the walls as he stumbled through the house, arms outstretched. When the whole family were sufficiently horrified, he dropped down dead in front of them.

'That white hotel in Arniston, Terence. Take me there,' he heard her say, but found her eyes closed. Her body next to him was as still as the air in the bedroom. The clarity of those words lit up his thoughts, which came clear and fast, one on top of the other. For the rest of that day, they steered his actions.

*I need to book a room. Pack a bag. I have to get a car.*

With his heart pounding and his face numb, Terence slipped his legs over the side of the bed. He plonked his tog bag next to her. He rummaged in their closet, grabbed his best Adidas top, pulled it over his head. It smelled musty and a little sour, but tolerable.

Her side of the closet was neat. She had strewn the shelves with dried rose petals that picked up the colour of the polka dots on the curtains and the stripe at the edge of the duvet. Their bedroom was her pride. When his brothers visited, she would usher them and their jealous wives through the living room to it, pointing out a new set of linen or a curtain that matched the rug. 'It looks like a hotel room! So nice,' they would say. But when she turned her back, they rolled their eyes at one another and later, at the car, they'd whisper to him that she was too proud, trying to be something other than what she was. Somehow better than the rest of them.

The bag was packed. It held their jackets, a change of underwear, and socks. He dressed her in a loose-fitting summer dress, the one she always wore to the beach.

His mind left him and raced up and down the township street, knocking on each familiar door, crossing off his options for help.

*His uncle.*

He locked the front door, brushed the creases from his top, then strode to the top of the hill to rap on the blue door, three times, with evenly spaced pauses. His uncle parted the curtains and squinted at him through the window. Terence stepped into the glow of a naked bulb above the door, and hoping his face did not betray him, he asked his uncle for the car, offering to bring it back the following day. He would guard it like it was his own. He would check the oil and water, wash it and – as an afterthought that sealed the deal – promised to return it with a full tank.

The car sputtered down the road, dodging a dog and the pothole puddles left after a night-time shower. The mountains around the village were smudged against the last dark of the night, their outlines hardening with each increment of light. In the frosty silence of that early morning, the street was stirring. People trudged down the hill.

He bolted into the house, leaving the car idling.

*A beanie. Sunglasses.*

He propped a large pair of sunglasses on her nose and drew the black beanie over her head and ears. She would go in the passenger seat, and the bag in the back; if they were pulled over, this would raise the fewest questions. He grabbed the bag handles, then scooped her up in his arms. She'd grown heavy; two cases of beer.

He shuffled to the idling car. He tried the passenger door handle and whispered an exasperated *fokkit.*

It was locked.

He considered draping her over the bonnet while he unlocked the door, but returned inside instead to lay her back on the bed.

On his second attempt, he managed to strap her into the passenger seat.

The streetlight flickered onto a few familiar faces in the crowd passing by the gate. But it was too early, too cold, and they were on auto-pilot, looking straight ahead.

As Terence slid in behind the steering wheel, the first rays cleared the mountains. A delicate warmth spread through his body. Tyres spun, spitting gravel before they found traction on the tar.

At the intersection. Two minutes. Three.

A hoot from behind. In the rear-view mirror, a truck bore down on them, and in a gap on the freeway, he turned left.

They hit the speed limit. He glanced over. Her hand had slipped to her side, and he returned it to her lap.

*T*heir world consisted of their house, their street, the village, and the fruit farms with their packing sheds, which, like most of their jobs, went into hibernation for the winter. Cars on the national road sped by, oblivious to their existence and on their way elsewhere, warmer, with a beach and restaurants and hotels with staff in crisp uniforms. When they were kids, there was a comfort in the smallness of the village. The postman passed your house at the same time each day; you looked up from whatever you were busy doing to wave at him, and everyone was your neighbour.

For its size, and its distance from the next nearest town, the village was filled with a vague sense of other but, like all children shaped by a well-defined community, they were also bound to its fears and attitudes. The village moulded them into tiny people and, like Sunday lunch jelly, they tended to shiver once exposed to the outside.

Previous generations had never been to a restaurant; much less did they comprehend the rituals of staying in a hotel, and they were therefore ill-equipped to carry this type of experience onto their children. The past had already proved that walking through the wrong door, one reserved for others, could get you thrown out, humiliated, arrested. What if you said something wrong and they misunderstand you? What if you took the wrong chair? Ordered the wrong meal? The experience loomed as terrifying as a first day at school. So they simply passed on these feelings to their children instead.

During the summer holidays, Terence and his friends took these lessons and came to know where they belonged and where they did not. Come December, once the farms had shut down, their families would make the drive to Arniston, a fishing village dangling from the edge of the continent, and along a rocky stretch of coast they would pitch their tents at a campsite with a tiny café stocking essentials. There was no electricity, but there were hot showers and naphthaline toilets. Their designated swimming beach was a walk further south, down the road, past the hotel.

The Arniston Spa seemed designed for other people, wealthier, worldlier. It sat atop a slope that ran down to a pretty cove, with a chainless anchor leaning, lost, on its manicured front lawn. On weekends, swarthy cars pulled up to its whitewashed doors, spilling onto its terrace guests in dark sunglasses. Three storeys high with a flat, balconied façade, it whispered luxury. The east-facing building was as white as the fishermen's cottages to one side, and in the morning they all glimmered in the sun.

Each fading day, their group would pass the Arniston Spa on their way back from the beach, towels draped around their shoulders, shivering like skeletons. Curiosity occasionally prompted the children to act as if they were guests at this grand hotel. They would lock arms and mosey up its driveway with long strides and puffed-up chests, noses held high, giggles suppressed. Their play-courage never took them all the way to the entrance. At the last second they would turn and scatter back to the road, where they clutched their middles laughing, their exhilaration propelled by the release of a new fear.

As they took hold of themselves again, she alone would grow quiet in the midst of their chatter, stealing glances over her shoulder at the retreating hotel. Terence never understood the dip in her mood, neither had he the means to question its significance, and in time he forgot – until that morning.

*I*t will look suspicious if I carry her in.

A wheelchair. He would have to wheel her into the hotel.

There were supermarkets, petrol stations, and a clinic lined up in Bredasdorp's main road, the last town before Arniston. Terence considered the disability parking spaces in front of Pick n Pay. Maybe, under the guise of offering help, he could make off with a wheelchair. But he let go of the idea.

*The clinic.*

He reasoned it would be better to approach a nurse at reception, request a wheelchair for a patient in his car, then load it into the boot and drive off.

And that is just what he did.

Because Terence was invisible to her. She could not see him, had not seen him for a while, so it was easy for him to be a phantom of some sort, even while talking to someone. Afterwards, searching for the missing wheelchair, the nurse would have had trouble recalling their conversation, would doubt herself that he had even been there.

With her, with each passing day, he had learnt to play small. He had shrunk. *Don't sit on the bed, you'll crinkle the linen. Don't come in here with your dirty body and your stinky feet. Don't show any presence of you, anywhere.*

Bredasdorp was at their back. Big, cumulous clouds followed them to the ocean. Terence felt a breeze on his neck, as if from a soft, expelled puff of air, and rubbed the skin there. Her neck was also exposed, and he picked at the round collar of her top. His hand brushed her chin. He felt its cold, congealed muscle and recoiled.

'Almost there,' he said.

In the wheat field beyond, a blue crane raised its neck.

He dropped his chin. His eyes bore into the road. His mind drifted. The evening returned in snippets. He had gone to bed early. She had finished the last beers with two of her friends in the other room. The music was Saturday loud, but her ridicule of him was louder. In their tiny house, it was deafening, and he lay awake on his side, listening.

'No, what does he know? Scared of people. Can't get a word out. You know we only ever go to eat at the Spur? Says he doesn't like the food at the other places, but no, it's because he's too scared. English? Forget it. That's why we'll never go anywhere, he can't even say to go somewhere nice for the weekend. Shame. I must just get myself a sugar-daddy. From Cape Town.' She had laughed until the tears rolled. Her laughter grew louder until it poured from his ears, coming at him from every angle, and he had opened the windows to let it out.

After her friends had left and she had fallen into bed, he rolled onto his back and said to the ceiling, 'Did you have fun tonight?' She uttered a low moan, as she had taken to doing, as if her breath was too precious to waste on him. He had a habit of shrugging off her indifference, but it hit him like a mallet then.

So quiet now, he thought. Her lips, usually wet and pouty, were grey. A faint smear of freckles he had never noticed before lay across her cheeks.

The car chugged over a hill, then plunged onto a long, grey stretch of tar. The fynbos parted. Arniston shimmered into view. He slowed and their clouds raced out to sea.

*Leave her in the car. Check in. Settle the bill later.*

He left her in the car while he checked them in, leaving his driver's licence as security, and agreeing to settle the bill upon check-out. When he rolled her past the front desk, the staff smiled into the void between them. They met no one else on the way to their room.

Hours later, on their balcony, he stuck out his tongue to taste the air. A late-afternoon breeze tumbled with mists of sea spray. He sat with her clenched hand in his, a glass of beer in his other hand. The hotel shadow stretched across the lawn, creeping over and past the anchor down to the cove with its strip of sand, the grains at their brightest and sparkliest in the moment before dusk. For a while, Terence studied the languid waves tumbling onto the beach.

*T*hey had got married in a small ceremony. Afterwards, there was a party at a friend's place. There was music. There was beer. They braaied, and there was laughter. In the midst of it all she looked over at him, over the crowd, and in her smile Terence saw how much she loved him. How much of him she saw. He had held onto that smile for five years. It had since degenerated into scowls and sneers with each successive failure on his part – failure to find a permanent job, and their having to move house every few months. At their wedding, in his vows, words he had caught in that indefinable space between his body and his soul, he had promised her the world. And since, he'd given her nothing more than a room to drink her beer in.

'*I*'m thirsty.'

He brought the glass to his lips and sipped from it.

'I am thirsty. My fok.' It was both an order and an admonishment. He swung his head around, expecting to see her dark eyes on him.

He took another sip.

'I am thirsty. You getting married to that glass?'

What was her problem? He had brought her to this nice hotel. They were sitting on the balcony – Look! There's the anchor! – He was drinking a beer, yes. They were alone and enjoying each other's company. Now she wanted to come and spoil it with her demands, again. Only demands. Why is she talking to him? What is it with her? He was never good enough for her. He never matched her bedroom, her bedding, the curtains—

'I am cold. And I am hungry. I am thiiiirrrrsty.'

Fokkit. Terence jumped up, locked the bathroom door behind him. He fumbled with the taps, knocked them about, twisted the fancy knobs this way and that. Fokkit.

'Terrreence. Thiiirsty! Huuuungry!'

Fokkit, he thought. If she wanted beer, he would get her some. She would drink. And she would eat. He would feed her. He would pour beer down her throat, as much as she wanted, as long as it shut her up.

*Dinner. Beer. Fish and chips.*

Finally, he managed to get the tap running, splashed his face with cold water, then returned to the balcony. She sat etched against the pink sky and, for a moment, tenderness grabbed him. But he shook his head. There were things to do.

*T*he dining room was empty save for an elderly couple seated near the fireplace. Two waitstaff were idling about at the entrance.

He adjusted her sunglasses, then rolled her into the restaurant.

'Table for two?'

'Yes, please.' He took a deep breath and gestured to the wide windows framing the front lawn and its anchor. 'Can we sit next to the window?'

The waiter brought menus.

'Two beers, please,' he said.

'Castle or Black Label? We have craft beers also. On tap.'

'Craft b—? No. Black Label. Dumpies, thank you.'

The beers brought, he looked about him and seeing the staff distracted, reached over, grabbed her bottle of beer and guzzled half.

The waiter again.

'Two fish and chips, please.'

The waiter scampered off to the kitchen.

'Terence, I want praaaawnnnns.'

He flushed and looked about to see if anyone had heard.

The other waitress was at the bar. She had a hand cupped over her mouth, talking to the barman, both looking their way. It's nothing, he thought. People gossiped all the time. What did he expect in a place like Arniston, where at another table sat only an old greying couple, as old and grey as couples get – nothing to see here, move on – but they, fairly young, on a Monday? He knew they did not look like typical guests. You could tell by the way their clothes fit, by the tense expectation on his face and the grave grimace on hers, that their place was in the kitchen, or outside, tending the garden, but here, dining in the restaurant?

He took her hand, brought it to his cheek and mumbled, 'Nice weather.' He imagined it was what people talked about in these hotels.

Faint, bell-like laughter drew his gaze out the window. It came from a group of children ambling by. They were dark from the sun. They were playing tag and teasing one another, paying no attention to the hotel, but as they passed through its shadow, their laughter faded. Some pulled their towels tighter around their shoulders. After a few strides, they stepped back into the sunlight. Their jumping resumed. One boy bellowed louder than the rest.

*A bath and an early night.*

He pushed back his chair and left her to contemplate the view. Their waitress flinched as he stole up behind her, asking to take the meals to their room instead. Yes, take-away containers are fine. No, they won't need any sauces, thank you. On our tab, yes.

'My wife is feeling a bit under the weather, and has lost her appetite,' he said – and believed it. He had to believe it. The best lies are laid to rest the moment they leave your lips. They have neither a past nor a future. That moment, Terence had a simple faith, that whatever he did would be true and real and just. He rolled her past the waitstaff back to their room.

He ran a bath and got into the tub first.

*What now? Where to now?* Then, suddenly, and more pressing: *what if people find us? Will they kick us out?* His fears were irrational. They were paying guests, not some laaities who were chancing their luck, acting as if they could sleep in these beds and enjoy the views from the balcony.

Her joints had stiffened, and being seated in the passenger seat and in the wheelchair had locked her in this position, bent at the hips and at the knees. He mumbled words of gratitude for dressing her in the easy summer dress.

He slipped her body into the tub. He wiped her body with a cloth, and the warm water returned the colour, a deep brown, to her skin. Soap bubbles converged on her toes then slid down her feet, revealing the red paint on the tips of her toenails. Despite his care, she shifted; her mouth, then her nose slipped under. She stayed submerged until he looked up and noticed; he grabbed her head and pulled her face back to the surface.

Then her body was clean and he was calm. He carried her to the bed, laid her upon the towel he had spread out, dried her steaming body from head to toe, and towelled her hair.

During the night he turned, unable to sleep. Her snoring had kept him awake for five years and, that night in the hotel room, her silence did it just as expertly. He threw his legs over the edge of the bed, made his way to the bathroom to pour a glass of water, then took the chair next to the bed. The moonlight drenched their room in the dark blue of the sea; the bed, the cupboard and the walls seemed sheer, veils to a place beyond the hotel room.

She was on her side, barely lifting the sheets. It was as if she wanted to leave the linen undisturbed, as if by morning any sign of her presence needed to be erased.

*T*he pre-dawn chill was still lingering when he wheeled her through the lobby and out the front door, with the night manager at the reception desk engrossed in her phone.

It was a smooth ride down the path, curving past the anchor and crossing the road to the eight steps that led to the cove. There he engaged the brakes of the wheelchair.

He carried her down to the sand.

The sea was swaying from side to side.

Terence removed her jacket, slipped the dress over her head, rolled the socks from her feet. He undressed to his briefs.

He entered the orange ocean with her in his arms and walked towards the horizon until the water lapped against his slow-beating heart. Shadows tightened and loosened over her body. Sea water trickled in and out the corners of her mouth. He lowered his arms.

After a while she started sinking.

He had to leave her there, or she would never go.

She was drowning and he could not save her.

Moments or hours later, Terence left the surf and followed his long shadow up the path, back to the hotel. Standing in a pool of seawater on the thick carpet in the lobby and gazing about him, he felt everyone's eyes on him. He was visible.

# Broken English

*Adorah Nworah*

*A*beg, make una help me reason this story. My name na Muyiwa and I be cleaner for Wazobia Hotel. One day like this, I park my cart beside cast-iron door. Person don use something wey sharp, like divider wey dey inside math set, write 'Room 308' for the iron wey dey on top the door because Wazobia no get money wey them go use buy brass with room number, put for door. I come take deep breath, knock door.

And this room wey I dey talk, na the only executive suite wey dey for Wazobia Hotel. The room na the last room for end of the passage for third floor. The hotel na the unpainted three-storey building wey dey the back of Union Bank for Lekki. You go see am if you pass third roundabout, take left, then right, then another left again. I hear say Baba Wazobia, the army man, wey get the hotel no want paint am because him think say the scatter-scatter look, no go let area boy put eye for the hotel.

I dey see the way you dey look at me, dey laugh me. Na because I dey speak broken English, ba? You think say I no be important somebody, ba? Okay nah, make I show you I be important person. Me sef, I fit speak proper English, Queen's English, like Americanah. Make I clear throat first.

A dusty, army-green carpet ran the length of the dark hallway. Someone had left a mop and a bucket of greyish water beside Room 308. I decided I would vacuum the dusty carpet once I had finished cleaning Room 308. Then I would remove the bucket and the mop before I left that floor to clean the rooms on the other floors. I adjusted my yellow rubber gloves and took a last look at my cleaning cart.

Windex. Check.

Rag. Check.

Toilet brush. Check.

*I* shifted my weight from foot to foot and waited. No one came to the door, so I pressed my ear to the door and listened for a sound from within. I heard the muffled sound of a chair scraping linoleum, the rustling of a robe, and feet pattering. I stood with my back straight and my chest puffed, and ran my palms along the length of my rumpled brown uniform. I quickly went over the sentences I had rehearsed in front of the foggy mirror in the communal bathroom I shared with six others, somewhere in Jakande.

*Good morning kind sir. My name is Muyiwa Johnson, and I will be attending to your room for the duration of your stay. Please let me know if you have any questions or concerns as I clean your room today.*

But then I remembered the advice Nky-baby, one of the other cleaners, gave me. Stretch your vowel sounds. Oyibo can only hear you if you stretch your vowel sounds.

*Good mooorning kiiind siiir. My naaame is Muuuyiiiiwaaa Jooohnsooon, aaand I will be aaattending to yooour rooooom fooor the duuuuration of yooour staaay. Pleeease leeet meee knoooow if yoooou haaave aaany queeestiooons or coooncerns aaas I cleaaan your rooooom todaaay.*

See, I tell you say I fit speak Queen's English. No let this monki palm and glove fool you. I be engineering graduate, Lagos State University, First Class. I know book o, but no be that one go put food for table, abi? Two years after school finish, no correct job, nothing. All the correct job wey dey, rich man pikin don get am. Dem no even need suit and tie, commot house, go interview. Dem go just show for office, take job. Wetin smart man go do? Him go find apron, find rubber glove, find hammer; him go use them, break him English to pieces, because smart man must to chop.

That day was not like other days at Wazobia Hotel. Indeed, it was a very special day. At exactly twelve midnight, an Oyibo from America checked into room 308. He was an expatriate who worked for one of those oil companies dotting the Lagos and Niger-Delta skylines. Angel Gabriel, the hotel manager, told everybody that Oyibo would be at Wazobia for an entire week, and that everyone's job was to make sure Oyibo would be the first of many Oyibos to flock to Wazobia Hotel. He looked each of us in the eyes and told us that a lot was riding on this Oyibo from over the seas. After all, the Oyibo could recommend Wazobia to other Oyibos, or shut his eyes and make a hefty donation to Wazobia like that Oyibo who left a ten-million naira check beneath his pillow at the Sheraton.

I come dey listen well-well, dey nod like lizard. Anybody wey don tey for this city go know say Oyibo be blessing from above. The proof dey everywhere. It sticks out like a sore thumb: Lagos island with its decaying but majestic colonial architecture, Oyibo and their oil companies, buildings, expatriates, trucks, shopping malls, bribes, air pollution, mixed-race children, and the grass to grace stories about everyday Nigerians – cleaners and chauffeurs – whose luck took a turn for the better after assisting Oyibo with directions to Eko Hotel and Suites.

After the meeting, me and the six other cleaners discussed the Oyibo.

'Me, I just want to clean his room,' Angelica, a buxom woman in her early forties said. 'Jehovah Nissi, do it for your daughter abeg.'

'These Oyibo dey give tip well-well,' Lepa Lola added. 'My sister who dey work for front desk for Radisson say Oyibo give am $5 000 one time because him like her smile.'

We gasped in unison. Lepa Lola smiled till the corners of her lips reached her ears. I wanted to tell her there was no Oyibo to pay for her smile.

'And their rooms dey always clean pass Naija people room,' Oghenevwe said, massaging his tired arms.

I listened, nodding and taking mental notes. I had only had this job for a month, and was the youngest cleaner at Wazobia. Before this, I had been a driver, and before that, a busboy. The closest I had gotten to Oyibo were the Lebanese men who sold shawarma at inflated prices in Ikota shopping complex, and spoke English in exaggerated Nigerian accents. But Angel Gabriel saw something in me. Perhaps, he saw beyond the broken English to the dog-eared school certificate beneath my mattress. He pulled me to aside that evening and put me in charge of Oyibo's room.

Just like that.

'You this boy, you are very sharp and tidy,' Angel Gabriel said, giving me a paternal slap on the back. 'Not like all these other mumu-mumu cleaners. I know you will make a good impression on the man.'

Fast forward to the present moment. I ran my palms down my apron once more and had clenched my palm to knock again when the door swung open.

*Good Mooorning kiiind siiir. My naaame is Muuuyiiiiwaaa Jooohns-*
The words died on my lips.

I stared at the man in a lime-green bath towel that hung precariously from his waist. He stared back at me. I gawked at the cornrows on the man's head, at his dusky arms and belly, at the thick, curly hair that ran down his legs, at the rubbery texture of his kneecaps, and at his skin like periwinkle.

This Oyibo was as black as night.

He took a half-chewed stick out his mouth and flung it to a corner of the room. I watched as it flew across the bedpost and landed on a heap of clothes beside the bathroom door, and almost wanted to be back on the streets, peddling my certificate to everything in a suit. But I remembered I was not a very important person, not even with this English and correct use of tenses.

'How may I help you?'

Sometimes, English is not enough to capture my thoughts. Sometimes, it needs to be broken down, like that time wey I think say I go get good engineering job, and I don get job offer, but the day before I suppose start, they come cancel am because rich man pikin say him want the job. I call my mama, come dey cry, she come ask me wetin happen. I no fit speak the English until I broke each word into pieces because breaking English into pieces na the only thing wey dey hold me, make I no break bottle for this country.

'Oh, I'm sorry, sir,' I cried, bending my head in shame. 'I must have the wrong room. I was looking for the room of a Mr John Clark.'

The black man broke into a curious smile that revealed big white teeth. He stuck his hand out. I took the big, black palm between my palms and shook it.

'I am Mr John Clark,' the man said, in a strange, booming voice.

'Ah, but that's impossible, sir,' I said, shaking my head. 'Mr Clark is a white man,' I continued, running a hand down my left forearm as I spoke.

The man frowned, and took a sudden step towards me. I took a step back, just as I noticed the three identical horizontal lines on each cheek, tribal marks, no doubt. He could be a Bayo, or Akpan, or Emeka, an ethnically ambiguous Nigerian man jumping in and out of buses, traipsing the hallways of a government secretariat, pushing barrows in open markets, avoiding stampedes, cursing in traffic, popping Hennessy in a foggy Victoria Island nightclubs, sleeping on top of dog-eared certificates.

'Are you trying to disrespect me or sumn?' the man whispered, clenching his fists. 'Is this how y'all treat us Americans in this hotel?'

My thirty-something days at Wazobia Hotel flashed before my eyes: (a) Angel Gabriel handing me my aprons, gloves, Windex, and scrubs; (b) my first paycheck, seventy-five thousand naira, half of which covered the rent for my face-me-I-face-you in Jakande; (c) my mother, a wispy woman in Abeokuta who had recently been diagnosed with rheumatoid arthritis; (d) Aishatu, the girl I loved and her growing reliance on my bank account; (e) the gravity of Angel Gabriel's expectations.

But listen, my brain no fit make sense of black man who claimed with all his chest and teeth that he was snow, or warm milk, or chalk, or baby powder. My brain no fit digest that kind information. No let my name tag, Dunlop Slippers and sweat fool you. Na condition dey make engineer sweep floor, but him brain still fit put two and two together.

'Are you just gon' keep standing there or are you gon' tidy up this room?' Mr Clark asked.

'I have to report this situation to my manager,' I said, in what I hoped was a firm voice.

I turned my back on the so-called Mr Clark and began walking towards the lift on the third floor of Wazobia Hotel. However, like business in Wazobia Hotel, the lift moved at a snail's pace.

'Where the hell do you think you're going, boy? Think you just gon' walk out on me like I'm a nobody?' Mr Clark yelled, his voice drawing closer with each trickle of sweat now forming a pool in the hollow of my collarbone.

'Come on!' I muttered inside the lift's steel walls as I repeatedly slammed my fingers on the close button. But too late. Mr Clark slid into the lift with me just before the door closed soundlessly. My heart thumped in my chest. Mr Clark flexed his tattooed muscles and tightened the lime-green towel around his waist. Everything in this city was conspiring to break me. Even the lifts.

Just thinking about those seconds in the lift makes me want to break bottles, but that would only make me a thug, or an area boy, or a target for jungle justice or policemen, those rail-thin things who are prepared to eat anything, even a poor man with little meat – especially a poor man. So instead of bottles, I choose English. Curse English. What has English done for me? Curse you for sneering at the pieces of English stuck between my teeth. You go listen to this English. You go understand this English.

For inside lobby, Angel Gabriel dey shuffle paper behind front desk wey don spoil finish the time I rush in, dey breathe fast-fast. He come raise him head from the paper. Mr Clark charged past me and towards Angel Gabriel. He slapped the guilty-by-association front desk so that a red plastic flower vase filled with artificial hydrangeas toppled over.

'I wouldn't have your staff disrespect me!' Mr Clark cried. 'Do you know who I am? I am very important! Very important, you hear!'

Angel Gabriel come straighten him back. He come keep him arm for attention. It dey best to keep calm and remain polite because you never know which important person a guest fit have for speed dial. Just last month, some gangly guest we evicted for smoking cigarettes in a non-smoking room turned out to be the son of the Lagos commissioner for police. The commissioner come threaten to investigate Wazobia Hotel. He come threaten to shut down Wazobia Hotel by month's end. Angel Gabriel spent two whole days kneeling in front of the tall black gates surrounding the commissioner's compound in Lekki to save Wazobia Hotel.

'Angel Gabriel, sir,' I cried, rage seething beneath my skin. In this city, rage is always just beneath dermis, yes. 'This man dey claim say he be Oyibo. I only tell am say I wan confirm with you, because me I never see black Oyibo before.'

Angel Gabriel's mouth hung open. He himself dey expect Oyibo wey look like George Clooney, or Brad Pitt, or all them white men Nollywood producers dey put for movies when them one pretend say them dey shoot for over the seas. Him eyes come dey study Mr Clark, come dey note that him skin be as white as a lie.

'You not gon' do nothing about your staff disrespecting me, huh? You really gon' let this thing disrespect me?'

When you are a poor man in this city, your name is fool and mumu, and thing, and that one, and o' boy, and kssss, and who you be? – anything but your name. I am only Muyiwa to my mother and Aishatu, and even that depends on their mood.

Angel Gabriel is not like me. To him, Oyibo is whatever the hell it says it is, including black. And so he swallowed a large ball of spit and felt between his legs for his balls. They were still there. From a corner of his eyes, he caught the rest of his staff – cooks, cleaners, electricians, drivers – peeking from behind blinds and doors.

'My apologies, Mr Clark,' he murmured, bowing his head and his legs before Mr Clark. You see, when you are not a very important person in this city, you find yourself begging, and bowing, and kneeling all the time. 'The fool is very young and provincial. He has only ever seen Oyibo who are the color of Lipton with too much milk. He does not know you come in different shapes and sizes.'

Angel Gabriel punctuated his run-on sentence with laughter that mingled with the breeze fluttering in and out of the spaces beneath the lobby's louvers. He winked at Mr Clark like they were close friends basking in the glow of an inside joke. Then he turned to me.

'You!' he yelled. 'What the hell is wrong with you, eh? I give you a job and you repay me by dragging Wazobia Hotel through the mud.'

I bowed my head and willed the ground to swallow me.

'Open your mouth and apologise to Mr Clark before I give you a backhand slap.'

'I'm sorry, sir,' I muttered, my eyes on my feet as I stroked away the phantom pain left by the yet-to-be-delivered slap.

Mr Clark come dey eye me. He come dey nod him head the way politician wey dey television go dey nod their head when artists dey perform for them. I wan break bottle, but instead I gather English for mouth, dey crush am with the back of my tongue.

'Please sir. He's just a mumu,' Angel Gabriel continued, building momentum. 'He didn't know any better. Still so much learning to do. Please, e ma bi nu. Don't be angry, oga sir. We would do anything to rectify the embarazzment, sir.'

'Maybe I should look up other places,' Mr Clark murmured, eyeing Angel Gabriel. 'I hear Radisson Blu has the most impeccable décor.'

Angel Gabriel let out an audible gasp. 'Please oga sir. We will give you a fifty per cent discount for your stay. Please sir, don't leave us.'

'Very well,' Mr Clark said. 'You seem like a good man, so I accept your offer.'

'Thank you so much sir,' Angel Gabriel cried, wiping the beads of sweat that had started to form on his forehead with a handkerchief.

Angel Gabriel come dey smile for Mr Clark, he come dey

stretch his trouser pockets. He come dey eye Mr Clark's pocket for sign of naira, but Mr Clark don run comot to the elevator. Angel Gabriel sigh, then he come remember that na the patient dog dey eat fattest bone. Him come smile.

A week later, on a warm Sunday morning in the last week of August, Wazobia Hotel waved farewell to our first Oyibo. Mr Clark handed his key fob to Angel Gabriel and shook his hand in that self-assured way men like him shake the hands of men like Angel Gabriel. Mr Clark patted Angel Gabriel on his back and Angel Gabriel cooed like a cat. Then Mr Clark walked out of Wazobia Hotel and into the Lagos sunrise.

He nodded at the small procession of hotel staff that had gathered beside the bright yellow cab waiting in front of Wazobia's grey walls to bid him farewell. Among the throng were cleaners and bartenders, their arms outstretched, their fingertips hoping to brush the threads of his garment, like he was a lesser known, but equally potent Messiah. I waved my certificate in the air and pleaded for a job at his company, even as I was jostled from side to side by the eager crowd.

Two women broke into song. Two more broke into dance, folding their hips and bending over backwards to meet the rhythm in the air. Mr Clark shielded his eyes from the sun. There was a curious smile on his lips that raised his tribal marks to the top of his ears. Then two simple things happened, the one following the other like bread on butter. Mr Clark got into the cab and murmured 'E kaaro,' to the driver, an old habit borne from living with Yoruba parents.

I broke English.

# Of Birds and Bees

*Davina Philomena Kawuma*

'*I* hate being a woman.'

'You don't.'

'But I do.'

'You don't. And get off the bed.'

'And go where?'

'Don't you want to know what we've paid for?'

Tangerine sighs and slips off the bed. We undress the mattress and step back. There are maybe eight stains, each having lost some resolve the further it has spread. One expects to find stains on these mattresses. At least we do. That's why we bring our own bedsheets.

'Looks like Australia,' Tangerine says.

I look away while she bends to sniff it. Where does she get the courage, her nose that close to the stains?

'Do you know how much body fluid these things absorb?' Tangerine asks. 'Why isn't there a Guinness World Record for this sort of thing?'

'At least there's no blood.'

Tangerine makes as if to say something, but then decides against it. She picks up the burgundy mattress cover, which has clusters of white flowers on it, and we make the bed. This time we spread the bedsheets we've carried on top of the monogrammed hotel bedsheets.

'Isn't it amazing how similar certain kinds of water are to spilt ink?' Tangerine says.

'What's amazing is how thin this blanket is.'

'I wonder who she was.'

'Who?'

'The woman who watered the flowers on this mattress.'

'Who says it's a woman?'

Tangerine smiles. 'Only women carry that much water in them.'

I roll my eyes and walk towards the cupboard that's fitted into the wall behind the bed.

'Men should be asking for a glass of our water,' Tangerine says, as she whistles her way into the en-suite bathroom.

I pry open the cupboard doors. 'Whatever you say.'

Tangerine has been going on about water since we watched that documentary, *Sacred Water*, which some French chap directed and some Rwandan chick, Vestine, I think it was, narrated. I won't say the documentary was meh. I'll just say I watched it the way I watch such documentaries: aware, the whole time, that people like me aren't the intended audience. Such documentaries are created by Bazuungu for other Bazuungu.

*T*he night of the screening, Tangerine was incensed. She complained all the way back home from the theatre. Everything about *Sacred Water* had annoyed her – that it was directed by a man, that it started out being about women but ended up being about men, and especially that the narrator called dibs on kunyaza and referred to it as 'Rwandan culture'.

'Even their word for water is our word for water,' she said.

'Meaning what?'

'Meaning we have a lot in common. Meaning I'm starting to think our differences are artificial. Meaning I was reading somewhere that the Bakiga migrated to Uganda from Rwanda, so in a sense they are as Rwandan as all the other people they accuse of being Rwandan. Meaning surely all this 'say you're one of them' talk is based on the idea that one can be purely something. Purely Acholi, purely Muganda, purely Iteso, purely Munyankore, purely Muhima. But is there such a thing anymore?'

'Is there anything that doesn't annoy you?'

'I guess this is what happens when everything – our history, our identity, our borders – is decided for us.'

I was by this time wondering if we would get a taxi. 'All this because some Muzuungu made a documentary about female ejaculation?'

'The English equivalent isn't female ejaculation. What's wrong with you? Why do you feed into these things? Just because that's what Bazuungu call it doesn't mean that's what it's called.'

I started to walk, motioning for Tangerine to follow. 'If you don't like the way Bazuungu tell stories, why not tell them yourself?' I almost added, 'All you ever seem to do is criticise. You don't actually write anything.' But I said, 'Obviously, that French chap also saw a wet mattress in Rwanda, and it interested him enough to want to make a documentary about it. Why hasn't a Ugandan or Rwandan made a documentary about that before?'

'Because it's normal to us, but anyway, that's not the point I'm making. The documentary might have been about women's pleasure, but it seems as if the only real point of that pleasure is for it to pleasure men. The women in the documentary are receiving pleasure, granted, but if the measure of that pleasure is the pleasure men receive from it, then what's new?'

I interrupted Tangerine when it became obvious that we'd never get a taxi, and it was getting later than late. I suggested we take a boda, which she agreed to. We went to her place, where she spent the better part of the rest of that night beefing about the documentary. The only part she liked, which was incidentally the part I disliked, was the idea that the water in question was worthy of veneration.

Leaving the memory of the sacred water behind, I shut the cupboard doors and assure Tangerine that nothing is lurking inside. This business of checking for dead bodies and porn and prosthetic limbs every time we arrive in a new hotel is tiring but completely necessary for someone like Tangerine, who has watched that TV show about the strangest things guests find in hotels one too many times.

I sit on the bed and watch her. She has trailed air freshener into the room, and is now sliding drawers in and out of the dresser next to the solitary window. I ask if she has found any false teeth yet. She shakes her head. Then she flops onto the bed and sighs.

'What's wrong?'

'I met someone. An American. Elinor Wylie.'

'Do you like her?'

'Very much.'

'And?'

'*Now let no charitable hope confuse my mind with images of eagle and of antelope … I am by nature none of these.*'

'Anha? What are you?'

'*I was being human born alone. I am being woman hard beset.*'

'See your life. What are you talking about, you? Mbu hard beset. Mbwenu, what hard beset?'

'*I live by squeezing from a stone what little nourishment I get.*'

'Stop that.'

'But it's how I feel.'

'You, who grew up in Kololo? Shyah! What stones did you ever squeeze? Nonsense.'

'It's how I feel.'

'Go away. The problem with you writers is that you confuse how you feel with reality.'

'How I feel is what's really going on. Don't you understand?'

'I'm hungry. What are we going to eat?'

*P*rior to the screening of that documentary, I'd heard reputable gynaecologists swear that there was no medical justification (or precedent) for 'female ejaculation'. And that what women supposedly ejaculated was merely urine. Still, of course I'd heard stories from classmates, and I'd read tabloids. So I hoped all those stories about squirting weren't urban legends, but believed that it, like most sex-related things, was in the mind. Maybe, as Vestine pointed out, it really did come down to the message(s) you sent to your brain.

Given how annoying she found the documentary, I didn't expect Tangerine to get into a sweat about, of all things, squirting. Imagine my shock when a few weeks later she announced that she was adding 'water-based foods', squashes, for example, to her diet.

'Don't be ridiculous. Do we even have squashes in UG?'

'Even if we don't, I'll eat their relatives.'

'And who might those be?'

'Pumpkins. Butternuts. Cucumbers.'

'Be serious.'

'I am being serious.'

I said, 'Come on, you know squirting isn't like breathing: not every woman gets to participate.' I told her that I genuinely didn't think women who didn't squirt were somehow 'less of a woman'. She said that was all very well but that she'd spoken to 'someone', someone she trusted, someone who'd apparently been with several women who had each squirted for days. Apparently, that someone had since confirmed that it wasn't urine, after all, but indeed a kind of sacred water. This someone is supposed to have rounded off the conversation by saying, 'If you've never seen a vampire, you won't believe vampires exist. But if you've seen one, in broad day light moreover, no one can convince you that vampires don't exist.'

Because I was in no doubt as to the identity of the 'someone' in question, as there was only one person whose constant reference to mythical creatures Tangerine didn't consider a weakness, I wasted no time in asking if Tangerine and Robert had finally opened up their relationship.

'Now you're the one that's being ridiculous!'

'It's a simple question. Just answer.'

'No, we're not in an open relationship,' Tangerine said.

However, it turned out that, get this, she had been 'practicing tertiary virginity for a while now'. I tried my best to hide my shock. Honestly, I didn't know such a thing as 'tertiary virginity' even existed in real life, but those are writers for you. It's like the rules bend for them or something.

She never once admitted that she was worried about what Robert was doing for sex now that she was a tertiary virgin, but then again, she didn't have to. I picked up on her anxiety when she asked if I thought it was possible for someone to watch too much porn. Personally, I didn't have a problem with porn. Porn was what got some of us through rainy mornings. While I agreed that everything should be done in moderation, Tangerine was still a bit of a prude, even three boyfriends later, so her definition of 'too much porn' was likely misleading. Naturally, I asked about her criteria of 'too much'. She said all she knew was that porn 'affected real-life interactions'. Then she went on to lecture me about the various ways in which porn affected 'the quality of a relationship'.

Tired of the equivocation, I asked her who it was that we were really talking about. She eventually confessed that she and Robert had fought about what she referred to as his 'porn habit'. Apparently, he didn't understand why she made 'a big deal out of it'. To him, it was just porn: 'You watch, you jerk off, you get on with your life, end of story.' Tangerine was, on the other hand, adamant that porn could never be 'just porn', and hurt that it hadn't crossed Robert's mind how uneasy his porn habit made her.

'There's another way to the island,' the receptionist says. Apparently there's a roundabout overland route that narrows into a long, wooden footbridge. We might have to take a boda for at least half the way, as the taxis that ply that route apparently take ages to fill.

'I want the water to take us,' Tangerine says.

The receptionist seems disappointed that I've let Tangerine have the final word. Still, both hands pressed to his lips, as if in prayer, he says, 'The water is always ready to take you, madam. But you're going to have to wait just a bit. The boat is still coming.'

Thinking that it really will take 'just a bit' for the boat to arrive, I tell Tangerine that I'm going to look around. She's to beep me if the boat arrives before I get back. I walk to the waterless pool and train my binoculars on a cluster of trees not far off. There's a noisy disturbance in a guava tree; two grey plantain-eaters are squabbling with a couple of common bulbuls over fruit. A little to the left, a great blue turaco and a grey parrot are watching the drama unfold.

Far across the hotel's courtyard, past the half-empty supermarket run by an Indian man, on the other side of a row of sleepy shops patronised by school-boys, the sky is starting to darken. I hope it doesn't rain.

I'm tempted to make a short trip along the fairly wide and

busy dirt road that runs parallel to the hotel. I think twice about this when I remember the walk we took on the afternoon of our arrival, when fewer than ten species (all of which are already on my life list) revealed themselves. On the same walk, Tangerine counted twenty-three cars, sixteen bodas and five bicycles; she's been studiously monitoring the traffic around here since we arrived. Apparently, she wants to establish 'an index of human disturbance'. She intends to pass all the information she gathers on to management. She's actually expecting to fill out some sort of questionnaire before she leaves! Writers are strange people, I tell you.

I hope it will be as easy to see birds on the island. Thankfully, trails have been cut into whatever has remained of the forest there, so I look forward to exploring the cleaner, quieter interior.

I return to the hotel's reception to find that the boat still hasn't arrived. Apparently it has taken the sound and meat guys. It turns out there's just one, never mind that the festival website boasts of 'over five ferries'. I used to lose my mind over such blatant deceit, but there's Tangerine to do that for me now. By the time 'just a bit' turns into one hour, and then two, she has demanded audience with the hotel manager at least thrice.

Generally, if my phone is charged, and I've carried headphones, I can wait for hours. Tangerine, on the other hand, slips quite easily into her 'Why do we strap time to our wrists if we are not meant to keep it?' mode. Since she's been drinking Uganda Waragi (albeit mixed with Minute Maid) for the better part of the morning, she's now morphed into the sort of person who thinks pacing up and down the entire length of the waiting area somehow hastens the arrival of a boat. At some point she even insinuates that the times on the wall – there are four faces to monitor the minutes and hours in Cairo, Lagos, Nairobi, and Cape Town – are hung wrong.

I ask the receptionist to bring Tangerine a bottle of water. Then, to pass the time, I suggest that she attempts one of those writing exercises she's always on about (write a poem about waiting without once using the word 'wait'; write a short story that's all dialogue; that sort of thing). My proposal is met with a side-eye and a middle finger. So I turn up the volume and watch my Trevor Noah clips in peace.

The boat finally arrives at 3-ish. You can tell it's a fishing boat. But it has an engine, and is much bigger than we expected, so we don't quarrel. We just get on and stand. There are many Congolese and Tanzanians on board. There's also a pregnant woman; we can tell she's Kenyan because of the way she pronounces 'bottle'. Since everyone in the boat is being nice to the pregnant woman, I decide to spread our leesu on one of the planks for her to sit on.

Tangerine has slipped into one of her brooding moods. 'The only time the world is kind to us is when we are pregnant.'

'See your head. You know that's not true.'

She gives me one of her looks, her heart in her eyes, but says nothing.

Look, if Tangerine needs to be overly sensitive in order for her to write as well as she wants to, that's her business. It's just that I refuse to believe that womanhood is the endless episode of angst Tangerine makes it out to be. Besides, she has had such a privileged life; what does she have to complain about? Her mother is a career minister and her father is a career diplomat; I'm talking next-generation tenderpreneurs with more connections to the first, second, and third families than a Uganda Telecom landline. What could she possibly know about angst?

She says nothing else during the five minutes it takes us get to the island, which turns out to be a proper island after all. By which I mean that it's a mass of land surrounded by water. I know how Ugandans can be; they say 'island', but you get there and it's a five-bedroom building with a sand-filled aquarium in the living room. For some reason, the fact that the island is in fact an island cheers Tangerine up. By the time we are helped off the boat, she is once again engaged in her favourite pastime, which is eavesdropping on random people's conversations.

We walk around, eating chips out of tinfoil, catching acts

between stages, and taking turns guessing the lyrics to 3 Doors Down's 'Kryptonite'. We run into people Tangerine knows while we skirt the cooking spaces and camping grounds and display areas. We bypass Bazuungu women worrying about bilharzia. Apparently, they've just discovered that the water in the makeshift showers is pumped directly from the lake.

'You'd think they'd mention it,' one of the Bazuungu says.

'Right?' another Muzuungu says. 'Like, it's one of those things you tell people.'

Tangerine laughs at the idea that the Bazuungu expected the organisers to have treated the water just for them. 'I wish I could be that self-absorbed.'

'You're a writer, aren't you? Give it time.'

Tangerine laughs and pulls me along. We stop by the percussion stall, where we learn interesting things about drums – how, for instance, certain rhythms are powerful enough to align the hemispheres of the brain.

'That makes so much sense to me because I write easier when I'm listening to certain kinds of music!' Tangerine says.

When there's nothing new left to see, we sit on the sand and watch the water. Lake Victoria, so-called because some Muzuungu chap 'discovered it', is calm. 'A child that's fallen asleep at its mother's breast,' is how Tangerine describes it. Aside from a few herons and darters, nothing else swells in the water.

'It was called Nnalubaale long before it was discovered,' Tangerine says.

'Everyone knows that. You writers are such poseurs.'

Tangerine laughs and lays her head on my shoulder; that's how much of a good mood she's in. We sit like this for such a long time that Tangerine eventually falls asleep. I continue to watch the water, which hasn't betrayed any of the hunger for which it has always been famed. It's hard to believe that, at one time, so many dead bodies had floated on this water.

Tangerine and I were children when Rwanda's centre stopped holding. I didn't know what things like 'genocide' meant. The one thing I'll always remember, though, the thing that carries back, clear as faith, is how unwilling people were to eat fish then. How simple things were then! How sensible it had all seemed to my child's mind – that one communicated one's solidarity, one's sense of tragedy, by refusing to eat fish. Sometimes I worry that what remains of that tragedy are the never-ending arguments about the source of the Nile. Maybe this is how people deal with tragedy, by reducing it to something more manageable, more breakdown-able; in this case, the mechanics of how people end up so far away from where they died.

Rwandans say the true source is River Kagera in Rwanda. Ugandans say the true source is in the part of Lake Victoria that's in Uganda. Aside from deciding who gets more tourism revenue, what does it matter? And what will it matter one hundred years from now, when nearly everyone that's alive today is dead? This is what I'm thinking when Tangerine wakes up hungry.

We decide to get more chips, and end up taking another walk. This is supposed to be the first day of a three-day rolex festival. The flyers have promised everything from nsenene rolex to sauerkraut rolex, but it's already five o'clock and there's no indication that there will be any live cooking performances. Tangerine eavesdrops some more. Apparently, one of the reasons she's come on this trip is to 'gather material' for a poem she's writing; she's been noting bits of conversation and sending them to her other phone as WhatsApp messages.

There's a smile on her face when she hands me her phone so I can see what she's gathered so far.

*Some things, like filial piety, you learn over the phone*
*Your problem is that you don't have favourites lol*
*Morning glory in the back seat of her car*
*If Adam were a robot, the world would still be a garden*

I hand her back the phone. 'Good day at the office?'

'You have no idea!'

By way of compromise, I suggest that we return to the mainland via the alternative route the receptionist mentioned. He said the bridge cut through a papyrus swamp. With some luck, I'll encounter and subsequently record my second papyrus endemic. (I'm currently dying to see the papyrus gonolek, which is threatened in the region and vulnerable in the country.) Like every good birder, I keep track of all my sightings. Of the 1037 bird species recorded in Uganda, I have seen and/or heard 565.

*W*e are in our hotel room, chilling, when the cotton arrives in two white buveera. Unrolled, unwrapped, unlike any cotton I've bought before. It seems incongruent, immoral even, that cotton should look like this. Yet when I touch it, it's as soft and silky as I've always known it to be.

I tip the bellboy and close the door.

'I'm sorry I'm being like this,' Tangerine says when I hand her the cotton.

'Don't worry about it.'

'Can you believe this was once our cash crop?'

I laugh. 'Isn't it still?'

'I can't remember.'

'Maybe coffee now. Or bananas. We can always Google it.'

'Looks like the thicker, grown-up version of that thing we saw a lot as children.'

'Satan's grandmother?'

'Yes. By the way, you can go back to the island without me if you want.'

'At this time?' I ask, knowing that I'm not going anywhere.

The plan was to return to the island after dinner. And yet here we are still. Tangerine has been feeling guilty about being 'a drag'. She's been wondering if, perhaps next time, she should travel solo. This trip has, for some reason, deepened her melancholia and propped her introversion. It's of course possible that she's one of those people who's better off travelling alone, but until she can prove this, I don't see the point of dwelling on it or letting it ruin our mood. 'We are already here, together,' I told her, 'so why not make the best of it?'

In the spirit of making the best of things, Tangerine started to look around for cotton only to realise we'd forgotten to pack any. We asked Sherry and Val from the second floor, but they didn't have any cotton either.

We met Sherry and Val last July at one of those expatriate-ridden parties where people discuss the merits of microwaveable American Garden popcorn in the same tone that they discuss cholera outbreaks. They are not strictly friends. I would say they are allies, if that's the word you wish to use, in that way people who won't have to endure each other for more than a few hours at a time tend to be. But we are not, the four of us, in any strict conventional travel sense, a group. We could never count as a single unit; Tangerine claims she would never fit correctly. Apparently, she's the wrong size, shape and temperament.

She admits to being slightly resentful of Sherry and Val's heightened need to share everything. She suspects their intimacy – she thinks they're sleeping together – lends them a, what's the word I'm looking for, 'receptivity' that she lacks. That may be, come to think of it, where the true power of sex lies: not in its intoxication, but in its ability to, as it were, open you up. She says maybe one of the reasons she agreed to this trip was that she thought it might be like sex for her; she hoped travel might make her 'less impenetrable'. Instead she now seems to be closing off and folding inwards, which makes it even more pitiable that the remote doesn't work. Tangerine says it's just as well. 'Did you know that there are more germs on TV remotes than in toilet bowls?'

Somehow the hotel rooms are connected in such a way that we can only watch what the receptionist is watching. And because the TV is mounted on the other side of the room, the only way to watch it, from where Tangerine is lying, is through a gauzy veil of mosquito net. I'm shocked she hasn't demanded to see the manager about the non-functional remote. I can't believe she's OK with allowing the receptionist to 'surprise' us, especially since 'surprise' means that smack dab in the middle of an episode of *Keeping up with the Kardashians*, the TV will blink and next thing we know we'll be watching *Border Security* or one of those formulaic Mexican soaps. Thankfully, the receptionist has yet to subject us to an English Premier League match.

We are this close to establishing why Juan Pedro – why must there always be a Juan Pedro? – and Belicia can't marry, when the TV blinks yet again. We wait while the receptionist shuffles through several channels. Eventually, he settles on a Nigerian movie.

We watch the movie for a while until I rise in protest. 'But Nollywood also! Apaana!'

They never give us a movie in which a 'kingdom' comprises more than fifteen people. And by the way that number is invariably inclusive of the king, the queen, the prince, the princess, miscellaneous scheming palace officials, and the people whose job it is to fan – with oversized feathers attached to the end of a long, wooden rod – members of the royal family.

Tangerine laughs and turns off the TV. We consider our options. Returning to the island at this hour seems foolhardy, especially if we're going to have to use the fishing boat. We agree that we will shower, go down to the restaurant for dinner, and then chill in the bar. We also agree that Tangerine, who is now scratching her scalp furiously and blaming the dust, will shower first. Still, I follow her into the bathroom. I like to watch the faces of people I'm talking to. I tell her it's not the dust but the Amla oil and Indian hemp and Morgan's Pomade she uses. She says what she needs now is a 'properly hot' shower, inclusive of a thorough hair wash with her favourite shampoo. Unfortunately, the heater in our bathroom doesn't work. If we want hot water, we have to shower before the cask in the bathroom loses what's left of the day's heat. At about seven, the best we can hope for is tepid water.

'If only I'd known how extra my hair would be in this place,' Tangerine says.

I watch while she gathers her faux dreadlocks into a ponytail.

She bends to wash her face with the small bar of Imperial Leather soap. Then, using a small ball of cotton, she starts to rub cleanser onto her face. She employs the circular motions favoured by the glowing women in beauty product ads. This is why the bellboy had to go all the way to town, by the way; so that Tangerine would be able to cleanse her face. She assures me that this isn't vanity. That she really does need 'purification', if only of her face. Apparently she has imagined, possibly even felt, dust permeating her skin and seeping into her blood vessels, and that this has somehow 'killed her vibe'.

'You know how people say cleanliness is next to godliness?' she asks.

'Anha?'

'Well, cleanliness is also next to self-assurance. And calmness. And coolness.'

'Cleanliness is next to self-assurance? Uhm, is that a real thing?'

'It is to me.'

'Right.'

'It's like entering bed with dirty feet. You can't sleep properly.'

'Maybe if you're not super tired.'

'Anyway, you can't have legit fun if you feel dirty. You get?'

'Mhhmm. I think you should be able to have fun regardless. But whatever.'

She examines herself in the mirror, and then turns to me. 'By the way, do you think my breasts are too small?'

Oh God. What is this? Ours has never been the kind of friendship that requires either of us to appraise some aspects of each other's physical appearances, so of course I ask where this is coming from. I mean, of course, in my heart of hearts, I have my suspicions. This is probably about the big-breasted women in porn videos, but I wait to see what she says.

Tangerine smiles sheepishly and says it would be nice to fill the cups in her bra. I tell her she's lucky her family has money. Now that she's allowed herself to get infected with Bazuungu problems, she's going to need money. Because, I mean, no offence, but the inclination towards plastic surgery seems to me a very 'first-world problem'. Just imagine a person like me. Where exactly on my version of Maslow's hierarchy of needs would a boob job fit?

Tangerine laughs and says she's not yet at a place where she's 'seriously considering' a boob job, but that even if she were, it'd be because she 'just wanted to see what life with bigger breasts would be like' and not because bigger breasts will please Robert.

I don't even pretend to believe her. 'Denial is a river in Congo. What else is new?'

She giggles and says shame on me. That it's a pity I'm questioning the sincerity of her motives. Isn't that what friends are for, though, I wonder. Who better than a friend to question your motives?

'Friends should be supportive.'

'Speaking of which, how's that award-winning poem coming along?'

A momentary freeze of Tangerine's hand is followed by a request for me to pass her the tube of moisturiser. One generous pinch of cotton later, she says the poem is 'dabolyuu ai pee.'

'Meaning what.'

'Work in progress.'

'Why didn't you just say that? Why invent an acronym?'

'Because,' she says, chucking the used cotton into the bin, 'I'm a writer. I invent stuff.'

Sometimes, I swear, I can feel my eyes rolling all the way to the back of my head. 'So, are you going to show me this poem or not?'

Tangerine hesitates. 'But don't jinx it.'

I laugh. 'Don't be silly! How would I jinx it?'

She says her phone is on the bed, beneath one of the pillows, and that if I fetch it for her, she'll read me what she's written so far. I tell her I want to read the poem myself. She asks if I know that poetry was initially meant for the ear and not for the page.

'Not now, please. Not another lecture on new approaches for analysing the perceptions of and attitudes towards performance poetry within socially mediated online spaces in Kampala and their impact on the Ugandan psyche.'

Tangerine laughs. 'Look at you! That's not how I sound.'

Tangerine knows I can't stand the faux American accents and 'intellectuality' of her performance poet friends. Why she keeps trying to plug me into that scene is beyond me.

'Okay, okay. Fine. But just know that I'm making an exception. I don't usually let people read my unfinished work.'

'Blah blah blah.'

It takes only a few seconds for me to retrieve the phone, but by the time I return to the bathroom, Tangerine has adopted a theatrical pose in front of the mirror. In the spirit of being a supportive friend, I supress my laughter. I however make it clear that I won't stay if she insists on performing her poem for me. She side-eyes me, but unlocks the phone nonetheless. After much tapping of the screen, she hands me the phone.

I swipe the screen to enlarge the text:

*It might be my strange taste—*
*warm shadows for the geckos*
*—boards to tame the restless mice*
*stoles for the unripe wetness*
*but the house seems ready*

*Go*
*Sugar-filled ride through slow —*
 *bodies*
*Bring me a woman*
*soft — watery*
*quickfooted but homesteady*

*Come*
*Rain-fed viscera, gifted by nature*
*—the world is still a garden—*
*This is your body, which will be given up for—*
*Morning glories*

*Go*
*Banana-growing minute*
*moonward sleep – bent by bad-boned tree*
*householed skin loose with beat of drum*
*joints athrum – with respect*

*For the gates of men shall prevail*
*Still—*
*Respite from homemade dailiness.*

I look up from the phone to find Tangerine watching me. 'What do you think?'

'Well, you certainly have strange tastes. I mean, that's never been in contention.'

She laughs. 'Silly! I meant do you like it?'

'Do you like it?'

'Yes.'

'Then I also like it.'

# Slow Road to the Winburg Hotel

*Paul Morris*

*J*akes stood near the road sign. Above his head, the letters spelled 'Three Sisters' and the arrow pointed left. There was a rumble in the distance, but from the wrong direction, so he walked back onto the gravel that met the tar and sat on his pack. Two hours.

He sat in the sun because in the shade, the wind cut cold into his skin. It hummed through the barbed wire that lined the N1. It had stolen the wet from his lips, leaving them broken and sore. The road began to hiss. He stood up. A car from the right direction. Going north. Jakes put his arm out and his thumb up. He wore what he imagined was a friendly, hopeful look on his face. The road roared. The car sucked the sound with it, and he was left with the Karoo wind in the scrub and the distant rattle and whistle of a clapper lark.

He walked away from his pack. Towards the road sign. Someone had used a knife or a nail or maybe a shard of broken beer bottle to scratch: Three Sisters the hitchhiker's graveyard.

Never hitch to a timetable. He knew this from when he used to hitch everywhere. He was too old to be doing this, but his rusting bakkie had packed in at Worcester. He could have tried to fix it. He could have called Mikey. Mikey would have driven up from Paarl when he finished work. But there was no time. He needed to be in Winburg. As long as he was at the hotel by tomorrow night, it didn't matter how he got there. He'd fix the bakkie on the way back.

After a while, a man walked up the road from Three Sisters. He wore new jeans and a clean white shirt under an open windbreaker. His shoes were black and they shone in the winter sun. The man said hello. Jakes nodded. He hoped the man got the fuck-off vibe. Then he felt bad for thinking that way.

'You need to stand about a hundred metres that way.' Jakes said, sticking his chin northwards, away from the approaching traffic. A truck came into view. Six cars jostled in its slipstream. He stuck out his thumb. Hopeless, though. No one picks up two men.

One man hitching solo is ideal. A woman hitching alone travels faster. Though it's infinitely more dangerous for a lone woman. A man picking up a woman on her own is always likely to have an agenda. Even if it's just to leer hopefully for an hour or two. When a bloke picks up a bloke, both of them spend some time checking the other out. Trying to work out whether the other is a psycho killer or something. There's a kind of equality of suspicion.

The road was empty for a while. The wind grated his face, and plastic fluttered in the barbed wire behind him.

'Bru. I've been here for hours. We need to stand well apart. I don't want to doss under a bush tonight, okay?'

The other man's lips moved into a slight smile. He didn't move.

A windscreen glinted in the distance. It was a dark blue car. Jakes saw that it was a BMW. Drivers of expensive German cars usually didn't want road-soiled passengers on their leather seats. The car drew closer, and the other man reached into his pocket, and held up a fifty rand note.

'Hey, what's with the bucks, bru?'

'How you getting a lift without showing money?'

'But I'm hitching. That's the point. You travel for free. If I wanted to pay, I'd catch a bloody bus.'

The man smiled again.

'What's so funny?'

'Nothing, my brother. Nothing.' The man shook his head and focused on the BMW, which streamed past and left them blinking grit.

'C'mon bru, tell me.'

'Okay. How long have you been here now? Hours?'

Jakes nodded.

'Getting a lift takes a long time. But with money, it is quicker. Rich people don't give lifts. Poor people with cars can't afford petrol. So we give some petrol money. Lifts are quicker. It's simple.'

Two trucks, one tail-gating the other, hammered towards them. The tail of cars behind them took the chance the long, flat straight offered, and began overtaking. None of them stopped, they all wanted to get away from the trucks.

Some cars passed going the other way. Then it was just the wind again. A white spot in the distance grew into a Toyota Tazz with a grey wake of burning engine oil. Jakes raised his thumb. Hopeless. The other man raised his fifty-rand note.

'Bru, put your bucks away, man. Hell…'

The man ignored him, head turned towards the approaching jalopy. Mandela fluttered between his fingers.

The engine pitch lowered. The exhaust spat and crackled, and the brakes squealed. The Tazz stopped twenty metres beyond them. It had one brake light, and an arm beckoning from the passenger window.

'Well I'll be buggered.' Jakes watched the other man trot up to the car. The guy had poached a lift by waving money around. It wasn't in the spirit of hitchhiking at all.

The man bent over and spoke into the car. He opened the back door and tossed in his holdall. He turned to Jakes. 'Want to come? There's space.' Jakes shouldered his pack and hurried over to the Toyota.

The passenger was skinny with a gold front tooth. 'Where you going?'

'Winburg.'

'Can take you as far as Gariep.'

'Okay.'

'Fifty.'

'Sorry?'

'Fifty bucks. Petrol money.'

From the driver's side came a deeper voice. 'En olie. Die ding drink fokkin' olie.'

'I'm not paying for a lift. I'm hitchhiking. Since when did hiking cost bucks? If I wanted to pay for petrol and oil, I'd have caught the flippin' bus, bru.'

'So catch the bus then.' Skinny turned to the driver. 'Let's go.'

'Okay, okay.' Jakes shoved his pack to the middle of the back seat and folded himself into the car. Stale beer bottles on the floor, a smoke smouldering in the ashtray between the front seats.

Jakes paid Skinny. It felt like surrendering to bad fortune. The alternative was to sit on his pack listening to the wind in the scrub, worrying about whether he'd make it to the hotel in Winburg in time.

The men in the front closed the windows. The skinny one lit a smoke from a dog-end in the ashtray. He had gold earrings. The number 26 was tattooed on his hand.

'So what's in Gariep?' What else do you say to ex-convicts? *Who did you shank to earn that tat, bru?* No. But the question came out, and Jakes wished he'd just kept quiet.

'What's in Gariep?' repeated the big guy behind the wheel.

'Ja.'

'A big fuckin dam is in Gariep,' said Skinny, and both men in front laughed. They looked at each other like it was the biggest in-joke. Jakes didn't want to know. He looked out of the scum-streaked window. Brown empty land rolled by. Crooked scrapes clawed across the flats where water flowed once every fifty years. Broken hills stood isolated in the veld. It was an awful, hard-arsed place. He'd go mad here. No sea for hours in any direction. He thought living in Paarl was bad. Here, there was nothing but dust and dirty-brown sheep.

'Business,' said the big guy and shared a grim smile with his gold-toothed associate.

'Oh. Okay.'

On the seat next to him, the other hitcher gazed out of his window.

The smoke was giving Jakes a headache. He was going to smell worse than his slept-in clothes when he got to the hotel. He wondered whether he should wind his window down a crack to get some clear air. He wondered whether he should ask first. Then he saw that there was no winder, just the spindle that the thing had once been attached to. Jakes closed his eyes and tried to imagine what the hotel would be like.

He'd never been in a hotel before. He'd only driven past them in Cape Town. Shiny cars dropping people off and picking them up. Or in the movies, all polished and plush, with people calling guests sir and madam, and being very nice. He called people sir and madam in his job, too. But taking money and cell phone numbers from customers at the car wash was nothing like working in one of those hotels. That he knew for sure. He thought he should be realistic, though. Winburg probably wasn't a big place, though he really didn't know. He just guessed because he didn't think there was much in the Free State apart from Bloem.

The smoke and collapsed back seat contrived with the lack of space to keep him awake. Next to him, the other hitcher was still looking out of his window.

'So what happens in Three Sisters?' Jakes asked him.

'Sorry?'

'Three Sisters. What's it like to live there?'

'I don't know. I don't stay in Three Sisters.'

'Oh. I thought...'

'I just slept there last night.'

'Okay. Like at a hotel or a B-n-B or something? Do they even have stuff like that in Three Sisters?'

'With a woman.'

Skinny Man turned in his seat, fag in hand, gold tooth displayed in a grin. 'Hey my bra, you scored in Three Sisters?' His laughter was full of phlegm.

Jakes ignored him. 'Do you have a girlfriend there?' he said to the other hitcher.

'No. Not a girlfriend.' The other hitcher looked out of the window again.

'Nay, not a girlfriend,' Skinny persisted, 'Just a hot little Karoo sussie looking for a piece of the big city. Maybe she wanted to learn some new moves van die Kaap af, nê?' His laughter sounded like dirt and bad intentions.

'She was nice. She was in the bakkie I got a lift in. She was very nice. Very friendly.'

'Ja,' said Skinny, 'very friendly wyfie that one. And the two of you made lekker politics in her nice warm Karoo bed, ne? Ja!'

Skinny reached down between his feet and came up with a quart of Black Label. He opened it with his teeth, took a long swig and passed it to the driver.

'So what do you do for a living, then?' Jakes said to the other hitcher

'I'm unemployed.'

'Bummer.' Jakes shook his head. The car drifted into the oncoming lane as the driver tilted his head back to take a slug of beer.

'What did you do before?'

'I was in Sun City.'

'You were in the hotel business. Cool.'

Skinny and the big guy laughed, and Skinny turned in his seat again to look at the other hitcher. The big guy studied him in the rear-view mirror. The hitcher went on looking out of his window.

'What were you in for?' asked Skinny.

'Murder,' said the hitcher, still watching the vast Karoo scroll by.

Jakes looked from Skinny to the man next to him and back again.

'Hey bru, what do you mean, murder? You said you worked at Sun City with the casinos and golf and the topless dancing chicks and shit.'

The laughter from the front got out of control. The car weaved and the driver shoved the quart bottle between his thighs so he could steer and wipe his eyes at the same time.

'Jirra,' said the big guy, 'if they had topless cherries at Sun City, the murder rate would go through the roof.' He turned to Skinny. 'How's this laanie? Different planet or what?' They laughed again.

'Planet whitey.'

'Ja! Planet whitey. Good one, my bra.'

Jakes frowned.

'It's a prison. Sun City is what they call Johannesburg Correctional Facility,' said the other hitcher.

'Oh.'

Jakes turned to look out of his own window. He thought about the 26 tattoo. He wondered who the man next to him had murdered. Skinny wound down his window and tossed the quart bottle into the scrub.

'Hey, there's money on that bottle!' said the driver.

'Fuckit, forgot,' Skinny said, reaching down for another. There was the sound of teeth on metal. 'Hey,' he said and took a long drink before passing the bottle to the big guy. 'I bet you were innocent of the crime too, nê! Everyone's innocent in the tronk, laanie, every-fuckin'-one.' He laughed. 'Hey, laanie, you haven't been in the tronk. I can tell.' The big man was enjoying this. His belly bounced with silent laughter. 'But maybe you're on the run. Did you pop someone you caught naai-ing your wife?'

Jakes never knew what to do when he was the joke. He managed a weak smile and shook his head. It was like when Mikey and the guys ribbed him around the braai, sinking a few beers after work behind the wash area while the fire burned. It was always him. He was the running joke. They were his work mates. Mikey was his friend. He could either just take it, or tell them all to get lost. And then where would he be? No friends. That's where he'd be.

This was different. Skinny was a member of a prison gang. The guy next to him had been in Sun City. And not the one with the topless dancers.

The day ended quickly with a sunset of brilliant red, and then darkness. Occasionally, lights reflected in the rear-view mirror, shining a rectangle on the big guy's face. Cars overtook them. Trucks overtook them. The Tazz was doing eighty-five, maybe a hundred downhill. Everyone overtook them. The big guy never moved over the yellow line.

'I need a piss,' the big guy said, and pulled into a picnic area. Broken glass caught the lights as they bumped onto the gravel. Something scuttled from under an overflowing bin.

'I can switch off, nê?'

'Ja, switch off. We got help now.'

'Help for what?' asked Jakes.

'Push start. The battery's fucked.'

'Oh.'

They lined up along the barbed wire at a respectful distance from one other and pissed. Jakes smelled rotting fast food from the bin and the dull stench of human shit. Somewhere far beyond the fence, he heard the lonely call of a night bird. He zipped up and wiped his hands on his jeans.

There was no moon and the stars poured across the sky. It reminded Jakes of when he was a kid and his old man had taken him fishing to Eland's Bay. It was only the once, but he'd never forgotten it because it was just after his mother had abandoned them for good. He remembered sitting on the beach at night with his dad, close for warmth and looking up at the sky while the old man baited a hook. The sky was peaceful and frightening, but he had felt safe with his father next to him. He must have been ten or eleven. His father told him everything would be okay. They would make a life, just the two of them. That sometimes a husband and a wife didn't love each other anymore. But that didn't mean that Jakes wasn't loved. Maybe one day his mother would return to tell him that herself, he'd said. His old man died a year later. That was when he'd been taken to his aunt in Worcester.

The 26ers leaned with their backsides against the bonnet sharing a cigarette.

'Where's the other guy?'

'Over the fence.'

'What?'

'Climbed over the fence.' Jakes looked at him blankly. 'Hy't gaan kak, man.'

'Oh.' Jakes gazed into the darkness, trying not to imagine the man squatting in the scrub.

The wind had dropped. Now it was just cold. Something rustled in the rubbish next to the bin, and in the distance was the piping call of the night bird again. The cooling Tazz ticked.

'So why you going to Winburg?' Skinny blew smoke with the

question.

'I'm going to the hotel.'

'Ja, so you said. But why? Winburg is a hole, bra.' He chuckled.

'I'm meeting someone there.'

'A cherry?'

'What?'

'A woman?'

'Oh. Yes, a woman.'

This was the first person he'd told. Mikey, his friend at the car wash, thought he was going to visit his aunt in Worcester. If Mikey had pressed him, Jakes would have told him exactly where he was going and why. Jakes thought it was a kind of flaw he had: telling when asked. He wasn't a particularly honest person. If he was honest, Jakes thought, he'd have corrected Mikey. He'd kept a deceitful silence instead. Now he was worried that Skinny would keep asking questions, and he would keep answering them.

'You know,' said the big man, 'the night is very beautiful in the Karoo.'

'Ja,' said Jakes, surprised. 'I was just thinking that.'

'You're inside most of the time. And even if you could see the sky, all those spotlights. It's too bright.' He passed the smoke to Skinny. 'I missed the sky when I was in jail. This Karoo is very beautiful. One day if I leave the Cape I'll come here. One day if I've got money.'

'Jirra my bra. Don't get carried away now. Los maar the poetry and concentrate on Gariep.' Skinny flicked the sparking butt onto the gravel. 'And anyway, if you could see the sky in the tronk, you'd better look out and not up. Stop looking over your shoulder and someone would lem you, my bra.'

'We should go,' the big guy said. 'Where's the other one? Is he back from his kak?'

'I'm here.' The other hitcher was sitting in the back of the car.

'Nog a drankie first, my bra. And our new tjommie can tell us about his wyfie in Winburg.'

'No bra, we go. He can tell us stories about his woman when

we're moving again.' The big guy dumped himself behind the wheel. The car listed. He turned the key in the ignition. The starter motor turned twice. Sick and slow. Skinny shrugged.

'You never know,' the big man said.

The other three pushed the Toyota until it gained some speed. The driver popped the clutch. The car jerked, coughed. They pushed until on the third try, the car stuttered, revved and pulled away from them.

The big guy kept the revs high, and the men jumped in. The Toyota left the lay-by in a cloud of smoke and dust.

Skinny bit the cap off another quart. 'Pushing cars makes me thirsty.'

Jakes watched the black spaces the hills made on the horizon move in slow progress. The lights of oncoming cars lit the interior of the Tazz from time to time. A black Audi overtook them at twice their speed. Their car shook and the big guy cursed quietly.

Jakes had looked up the Winburg Hotel on Mikey's computer. There wasn't much to see. The bar looked nice. It was open-air with a thatched roof and some tables. Jakes thought it would be a good place for a few beers. He'd sit at the table rather than the bar. They'd be able to talk better there. He wondered what she'd be like.

'So what's she like?' Skinny asked, turning to look over his shoulder at Jakes. Jakes felt a nick of panic. He wondered if he'd spoken his thoughts out loud.

'What?'

'The woman in Winburg. The mystery lady. Is she special?'

'I suppose.'

'Only suppose?'

'It's not simple.'

'Of course not!' Skinny gurgled, and the big guy sniffed approval.

'And you?' Skinny said, pointing his chin at the other hitcher. 'You said you're on your way to Senekal. Another shithole. Must also be a woman, nê?' The two men looked at each other. Their shadowed faces were lit by the headlights of oncoming vehicles, then smudged dark again. What Jakes couldn't see, he could feel.

The other hitcher turned to face the Karoo night.

'Hey!' Skinny said. 'I'm talking to you, bra.'

The other hitcher turned slowly to face the man in the front seat. 'It's not your business why I'm going there.'

'Jirra, this one's hardegat, nê? Did you hear that? We give him a lift and he comes with this…' Skinny searched for the word, 'with this disrespect.'

Jakes felt his heart beating.

'Los it, man,' the driver said.

'Nay, fok! He mustn't come with this kak now. We give him a lift all the way to Gariep. I'm making conversation. An answer would be polite mos, nê?'

'Remember our conversation,' said the big guy.

Skinny ignored him. 'Hey, I asked you a question.' His voice had risen. Jakes felt spit land on his lip.

'Fuck you,' the other hitcher said quietly.

Skinny moved quickly; Jakes just made out the pale blade in the darkness as it went to the other hitcher's throat. As the man blocked the attack, his own hand moved a knife to Skinny's throat. The driver shouted a curse and the car swerved. The tyres changed their humming as they hit gravel. The Tazz lifted two wheels off the ground before slamming to a halt in a ditch.

It was quiet for a moment. The car was the right way up. Jakes opened the door and scrambled out. As he did, something fell at his feet. He looked down. He couldn't see anything at first. Then a truck crested the rise behind them, lighting up a pair of knives. Later, he would wonder what the chances were of both weapons landing in his lap when the car hit the ditch. Without thinking, he picked them up and hurled them as far as he could into the Karoo night.

Skinny scrambled round the front of the car, and the hitcher was getting out of his back door. Jakes could feel the looks on their faces. 'Hey! Jou ma se…'

The big man moved quickly for his size. He snatched a fistful of Skinny's clothing and shoved him back a step by extending his long arm. With his other arm, he pointed at the hitcher. 'Enough!'

When Skinny stopped struggling, the big guy pushed him away a few paces. 'Enough,' he said again, this time, quietly.

Jakes stayed on the other side of the car. All he could hear was the breathing of the three men and the singing of a bird in a tree across the road. The cold, and the thought of the knives, forced a shiver through him. The horizon revealed the moon, bright and silver. Blood hummed a rhythm in Jakes's ears. He thought it might be best to get his pack from the back seat and slip into the darkness. The blades, the violence, the anger were too much. He wanted to be showered and sitting at that table next to the thatched bar when she walked in.

'You two need to make peace,' the big guy was saying.

'Fuck that. He can walk,' said Skinny.

The other hitcher took two steps backwards, never taking his eyes off Skinny's shape in the darkness. He reached into the car and took his bag off the back seat.

'Wait,' the big guy said.

'Let him go, bra. I'm not riding with him any further. I'll lem him.'

'You're not cutting anyone. You made a promise. To everyone. Remember?'

'He disrespected me…'

'You promised.'

A van slowed, geared down, the driver perhaps thinking to help. Its lights caught the men and the Tazz in the ditch. Then it sped up again, the shape of the group in the ditch warning the driver off.

Jakes took his pack off the back seat and hoisted it onto his shoulders. He started walking south because the other hitcher had made to go north. He didn't want to travel with a man who'd pull a knife. A man who'd murdered.

Jakes walked, hoping he'd go unnoticed.

'Hey!'

Jakes kept walking.

'Hey, you. Just wait.' It was the big guy. Then he turned to Skinny. 'Tell him, bra. You must ask him nicely. They're leaving because of you. And you promised everyone remember.'

'Fuck him. Fuck them both.'

'Well bra, we're both screwed if you don't get them back. We're never going to push this thing out of the donga on our own. And then we're not going to make it to Gariep, and we won't finish the job. Then when I get back, my name is gat. And you are completely and utterly naaied.'

'Jissus.'

'Apologise.'

'But…'

'Do it, bra.'

Skinny walked in a tight, frustrated circle. He kicked a stone, which clanked off the front wheel. 'Okay.'

'What?'

'Okay, I'm sorry.'

'Don't tell me. Tell them.'

Skinny raised his voice so that the men walking in opposite directions could hear. 'Sorry. I'm sorry, okay? Just stop. Let me tell you.' Then under his breath, 'Fokkit.'

Jakes stopped, even though he thought he should keep going. The other hitcher was further away, and the lights of a truck caught the white shirt collar that showed above his windbreaker. The man raised his arm. Jakes guessed that Mandela fluttered between his fingers. The truck geared down and stopped. The other hitcher scaled the steps into the cab and was gone.

Jakes stood, indecisive. The road to the south shone grey in the moonlight. To the north, the red lights of the truck grew smaller. He zipped the parka to his chin and pulled up the hood.

'I think I'm gonna go.'

The big guy walked a few paces towards him. Jakes backed away. 'Look bra, if you want to go, that's fine. Just help us push the car onto the road. Please, man.'

Jakes looked at his boots. 'Your friend's a bit extreme, bru. I mean, what if I say the wrong thing? He might get pissed off with me like he did with the other guy. I don't want trouble.'

'He won't. I'll make sure. He's not like he used to be.' He turned to Skinny. 'You won't make any more shit, will you?'

Skinny forced out a no.

'Jeez bru, what did he used to be like?'

'Don't worry. He knows what they'll do with him if he messes this up.'

The big guy walked around to the other side of the car. 'Ag, man!'

'What now?' Skinny asked.

'Flat tyre. We'll have to unload to get the spare.'

Jakes looked up the road. Vehicle lights ghosted from the other side of the rise, then broke over the hill as two blinding headlights. He turned to the car where Skinny and the big guy were heaving out a pile of boxes. He tried not to think about what might be in them.

Skinny hauled the spare out. Jakes walked towards the car. There was a box to one side he missed seeing in the dark. His foot caught it and he sprawled into the rest of the cargo, knocking over the pile and spilling the contents onto the gravel.

'Sorry, sorry. I didn't look. My eyes are closed.'

'It's fine,' said the big guy.

'Put whatever it is away, bru. I won't look.'

'It's fine. Open your bladdy eyes, man.'

Jakes sat back on his heels and opened his eyes even though it was a bad idea. What would they do to him once he knew what they were taking to Gariep? Once he'd pushed them out of the ditch, they wouldn't need him anymore. Maybe they'd let him go. Or maybe Skinny would lem him and leave his body under a bush in the veld.

He stared. 'Books?' he said.

'Ja,' said the big guy.

'Just books? Like, no drugs hidden in them or anything?'

Skinny laughed his muddy laugh and the big guy joined in. 'Have a look,' said the big guy.

In the moonlight, he saw novels and biographies.

'Come, let's get this tyre changed.'

While Skinny wrestled with the wheel spanner and turned the cold air blue with every stubborn nut, the big guy explained. Skinny had come out of Pollsmoor prison and gone straight back to work. The community, as the big guy called them, had caught him climbing out of a window with things that didn't belong to him. 'They were going to kill him.'

'Ja, for sure,' said Jakes, 'I would have wanted to as well.'

'No bra, they were going to actually kill him, to beat him to death.'

'Sjoe, man. That's hardcore.'

The big guy had stopped them. He'd turned from gangster to community worker himself, and figured he could turn Skinny around too.

'So the people told him to do good deeds until they were satisfied. To take the donated books to Gariep for their new library. I'm overseeing his rehabilitation,' he said, grandly, hands on hips.

Jakes felt his relief bubble into a giggle then laughter. He laughed until the tears rolled and his belly hurt, and the others joined in.

When they'd finished, Skinny crouched, still grinning broadly, and began to fit the spare. 'Listen laanie,' he said as he tightened the nuts, 'now tell us about the woman from Winburg.' And Jakes told them everything.

*J*akes threw his pack onto the gravel and jumped off the open bakkie. He was stiff from hunching down, trying to keep warm. Akkie and Granville had dropped him at Gariep as the sun rose over the hills. They'd exchanged names once Jakes realised Akkie wasn't going to lem him. Then one lucky lift had got him to the turn-off for Winburg.

He would make it to the Winburg Hotel on time. He'd meet

her after all. The woman he'd found on the internet after months of searching on Mikey's computer. Maybe she'd be as nice as she'd seemed in her messages. His mother, who'd walked out on them a year before his father had died. Maybe she really was sorry. His old man had always said that forgiveness was a good quality. Jakes thought he'd give it a try.

# Maintenance Check

*Alinafe Malonje*

*B*attling anxiety looks and feels exactly how it sounds –
like a war – and like a soldier unqualified for spontaneous
battle, Mwai was never ready. Her life was always on the move,
always evolving; the time for making long-term plans and having
far-reaching dreams had come and gone, the rise and fall of the
world had taken those away from her one by one. So she stopped
dreaming of the future, and took her dreams one day at a time,
going with the rise of the tide, with the hopes that a dream
cultivated for a shorter period was less painful to lose.

At first she treated any inconveniences she experienced like
birds pecking at the side of a house: insignificant until they grew
in numbers. When this didn't work, she tried a new approach. Her
problems became like water dripping into a bathtub in the dark
hours of night: irritating, but only if you could hear it. She locked
that bathtub in a room inside herself, a room remote and deep
enough that she didn't have to hear the drip, drip, drip of her pain.
The more pain caught up with her, the more rooms she created
within herself, where she could never run out of space.

*L*ike a hopeful farmer in a drought, I was always ready for things
that never came. I lived standing in front of doorways that gave
me multiple entrances into Mwai's life. I never opened any of
these doors, always believing if I entered too quickly, too loudly,
without warning or without invitation, I would be escorted right
out again. So I waited. I waited and I watched as she shut herself
up in rooms. It was painful and yet fascinating to see.

I had begun to think of her as a hotel, one of those prestigious
hotels where one needed to book months in advance to guarantee
a room. One of those hotels to which everyone wanted to gain
entrance, but few could afford the prices, and even fewer had
access to the currency required. In my eyes, she was exactly
like that. I knew that was never her intention, though. She had
just hidden so much of herself from the world that the mystery
attracted the exact attention she was trying to avoid.

I had watched from a distance as many a guest walked up to her at the front desk to request a room. Some guests were outgoing, others were reserved. Every time I expected her to turn a guest away, she would grant them a room, and every time I thought she would let someone in, she would turn them away. She was an enigma. How could someone want the peace of solitude while simultaneously yearning for the intimacy of company? By watching as she checked multiple guests into her hotel and checked others out, I hoped I could decipher the currency one needed to enter the hotel that was Mwai.

*A*fter years of waiting on the sidelines and watching as the hotel both grew and withered, I decided to try my luck. On a cloudy day in February, I approached the hotel. I tried not to linger too long at the entrance, but its expansive nature was so daunting I couldn't help standing back to watch it for a moment.

It sat on the side of the road in a part of the city that was neither affluent nor poor. It was a high-class hotel in a middle-class area, and it managed to invite wealthier guests into a neighbourhood they might not have seen otherwise. It towered over its surrounding infrastructure in a way that was more complimentary than intimidating.

Standing before the beauty of Hotel Mwai, my fears of being turned away resurfaced, so I stuffed them down and walked through the doors. I was met with the faint scent of coconut oil and tender hotel music, and the momentary panic I had felt outside faded. Standing at the front desk was none other than Mwai herself. I didn't know what to make of her being the receptionist of her own hotel. I couldn't decide if it spoke to her humility or her lack of self-awareness. Her hair sat on her head in a pineapple, and despite the dark weather, her skin still managed to glow.

'Welcome! You must be from the maintenance company,' Mwai said to me before I could get a word out. It wasn't a question at all; it was almost as if she was giving me direction.

'Uh, yes I am, how can I help?' And just like that, I slipped into a role I wasn't expecting, but one I assumed this hotel needed. I also began to think that this would be the only way I could stay. Her eyes lit up at my response, but I sensed hesitation.

'That's great. Let me show you around the hotel, and you'll see how to help me, because I'm at a loss at the moment.' She called for someone to replace her at the front desk and began leading me down a corridor. I followed her hesitantly, unsure of how much help I could possibly be, but glad that this charade allowed me a tour of the hotel, something I had only ever dreamt of before.

'What exactly is the problem?' I asked her, becoming more comfortable in my role.

'I'm not sure – I was hoping you could tell me. I've had some complaints from the guests about a perpetual dripping noise. I can't hear it myself if I'm honest, but maybe you can help me locate the source.' She paused in the middle of the hallway to look at me as she said this. She was brushing this maintenance check off as routine, but I could feel her urgency.

*T*he conference rooms were the first places she showed me. The rooms were packed with people, some of whom I recognised from my years of watching Mwai. There were former classmates, colleagues and distant relatives. Something told me that these rooms hosted the most people, and something else told me they were probably the most beautiful rooms in the whole hotel.

I eyed the crowd seated around various tables, and concluded that these were the people who only saw the parts of Mwai that were on show, the parts of herself that she presented willingly. The rooms were spotless, with golden chandeliers dangling from the middle of each ceiling, each one adorned with clear crystals that clinked together ever so delicately, resulting in a distant symphony that echoed throughout the rooms. As beautiful as the chandeliers and their accompanying sounds were, I knew they were a distraction, because behind that echoing music I could hear a faint drip, drip, drip. The minute I heard it, my head turned towards Mwai to see if she had noticed it as well, but she was already staring at me. The look in her eyes was inquisitive, as if she had been waiting for me to notice something.

'Did you hear something?' Her eyes were trained on mine, almost willing me to speak.

'I'm not sure. Let's move onto the other rooms.' I wasn't sure why I didn't tell her I could hear the dripping. I told myself it was because I was trying to prolong the tour of the hotel for as long as possible.

*T*he kitchen was well used and well lived in. Entering it brought a smile to Mwai's face.

'There aren't many people in here,' I said, partly an observation and partly a question.

'I suppose this is my sanctuary of sorts, not because it's special or intentionally exclusive, that's just the way it happened,' she said, running her hands along the surface tops. 'This was a room I was pushed into from a young age regardless of whether I wanted to be in here or not. I always wanted to resent the kitchen because I had never had the chance to choose it on my own. Instead I longed for the chance to stand in this room with a floured apron and a rolling pin in my hand. I longed to be the reflection of my mother, but when I was pushed in here to be just that, a conflict began brewing in me. I wanted to choose it myself.'

The drip, drip, drip began again, fitting into Mwai's monologue. 'Sometimes I wonder if I love this room because I gravitated to it, or because I was conditioned to.' She paused, and I wanted to urge her to continue, but I didn't want to interrupt her train of thought. I hadn't expected her to share such intimate details of her life; it was as though she had forgotten I was there.

'Anyway, whether I chose this kitchen or was forced into it is moot, because what is a hotel without a kitchen, anyway? To be a hotel in Malawi is to realise that a hotel without a kitchen isn't as valuable as a hotel with one. I guess to be a woman in Malawi is the same.' The dripping sounds intensified.

૮૭

*S*he led me upstairs to the bedrooms. I didn't realise until we were headed there, but these were the rooms I had been waiting to see. The first bedroom we looked at was one of the deluxe suites. The bed was crisply made and the mini-bar was freshly stocked. It was an impressive room, but I couldn't help feeling a little underwhelmed. With what I had seen thus far, I expected more. This looked like your average hotel bedroom. The air was thick and damp, as if no one had slept in this room for a while. I was confused. From what I knew of the hotel, it had entertained a number of guests throughout the years, so why did it seem like it had been ages since anyone had checked into this room?

'Does the hotel not get many overnight guests?' I blurted out. Mwai didn't even flinch at my question.

'Not as of late. We get plenty of customers in the restaurant, and even more renting our conference facilities, but it has been a long time since anyone has stayed in these rooms.' She sat on the edge of the bed. I sat next to her. We were silent for a moment, letting the sounds from the street below filter into the room. The hum of traffic, the sounds of vendors selling mandasi, and the voices of mini-bus conductors shouting out their destinations kept us company until Mwai spoke.

'The first guest came when I was old enough to know better. He walked up to the front desk with the confidence of a man who knew the value of his currency. I had decided long ago that the preferred mode of payment was an open mind stemming from intellect and decorated with humour. I knew this hotel needed a guest who could bounce through hallways that too often kept people grounded, a guest who would open the windows to a room that had gone too long without dusting. That first guest offered crass humour, rough edges and a pretty package as payment instead. It wasn't what I expected, but novelty has a way of fooling you. Novelty will transform a guest unworthy of a five-star experience into a client fit for the deluxe suite. He waltzed right in, dragging his luggage, and at the time I never even questioned it. I had forgotten that a prestigious hotel doesn't allow guests to drag muddy baggage through pristine foyers, but in a season where patronage is low, even a prestigious hotel is forced to settle, so that's what I did. To be a hotel in Malawi is to master the art of faith, faith that this season does not determine your worth. To be a woman in Malawi is just the same.'

I regarded Mwai's profile as she stared ahead. Hers was the kind of beauty that you grew to appreciate. The pineapple she had gathered on her head left room for a few curls to spill over her forehead. Her skin had the same shine as dark roasted Satemwa coffee beans.

By now, the dripping had taken the place of the hotel music as background noise. I wasn't sure when it had begun, or if it had just been going on since we left the conference halls.

'Can you honestly not hear the dripping, Mwai? It sounds like something's leaking,' I asked.

'No. Something's flooding,' she said as she fingered the bed covers. I wondered what she meant: if she knew that something was flooding, why hadn't she said so? Surely if there was a room flooding in the hotel, we should be hurrying to fix it.

'Do you want to see the next room?' Her voice had lost its bright and welcoming tone, but I continued humoring her.

'Yes, let's see the next room.'

*T*he final room we wandered into was the restaurant, dimly lit by lightbulbs that cast a burgundy tint. It was almost full, and we took our seats at a table in the centre of the room.

'I've always felt that eating with someone is an intimate experience. Food, like language, has the ability to carry a culture and make a person feel closer to who they are, or even who they're trying to be,' she mused.

At some point during this tour, the Mwai from the front desk had disappeared – or rather, she had transformed into something else. I no longer felt that I was being shown around the hotel; I felt like I was talking to the hotel itself. I was a stranger turned maintenance worker: why did Mwai feel the need to explain herself to me? Why did she feel the need to explain herself at all?

I looked through the menu and was both impressed and confused by the multitude of cuisines the restaurant offered. I was accustomed to restaurants that chose one cuisine or concept that linked all their meals. I couldn't, for the life of me, figure out what linked these offerings. The menu ranged from Malawian dishes such as 'Nsima with Chambo fresh from the Lake' and 'Chicken Kwasukwasu with rice', to Italian pasta and pizza dishes, to Chinese noodles and various fast-food options. All the choices looked delicious, but it wasn't exactly a cohesive menu.

'I think eating different food around different groups of people is like code-switching with your palate. I didn't realise that's what I was doing when I was younger, so I insisted that my family eat pizza when my American friends came over. But I was making my Africanness more palatable. I wish I had been stronger. I wish I had been the one to make an impression on others instead of always being the impressionable one.'

I watched Mwai speak and couldn't think of what to say in reply. I looked around the restaurant at the variety of faces. I had always known that Mwai had spent a lot of her life around an international crowd, but seeing them all in one place was more daunting than expected.

'The diversity in this hotel is beautiful, Mwai. If this is representative of the access to the world you have had over the years, it's no wonder the hotel is so popular. It's full of culture,' I said, still looking around at the mixture of people in the room.

'One can be full of culture without ever interacting with other cultures. I feel like meeting all these people and living in a constant state of conscious and unconscious code-switching is what made me lose my culture.'

I snapped my attention back to Mwai, but she was gone. I was by myself at the table.

*I* wandered around the hotel alone. The dripping noise was at its loudest now, but it came in waves. Sometimes there would be dead silence, then the dripping would start again. I wasn't sure if I was looking for Mwai, or for the source of the noise.

I found myself on the top floor of the hotel, in a corridor of locked doors. I could hear Mwai's voice in my head: 'To be a hotel in Malawi is to keep parts of yourself locked away even from yourself; to be a woman is the same.' I walked down the brightly lit corridor, the walls painted cream and trimmed with gold. This entire hotel was nothing short of beautiful. It almost confused me that something so beautiful could be so broken, but then I remembered that Mwai had always been a mix of contradictions.

There was a door at the far end of the corridor, and the closer I got to it, the louder the dripping sounded. I could see water seeping down from the top of the door and started running towards it.

I reached the door and twisted the knob, but it was securely locked. Even though I was being drenched by the water trickling down, I felt that if I pushed hard enough, the door would give. I needed to know where the dripping was coming from. I needed to know why the sound of water dripping could be heard only some of the time. I needed to know why the sound seeped into Mwai's sanctuary, why it sounded louder when she spoke of the unworthy guests who had entered the hotel, and why it was loudest in the restaurant, the heart of the hotel. I needed to know why Mwai acted as though she couldn't hear it.

'Come in, Mwai!' a voice shouted from behind the door.

I jiggled the doorknob and used my shoulder to push against the door.

'Mwai!' the voice called again.

I pushed again.

'Come in, Mwai!'

The voice was growing more persistent, and so was I. I put both hands on the wet door and pushed against it.

'Stop wasting time and come in, Mwai!'

I pushed.

'Open the door, Mwai!'

'That's what I'm trying to do!' I yelled back. 'I'm trying.' I stopped pushing against the pain and stood there, drenched, my eyes clouded with tears. 'I'm trying,' I said to myself.

I heard the sound of the door unlocking, and I tried the doorknob again. The door opened. The flood of water I was expecting never came. Instead I stood in an empty room, and the only water present were the tears running down my face. The flood was within myself. How could there be nothing in this room? Why had I locked 'nothing' away in the first place?

'Mwai?' I heard a voice behind me. I turned and saw the Mwai from the front desk. How had I not recognised myself?

'I see you finally opened the door,' she said to me.

I placed my hands on her cheeks and stared into her familiar eyes. 'Why didn't you tell me?' I asked.

'Tell you what? Who you are? That's not something I could have told you. I had to show you. I had to show you why you left yourself, in order for you to come back.'

'I still don't understand. How could a room full of nothing have caused me so much anxiety?'

'It's not nothing. It's just that you never confronted all those moments that made you doubt yourself. You convinced yourself they were nothing, when really they made you feel like nothing.' She put her hands on my hands and looked me in the eye. 'You need to check back in, Mwai. Trust that your pain is not irrelevant, and check back into yourself.'

The dripping had stopped. I did as I was told, and checked back in.

# The Jollof Cook-off

*Nkiacha Atemnkeng*

'*M*ost wars last years. This one has to be over by dinner.'
*War of the Buttons*

The egg-yolk sun sank into the bluish green waters. Groves of coconut trees became silhouettes, swaying in the wind. Hundreds of them lined the shore. The sea's gruff currents crashed against the sandy beach, the retreating waves leaving a fine mesh-work of brown seaweed and coconut fruits at the feet of the trees.

Two muscular horse riders, soldiers in the Nigerian army, jerked in the saddles of stallions chopping their hooves on sand on their way to their stables. They waved at the manager of Coconut Grove Hotel, and at four chefs relaxing in hammocks tethered to coconut trees, drinking coconut juice straight out of the nuts with straws. Everyone waved back at the soldiers, who smiled and rode on.

The manager tilted his head in the direction of the chefs. 'Akwaaba,' he greeted them in Twi, adjusting the collar of his shirt. He extended his right arm and shook hands with each of them. 'Welcome to Ghana once more. My name is Kweku Sankaa.'

'Thank you,' they beamed back.

Sankaa had not been present when the chefs had arrived at the hotel. He spoke in a hoarse voice, sometimes with exaggerated gestures. He didn't look into their eyes for too long, taking quick squints at their faces instead. He said he was a small jack-of-all-trades, who did a few other things at the hotel, like maintaining the electrical equipment degraded by the salt-laden moisture in the atmosphere. He occasionally mixed shots at the bar. In fact, it was during one of his mixing sessions that the idea of inviting them there had struck his boss, the hotelier Madame Appiah.

It had been a BBC Jollof rice debate that had inspired her as she drank piña colada at the bar. She had smiled when a Ghanaian food lover claimed that the best Jollof was Ghanaian Jollof. A Nigerian had said nada to Ghana, Naija cooked it best. A Senegalese informed the others that they had invented Jollof rice. Other Jollof-cooking nations simply copied their benachin. Even Sierra Leone laid claims to the Jollof throne.

Madame decided to invite some of the best chefs in West Africa to Coconut Grove Hotel on an all-expenses-paid trip to compete in a Jollof cook-off. The winner would walk away with a two thousand dollar cash prize. She had invited chefs from Sierra Leone, Gambia and Liberia too, but they had been unable to make it to Elmina. So it was going to be a four-nation cook-off.

Four guards ushered the chefs along the footpaths covered with coruscate white shells that dissected the grass lawns stretching to their rooms. Neon-lit lamp-posts illuminated the sidewalks. The chefs admired pictures of Kofi Annan, Serena Williams and Bono on their Coconut Grove Hotel sojourns, displayed on the notice board at reception. A map of Africa on the wall was painted in the colours of the Ghanaian flag.

They approached a series of white, one-storey buildings with Greek-styled colonnades and ox-blood roofs, tucked apart but in symmetry within the terrace of lanky coconut trees. And the accommodation was ripped straight from the pages of the travel guide. Furnished family bedrooms with king-sized beds, 24-hour room service at a dial, laundry pick-up, spacious balconies adorned with flower vases, pizzas in piazzas.

Sun rays knocked on the doors of the resort the next morning. Sankaa led the chefs to the hotel's main piazza under a bamboo roof for breakfast. They passed by the peacock's enclosure and admired its colourful tail. It made a call. Sankaa said he always thought its mating cry in the mornings had replaced the crow of a cockerel.

The Cameroonian chef, Fese, commented that the hotel was fraught with nature – the sea and the sun. Yaa Lulu from Ghana confessed that she had never experienced such comfort before. She had had the loveliest of nights. Adebisi, a Lagosian, confirmed that it was indeed a dreamy destination. Saraitou, the tall Senegalese with brown eyes adjusted her hijab and smiled, but said nothing. Nevertheless, she considered the hotel to be a jardin botanique. She had lodged in fine hotels like this from a young age, sometimes with family, sometimes by herself.

A young waitress came to take their breakfast orders, eager to please. The crunchy smells of pastry, cakes, eggs, black-eyed peas, bacon, tea and fruits pricked their nostrils. Yaa Lulu thought it was strange that she was a cook being served by another cook. She came from humble origins, and had worked very hard over the years to succeed as one of Ghana's best chefs. She had been a waitress herself once, in an Accra hotel where rich businessmen kept putting their hands on her bum. They told her that she was beautiful and curvy. Now and then, as a famous chef, she met some of these men, who had completely forgotten their former habits. One had even offered to invest in her business.

Saraitou remembered her three-hour bus ride from Accra to Elmina – the sea of posters that displayed old, smiling, dead people in places like Winneba and Cape Coast, more celebratory than mournful. Sankaa narrated some of the funeral stories for which Ghana was known. Some rich Ghanaians organised funerals that lasted days, and buried the dead after months, in stylish coffins that ranged from airplanes to cars. Saraitou gasped. Such ceremonies were not considered possible in her middle-class Wolof Muslim family back home.

Fese talked about a girl she had seen by their bus window, who had been offering huge African land snails for sale in a bowl. The sheer size of those molluscs had astounded her. She had never seen Congo meat so big – except in lovers, of course. Like her former flame from Kinshasa, MBazooka LeGrand Truc.

'Chai!' she exclaimed. 'Congolese men are the best hung and most endowed in all of Africa.'

The table exploded with laughter. Yaa Lulu liked the Cameroonian Pidgin nickname for snails – Congo meat. She informed Fese that those snails didn't taste very good. She needed to spice them for two to three days with marinade before they would taste anywhere near small-sized garden snails. Fese giggled at the joke; a bonding spark ignited between the two women.

Adebisi didn't eat snails. She snapped right through their conversation. 'So, when will the cook-off begin?'

Everybody glanced in her direction.

'I think your question is pointless,' Fese retorted. Saraitou didn't say anything.

Yaa Lulu sensed the tense air. 'Can you please let it pass?' she urged, as Adebisi opened her mouth.

The Nigerian exhaled. She stared at four fishing canoes in the sea, paddled by bare-chested men. The chefs sniffed the raw smell of fish, prawns and lobsters from the morning's catch. The waitress stepped to their table. 'Breakfast is ready.'

The chefs made lists of all the ingredients they would need, which the hotel staff bought from the Elmina market. Next, they prepared their ingredients – cleaning, peeling, chopping – and stored them in different fridges. 'The creativity employed in choosing your Jollof ingredients is so important that it is the first step in fighting the Jollof war. You could win or lose the war from that battle alone,' Sankaa boomed.

After completing this important task, the chefs enjoyed the delights of Coconut Grove. The two Nigerian soldiers taught Adebisi how to ride one of their horses. Fese admired the crocodiles in the small pond and swam in the sea. Yaa Lulu played golf and relaxed in a tree house in the fruit garden with a cookbook. Saraitou paid a visit to the Elmina slave castle. She cried when the castle guides told her the horrible stories about the place. 'How can a slave castle be a five-star tourist attraction in modern times!' she exclaimed, wiping the tears flowing down her cheeks.

Madame Appiah arrived in the evening, while the chefs were drinking shots of Art Basil at the bar. Saraitou thought Madame Appiah looked like her mum's rich friend who owned the Koranic school she attended in Dakar. Adebisi wondered from where she had got the money to set up such a fine place. Yaa Lulu found it hard to believe that she was finally meeting one of Ghana's richest women. Madame Appiah made Fese think of the lavishly dressed women who had travelled first-class on the *Titanic*. She fantasised about poaching the rémé's fashionable clothes back to Limbe.

'Food tells you a lot about a culture, a lot about a people,'

Madame started, quoting Trevor Noah. Her plan in bringing them together was not just to pick the best Jollof cooking chef, but to also learn about their different cultures.

The judges – a team of food experts from across Africa – had already arrived. The chefs would also be cooking Jollof as lunch for a group of Kenyan medical doctors currently staying at Coconut Grove. They were eye specialists on a month-long visit, treating the ailments of many of the town's patients in the nearby hospitals. They couldn't wait to relish that one-pot delicacy prepared by some of the best Jollof chefs. Many would be tasting it for the first time.

'I didn't know Kenyans don't cook Jollof,' Fese said.

'Kenyans cook Jollof. They call it pilau,' Yaa Lulu replied.

'Shey, na that rice wey yellow as if them paint am with food dye? Abeg! Make e sleep for on top pillow, no be Jollof!' Adebisi said. Everybody laughed, except Yaa Lulu, who asked Adebisi not to attack pilau again.

'You always run away from wahala at the slightest opportunity. Can't you be blunt?' Adebisi asked.

Yaa Lulu sighed.

'Jollof rice is a West African affair,' Adebisi boasted.

'Eh heh!' Yaa Lulu exclaimed. 'I can even live without our Jollof. My country has a lot of food variety. I have been to Kenya to cook. One thing I don't understand about that country is how a whole nation survived since independence without eating yams, plantains and soups. Most Kikuyu food is either boiled or fried with just salt, finish. Kenyans are like the white people of Africa.'

Everyone laughed again.

'That means Kenyans probably eat for sustenance, not enjoyment, noh,' Fese chipped in.

Sankaa led the chefs to the hotel kitchen at midday. They entered the kitchen and admired its ornate pantry and furnishings. State-of-the-art machines stood in every corner: ice cream and baking apparatus, grills, fryers, blenders, pressure cookers, ovens and fridges. Madame Appiah glanced at her Hublot watch as the chefs put on aprons and caps. They took the bowls and plastic bags containing the ingredients they had prepared out of the fridges.

'Ready?' Madame asked. She looked at her watch again and shouted, 'Start!'

The long-awaited Jollof cook-off had began. Cooking time – forty-five minutes. All kinds of cooking styles, techniques and ingredients could be used.

Adebisi opted for strong garlic, red pepper, onion and ginger constituents. She brought out two canned tins of tomatoes from a plastic bag, held the key of the first can's lid and peeled it off.

Fese gasped when she peeked at Adebisi. 'How can you cook Jelof rice with tin tomate?'

Adebisi watched as Fese produced four red and plump tomatoes. But when she unveiled her chopped carrots, green beans and tiny dices of spiced beef, Adebisi giggled.

'I'm wary of any Jollof that is cooked with carrots and green beans. How does that even sound to the ear?'

Yaa Lulu ignored Adebisi, closed her eyes and said a short prayer before displaying her ingredients. A lot like Adebisi's, but with a nice twist of prawns, shito and red sauce.

All eyes turned to Saraitou as she took out her condiments from a bowl – deep fried pieces of fish, a small cabbage and two bay leaves. No tomate! The other chefs creased their foreheads into furrows. They had never imagined a Jollof recipe without tomatoes.

'That is like Senegalese music without Youssou N'dour,' Yaa Lulu said.

But Saraitou exuded poise in the manner in which she started and went about her unique cuisine sans tomate. So much so that the other chefs doffed their hats at the way she deftly prepared her riz sauté.

Then they all engaged in their own catering work. Knives incised and sliced. Chopping boards were pecked. Blenders ground. Cooking spoons spliced spices. Lifted and nose-dived the brews into shallow-frying pots, releasing mouth-watering scents.

They were painters at work, dipping their dyes into pots of rice. All in a bid to jollify Jollofs.

Saraitou threw a coup d'oeil at the others. She frowned at the sous-classé redness of her neighbours' Jollof. She preferred that whitish-yellow texture of her benachin, beautifully littered with the verdure of cabbage and bay leaves, like little green tattoos. She watched Yaa Lulu rouge the rice, precipitated by her red sauce.

'Damn it,' Adebisi thought. She wasn't there to bow down to all that originality nonsense about Wolof Jollof, or look up to God in prayer for her victory like Yaa Lulu. She was there to win the Jollof war, period. She needed that prize money.

Madame Appiah observed each Jollof nation as they brought in their unique twist of ingredients. Each country had its own version, laden with cooking innovations, marked by the inclusion or exclusion of seafood, beef, green plants and deep-fried fish. She had heard that some cooks even added okra and deep-fried ripe plantain.

Adebisi went for the hot and spicy feel of Nigerian Party Jollof, inspired by her strong ingredients. Fese envisaged a peppery and far less sticky gastronomic delight: Birthday Jelof. Yaa Lulu cooked a salty-sweet one-pot dish, with a nice dose of her prawns. But Saraitou toned down all the spiciness in her riz sauté, imparting only a subtle, perfumed aroma that excited the nose. Her benachin had a light flavour, with just enough pepper and unctuous seasoning.

The pots of Jollof boiled and bubbled, releasing piquant vapours each time a chef opened a lid. The sweet food aromas stung Madame Appiah and her manager's nostrils, and saliva flowed around their mouths. The rice cooked to readiness in due time: Madame said it was the magic of Jollof rice.

Fese worked with concentration. This was her final of the Africa Cup of Nations. She hoped she would win for pride, just like the Indomitable Lions. She didn't pray, even though she was Christian. She didn't think a prayer would make her win: her God-given skills would. She shook her head as she watched Adebisi from the corner of her eye. Weeeh! Rice was probably a Nigerian staple. They had all sorts of rice meals over there, lamenting like babies yanked from the nipple whenever rice was unavailable.

She wondered why Jollof rice was so popular in Nigeria, when their Ofada rice tasted better. She had told many of her Nigerian friends that they should adopt Ofada rice as their national rice dish instead. Their preference for Jollof didn't make much sense. A food writer once told her that it was like a parent showing off their less skillful child in a talent contest, leaving the more talented sibling to watch from the audience.

Yaa Lulu fidgeted nervously when she looked at Saraitou. Adebisi felt she was lagging behind when Fese switched off the flame. Her dish had been the first to be ready. Forty minutes. She opened the lid with her left hand and stared into the pot.

'I cook ma Jelof yi komot one one,' Fese mumbled to herself.

Adebisi looked at Birthday Jelof and sighed. 'Cameroonians should stop that rubbish of green beans, carrots and what-not. It looks like the Spanish dish paella,' she said.

Saraitou grinned. Yaa Lulu walked towards Adebisi, shaking her right index finger repeatedly towards the plump woman's forehead. 'Can you stop all the hating, for Christ's sake?'

The Nigerian chef made a face. The Jollof duel between them had always been a fierce fork-against-fork fight.

'Eh yah, see who just became bold, with your tasteless Jollof,' Adebisi hissed. Yaa Lulu widened her eyes. Saraitou halted her work and stared at Adebisi. Madame Appiah froze. She and Sankaa glared at the chefs.

'Don't insult her Jollof,' Fese instructed from her corner in defence of her friend. She really liked the Njanga rice scent of the rouged crustaceans in Yaa Lulu's Jollof. Saraitou switched off the cooker.

'Mind your business,' snapped Adebisi. 'Please go and be cooking your dog meat sha. Maybe when the guests reject your Jerof, you can put it in tins and sell it to rich white people in Douala.'

Fese made a throaty, dismissive sound. Her fingers gesticulated. Her voice levitated. 'With ya wowoh Jollof! Go and cook Ofada rice.'

Yaa Lulu took off her food from the gas. She walked towards Fese, knocked her hands together as if in prayer once more, and did a palms-up in front of her body.

'M'adamfo nya abotare kakraa.'

Fese tilted her forehead and peeked at at her friend, confused about what she had just said. Yaa Lulu realised that she had spoken Twi instead of English, or Pidgin English. She giggled. Although Fese didn't understand her friend's Twi plea, she understood her please-calm-down gesture. Moments later, Fese smiled.

Madame Appiah stared at Adebisi. She seemed non-committal. Not sorry. She asked if she had finished cooking. No. Adebisi opened the lid of her pot. Vapour whiffed. Her Jollof still needed a few more minutes to dry off. Time up. She switched off the gas. Madame Appiah asked both Adebisi and Fese to approach her. They obeyed.

'I don't want to hear such unprofessional language from any of you again. Are we clear?'

'Yes, Madame.'

*T*he guests sat around the mahogany table in the hotel's main piazza. A waitress served snacks, small bowls of chin chin and groundnuts. Hors d'oeuvres of pepper soup and fruit salads followed. The guests nibbled, drank wine and chatted over the loud tune of Fuse ODG's hit, 'I need Jollof'. The doctors from Jollof-starved Kenya were ready to savour the delights of the famous one-pot delicacy.

They relived epic moments from Jollof wars. The Nigerian Minister of Information's flop, when he said Senegal cooked the best Jollof rice live on CNN. It had led to a legion of Nigerians mauling him online. Mark Zuckerberg saying Nigerian Jollof tasted delicious during his Nigeria trip. The wonderful Jollof-inspired Afro Pop hits. The never-ending Jollof debates in the media and online.

The doctors and judges cast glances at the hotel's other guests, taking lunch in the small piazza opposite the bar. The two Nigerian soldiers strolled along the beach with backpacks and AK-47s.

Two waitresses made two trips to the guests' table. They brought four bowls of food covered in metal foil, marked A, B, C and D. When they unveiled the bowls, everybody basked in the marvel of Jollof. The four constellations of rice made the picture-perfect West African Christmas card, the reddish-yellow hues like the tropical sun setting at dusk in its orange splendour.

Fese's Birthday Jelof featured green beans, chopped carrots and tiny dices of spiced beef. Like her green, red, yellow national flag. Ghanaian Jollof consisted of big, bold eminences of reddish rice grains amid mashed prawns. Nigerian Party Jollof entailed thin strands of orange Uncle Ben's rice. And Benachin was a whitish-yellow riz mélange of fish, cabbage and bay leaves.

The waiters set coconut-shaped plates and cutlery on the table. But none of the guests were told which Jollof was which. Bon appétit. The doctors served themselves, taking a voracious bite out of every Jollof dish. The sweet rice danced joyously in their mouths, to the tune of their saliva-inducing tongues, entertaining their taste buds.

The guest judges ate too, but their taste buds served a different purpose, contrasting rather than tasting. Their tongues navigated the undertones of the spices. How they blended to form a choir of culinary sensations: conductors leading that beautiful choir, in a church that preached the gospel according to spice.

Madame Appiah had learnt a lot from the chefs. Lesson one: in the business of taste buds, everyone blew their own trumpet. She saw Adebisi as a condescending chef. She thought Saraitou was confident, Fese was combative, and Yaa Lulu was hospitable.

The four women were ushered to the table after the guests had eaten, amid great applause. A photographer took a picture of them. Madame Appiah made a speech in which she said the picture would go straight onto the wall of the reception area.

Those present were all chefs par excellence. She was going to work with them over the next couple of days to produce the definitive West African Jollof cookbook. She concluded by inviting them to taste the work of their hands before the chief judge announced the winner.

The chefs dished small amounts of food from the Jollof dishes. The chief judge rose with his envelope fifteen minutes later. The music ceased. Cutlery and wine glasses were abandoned. Silence engulfed everybody around the table. Even the ocean waves seemed to have stopped washing against the shore. Many guests from the small piazza moved to the main one. The two Nigerian soldiers, attracted by the atmosphere of anticipation, jogged to the main piazza.

The chief judge pulled out a card from the envelope towards his chest, so nobody could see the name of the winner inscribed on it.

'And the winner of the Jollof Cook-off, organised by Coconut Grove Hotel, is…'

He paused for effect. Someone on the table started to wail. Everybody looked in Adebisi's direction. She had abandoned her unfinished plate of food and was weeping profusely. The small crowd fidgeted. Three doctors rushed to her side, comforting her. They asked if she was okay, but Adebisi didn't answer. She only continued to sob.

'What is wrong with you?' Madame Appiah yelled, staring daggers at Adebisi. The chef could not speak. She desperately needed money so that her son could have an operation. When she heard about the contest, she decided to raise the funds by winning.

Not sure she was going to win, she had sought help from a Babalowo. The man had given her a food charm to include in her food when she finished cooking. A potion. He told her that any jurist who ate her charmed Jollof would judge in her favour. But Adebisi had failed to include the potion in her dish – there hadn't been any opportunity. Madame Appiah and her manager's eyes had been pinned on them, especially Sankaa's. He had taken quick squints at every one until they left the kitchen. Adebisi had been too scared of being caught en flagrant délit.

Now she was panicking. 'I just received news that my son is ill,' she said. 'He has to undergo a medical operation.' But she didn't add that she didn't have the money to take care of his medical expenses, neither did she mention the potion. People gathered around her, consoling her, including Madame Appiah, who had just learnt another lesson in her cook-off: human relationships were like Jollof rice. They were only as good as their ingredients. An idea popped into her head.

The chief judge stood rooted to the spot, staring at Adebisi in sympathy. He didn't know whether to proceed or not. One of the Nigerian soldiers coughed. A few people glanced at him.

'Dis una Jollof war na some jolly conflict eh. See as y'im dey really bring us Africans together. No be like the kind wars wey we dey fight.'

'May I have your attention, please?' Madame said. Everyone turned in her direction.

'Chefs, you have all done a great job here. In fact, your Jollofs tasted so good you could have all been named Joliffe at birth.' Most of the diners picked up their cutlery and clinked their wine glasses. Others cheered her punch line.

'Thank you, Chief judge, I will take it from here. I will announce the winner myself,' she said, glancing at him. The judge complied with a slight bow.

Madame spoke again. 'And the winner of the Jollof cook-off organised by Coconut Grove Hotel is...' Cemetery silence filled the air as she halted.

'Can we pause for a commercial break now, please?' called out the second soldier. Every one burst into laughter, which thawed the tension a little. And it was back to business when Madame said it was a live event that was not being televised. She repeated her 'and the winner is...' and paused again for effect.

'There is no winner! You all did great, so every chef is getting the prize moneeeeeeeey!' she boomed, in an evocation of Oprah Winfrey on her popular talk show.

The chefs went ballistic, quickly followed by the cheering crowd. People screamed. They clapped and jumped. The chefs hugged, tension peeling from their bodies like husks from fresh cobs of maize. Adebisi ran towards Madame Appiah, shedding tears of joy, and they embraced.

Music began to play again – Sister Deborah's 'Ghana Jollof'. The Nigerian soldiers made playful thumbs-down gestures at the cheeky Ghanaian DJ. The guests laughed as they all swayed and nodded to the song. Yaa Lulu recited its teasing lyrics. Madame had orchestrated a magnificent end to the great Jollof Cook-off.

# The Tale of Two Sisters

*Tariro Ndoro*

*S*he is disoriented when she walks in. This isn't how she planned it all these years. She was meant to be triumphant as she entered the Grande Rambouillet, but instead she feels dizzy. It must be the heat, the contrast between the scorching outside and the cool interior. But she does at least feel relief. Here at last.

The staff fall over themselves to please her when she walks through the lobby doors. She has the confident look of Money and Importance. Plus, she has a body like Beyoncé. That is what she tells herself. Legs that go on and on and on, curves in all the right places. Curves her mother tried to hide under layers of baggy clothing, but you can't keep a lamp under a bucket.

'May I take your bags, ma'am?' She almost forgot she was carrying anything. By now she is so tired that she is beyond noticing any loads she carries, but the porters almost trip over themselves to get to her. Funny how they call you something different when your scent is extravagant and your clothes look tailor-made.

'Always make sure you look proper, even when you can't afford expensive things,' her mother used to say.

'...my name is Tomescu, I am the manager of the Grande Rambouillet, the finest establishment in Victoria Falls. Have you selected a suite, ma'am?'

She hears what sounds like a scoff, but there is no one close to her.

'The Celestial,' she says instinctively, noticing the way his face falters as she does so, yet how he recovers so quickly she never would have seen it if she hadn't been looking.

'Yes, ma'am. A very good choice. May I escort you to the lift?'

But she is parched ... and hungry. She does not remember when she last ate.

'I think I'll eat first,' she says and he melts into the background, making sure not to turn his back on her like she's royalty, yet not lingering a moment more than he's required.

'Ha! Too eager to please, that Tomescu. He came to us from the Jameson in Harare with the smell of scandal still hot on his heels.

Stole money or something. He does his best to give two hundred per cent, thinking mistakenly that we'll love him better for it, but Daddy preferred to have sullied staff members. All the better to blackmail them.'

Again she looks for the voice, but doesn't find it in the swanky foyer where everyone seems to walk with purpose. A crowd emerges from a conference room, and she is swept up and into the restaurant, her original destination. She decides to sit in the far corner.

They respect her nowadays, she thinks, as she walks into the restaurant they still call the Dancing Tiger – shoulders back, no slouching even though she is tired and dizzy. She spent hours and hours carrying her grandfather's encyclopaedias on her head, in the lonely house her mother built in Greystone Park. Up and down, up and down, up and down until her shoulders forgot to slouch and her hips remembered to sway. Deportment is important. She thinks of the adage and giggles inwardly, still the actress, still the little girl putting on her mother's dress and asking, 'Am I pretty?'

The waitress finds a table for her and she laughs inwardly again. How she once sat awkwardly, not knowing which glass to drink from, asking aloud which dish was the cheapest on the menu, and most of all (cringe!) handing the waiter dirty dollars, crumpled from hours in her pocket, instead of waiting for the bill. Now she chuckles at the overpriced 'local meals' pegged for tourists.

There are a few New Zealanders sharing her corner, the do-good backpacking type, but she can tell by the way they treat their waiter that the do-goodness only extends to their social media profiles.

'How I love to haunt those ones,' the voice comes again, and this time she is positive – positive that she has heatstroke or something (probably 'or something').

Lone woman sitting in a restaurant. She attracts stares. From the sort of middle-aged men who come to hotel restaurants to feel important. Her posture is regal today. It has to be. Or else the men travelling on business will take one look at her and mistake her for a bad woman.

She found that out in the early days. The way they came to her like tsetse flies to cattle kraals; having grown up sheltered behind a black electric gate, she thought: they must love me. Until one man asked how much she charged per hour. Then the wheels in her brain went round and round and arrived at an answer she did not like. So she sits regally, pretends she's looking down at her subjects … and the tsetse flies do not approach.

The irony: that her mother locked her in a tower. Mother was afraid of her body, her sexuality, she was afraid that the great wheel of history would turn and repeat itself. So she locked her daughter up. The tower was a grey wall, impregnable as the Wall of China. The only time she left its precincts was on weekdays when she was driven to school, and on Sundays, when she wore her most unflattering dresses to church.

'You must never lead the men to sin,' Mother said, as she threw her clothing on the bed, still determined to dress her like she was five years old. This was how she learned that a woman's body was a sinful thing; so she burrowed herself in colours like brown and grey and asked the barber to cut her hair so short, she looked like a boy. Mother approved of this.

What Mother would not have approved of, if she had known, is that at sixteen, her daughter came upon television the way moths discover light. That her daughter discovered that she was turning into a woman, and even with the thought of sin at the back of her mind, she discovered that she liked Pretty Things. And so, Tyra Banks's *Next Top Model*. She rushed through her physics assignments to glue her eyes to the TV to learn about fashion crimes and haute couture; and when she picked up her grand-father's encyclopedias it was not to learn about ancient histories like before, it was to beat her body into a great submission.

*I*n the Dancing Tiger, they are playing Ladysmith Black Mambazo in the background, the way they do in lobbies and aeroplanes before take-off. Because LBM has the monopoly.

'This is it,' she thinks, 'the claiming of my inheritance. My father's hotel.' And unlike every other hotel she's practiced in, this time she really does scan every surface of the establishment – as though it is hers already. 'So this is the hotel the great Daniel Changaira bought for three and a half dollars,' she thinks, wanting to be impressed.

Yet when she gazes around the restaurant, she sees that the carpet has not been vacuumed in a while, and the patrons look bored. Flies land on the food before it is eaten.

'They're slacking these days,' she says, and it occurs to her that she has spoken a thought that is not hers. A few heads turn, but she keeps sitting upright, knowing full well the importance of faking it until one makes it.

Daniel Changaira bought this hotel for three dollars in 1982 because the old murungu who owned it was tired of a place that reminded him of death. And how does she know the name Daniel Changaira? Because curiosity. Because the longer you hide things from your children, the more they want to know. Because there is an empty place on her birth certificate that says FATHER UNKNOWN. Because everyone in her class had a kumusha and a mutupo, and she too wanted a traditional home and a traditional name. Even though she knew she would never use them; she simply wanted to know.

Because she grew up an only child and spent all her time watching cop shows on Studio Universal and reading Nancy Drew paperbacks, and it wasn't strange for her to rifle through her mother's things when she was away at work, or on business trips and going to funerals and memorial services.

She found the name among old diaries, old letters, old trinkets. And the name made her look on the internet ... which was still new at the time, but then she was like Nancy Drew, so who was there to stop her? She hatched a plan, and began to diet, to exercise, to strut across the house with heavy books on her head (but only when Mother wasn't there).

'And what will you be having, ma'am?'

She is tempted to laugh again – she still feels like an imposter. Still remembers being six years old and pretending to be her cousin-brother, and all her aunts and uncles knowing it was really her.

Lone woman sitting in the restaurant. People watching, after all these years, and she is still pretending she is Nancy Drew, but this time it is the right hotel, the right time, and her heart lurches the way ships do when the tide is high.

'Crepe chicken,' she says, not looking at the menu. Not looking at the prices the way she did in those first days. That is what got her caught once. When the maître d' called the police because he thought she was soliciting.

'Crepe chicken for one, coming right up,' the young waitress says before sashaying away, leaving a wake of cheap perfume.

She is alone once more, gulping like a fish out of water, truly shy for the first time in years and years.

'I have a question,' she squeaks, to no one in particular – glad she is not white and that her blush is therefore not visible. Again, she feels the question is not her own.

*Once there was a woman who wanted a child, but could not have one alone. She dreamt of a family full of laughter and warmth. A family so far removed from the one she'd grown in that she believed in fairy tales. As the story goes, she walked into the Grande Rambouillet when she was only nineteen. She lost her cherry to a man who was older, as the story goes; he was as handsome as a snake-oil salesman. As the story goes, no one knew what happened until her waters broke one rain-drenched night. She had a child, but not a family. Knowing what the world did to women alone in the world who had daughters but no husbands, she erected a stone wall, reinforced with concrete, and employed nannies and gardeners and security guards and guard dogs to keep her baby safe; but it was to no avail. She named the child Ropafadzo and cropped her head, determined that history would never repeat itself.*

'Crepe chicken for one, with a side of teriyaki sauce,' the waitress is back, chirpy, young. Wearing a short skirt that is black and hugs her body like a barnacle. To be young and carefree like that again ... still, the question must be asked.

'Thank you, this is perfect, but I have a question...'

This time the statement is bolder, louder, refusing to be silenced.

'I said, I have a question.' Conversations hush and everybody stares at her. An apologetic smile from the waitress, and then the obliging mask of a stepmother asking a toddler what it wants: 'Yes, ma'am, how may I help you?'

'I was wondering, did, er, did a girl called Chenai Chiranga ever work here?'

And then glass shatters, and the restaurant is still as ice.

*Once there was a man who wanted success so badly that he killed his own daughter and left her body in one of his hotel rooms. It is said that his heart was colder than Manicaland weather, and though there were whisperings in Vic Falls (and the areas surrounding), the man never went to jail because he knew someone in the system, because he used juju on the investigating officers ... because, because.*

*I*n a hotel room, a woman discovers she is lying face down on a soft bed. The air-con whirs in the background, and she wonders how she got there. Right. She was in the Dancing Tiger. She asked a question that was not hers. The room began to spin, and she was helped from her table, the hovering Tomescu appearing at her elbow to escort her. But where, where was she now? The Celestial Suite: that was the clue. It's been a treasure hunt: the first clue, a name; the second clue, a hotel – but most importantly, this room, this hotel.

She gets up and looks around the room, ignoring the headache that threatens to split her in two. She stares at her reflection in the mirror, and the face that looks back is not entirely her own. Similar, yes, but not ... hers.

'Daddy would say, "They're slacking these days".' This time the thought that is not hers is not in her head, nor pouring out of her mouth without her permission. It is spoken, quite naturally, by the unnatural face in the mirror, which is similar to hers but not her own – same cheekbones, yes; same dimple, yes; but no scar near the left ear. So alike, they could be … sisters. This is Ropafadzo's last Own Thought.

જજ

*D*addy would say, 'They're slacking these days,' and he would shake his head. But don't be fooled; from the day Daddy bought the Ram from Tom Feldman for three dollars and fifty-nine cents in 1982 – all he had in his pockets, until the day heart disease and heartbreak finally claimed him in 2003, he accused the hotel staff of 'slacking these days'. He needed something to complain about.

Perhaps it was because he was the first black man to own the hotel, and, being the first, he was convinced that the staff undermined his authority simply because they were used to serving whites. But do not let my comment about Daddy buying the Rambouillet for three and a half dollars make you think it is a cheap establishment, oh no! Quite the opposite. Tom Feldman was simply in a hurry to leave the country after his wife and daughter had died in what he called the Rhodesian Bush War.

'I'm ready to leave, Danny,' he confided to my father, 'packed and ready. I just need a buyer for this wretched place. Too many memories, you know?'

Of course, he was the average strong and surly quiet man, but if you must know, they'd been sitting at a bar, and darling, people tell each other all sorts of things after the fourth round. All sorts. I can show you the exact bar stool Daddy sat on when he was pretending to be a good listener.

Oh, he laid it on thick, Daddy, asking all the right questions. What were their names? How old? On her seventh birthday, really? Haikona! He shook his head so convincingly that even I believed he felt bad for Feldman. At last, Tom Feldman got up, stumbled to his office and returned to the bar with two documents in his hands: the title deeds to the Grande Rambouillet Hotel; and an Agreement of Sale. It must have shocked Daddy that Old Man Feldman kept them in his office, but like I said, the man was itching to leave.

Daddy shook his head and said something about how he couldn't take the man's inheritance like that. Feldman insisted. Daddy shrugged, said, 'Well if you insist,' then gingerly signed the page and shook out the dollars and change from his pockets.

'Just one condition,' Feldman said, before handing the pen to the barman for him to sign as witness, 'I haven't paid the staff this month, so you'll have to tide them over ... and there is the issue of the taxes.'

Daddy tried not to look cheated. Which must have been hard. I mean, have you seen our father? People might not believe it, from the way he acted all braggadocio at PTA meetings, but he loved acting broke. Eyes together, brows furrowed, hands out, blah blah blah blah. But you know he's always crying about something – crocodile tears. He's the real cheat.

A list of people our father has cheated: my stepmothers, all five of them. In 1986, he started a Ponzi scheme. In 1987, he went to jail for it. Two weeks later, he strolled out like a man strolling on a beach. But the one thing my father never did was to kill me for juju. My death was an accident, but no one has ever believed that.

Ropafadzo watches the face in the mirror speak without opening its mouth, and is suddenly dizzy, suddenly tired, here in the Celestial Suite. She is stuck in the set of a Nollywood movie with its exaggerated vaudeville, but the truth is something more sinister.

'Sister, sister.' Where have you gone?

The sister walks out into the air for the first time in many years, the sun lighting her way. She is free, free! Apart from a few gasps from some old-timers, the entire hotel seems to continue on its merry way, the sweepers sweep and the cabaret sings as if the Titanic is sinking again, and and and, but she is leaving at last, and she never has to be bothered with hotel business again.

Ropafadzo can no longer move. Now she is forced to watch the cleaners in the morning. The Rambouillet belongs entirely to her and nobody else, but she is alone and no other voice speaks to her. She cries and yells and tries to move, but she is trapped between silver and glass. Sometimes she sees recognition in the eyes of the cleaning ladies, followed by screaming, running, and later, the smug face of Tomescu. No one else will ever manage the Grande Rambouillet while he's alive unless … unless a guest sleeps in the Celestial Suite. But no one ever does.

*Once there was a woman who wanted her inheritance so badly, she walked into a lions' lair. They say no one sleeps peacefully in the Celestial Suite. A woman who wanted so badly to possess what once was her father's that she followed a stray voice to a distant palace, and became trapped in its highest tower.*

# The Last Resident

*Jayne Bauling*

*H*e has lived too long.

The lift frightens him, and the stairs defeat him, even with their ornate dark wood banister to hold. He can't remember when the lift was installed; he thinks it may have been in the last three years.

So many things elude him, balanced by those that return to him clearly now, times and people he hasn't contemplated for over half his life. He finds this change to be one of the most disconcerting that age has brought. It is not the worst change, and some of the memories fill up the time between sleep and the few routine activities that divide up the days. Sleep consists only of fragments and confused wakings, and the activities are his meals in the dining room and tea on the terrace, as the new brochures call it.

He is the last resident in what is possibly the last residential hotel in this city once known for them.

There is nothing to remember or forget about his reason for the move to this south coast of KwaZulu-Natal. It was what you did when you retired. You chased warmth, clean air and a view, not anticipating the humidity, the wind, and the smells the wind brought. He had imagined he might take up line-fishing, picturing himself on some rocks, dashed by exhilarating salt spray. This was another thing you did in retirement – you found a hobby, like fishing or golf – but he was never a sportsman.

The move was a mistake he kept intending to correct, but the effort required was daunting. It was possible that a return to inland places would have been an equal mistake. Most of his circle had gone after their own sea or mountain views.

There had been a sea view to start with, in the cottage down the coast. He only came to Durban and the hotel when time's passage had balanced him between not yet needing care, but wanting someone else to do the work and perform the chores for which he felt too feeble. Electric switches especially had begun to haunt him: an empty kettle boiled dry, when just weeks earlier, it had provided him with cold tea when he forgot to switch it on.

The hotel is currently being renovated in stages. After he goes, it will be a regular hotel, with no residents, only transient guests. He has not given much thought to the manner of his departure. No one will come for him, should there be a need to be taken elsewhere, but he will be the last to go.

Mrs Cairncross – 'Call me Daffers' – left months ago. Her family came to fetch her. By now, his old friends and acquaintances must also have had people come for them, wherever their sea views were. They had married, many more than once, and had first and second families.

He has lived his adult life alone.

Other guests jostle him as they push their way into the lift. The tang of aftershave and the sweetness of perfume irritate his nose. They are young, they always are, all the versions of this morning's group, but they never use the stairs. They are in a hurry, on their phones, pulling small pieces of luggage on wheels. The longest any of them stays is two nights.

They never greet him. He doesn't think they see him.

The only greeting comes from Namhla as he enters the dining room that is now called the restaurant. She has been taking her turn asking for the room numbers of guests as they arrive for breakfast, but she doesn't require his.

'How are you this morning, sir?' She smiles at him as she asks, and she is new enough to her job for the smile to be real.

'Fine, fine, Namhla.' Some days he forgets that she is Namhla, and calls her by the name of one of her predecessors.

'Your table is waiting.'

He knows she says it to reassure him. There was a day he found a young businessman at his regular corner table. He stood helplessly until Namhla came to lead him to another place, soothing his agitation with the promise that it was just this once he would have to sit elsewhere.

Since then, she has seen to it that no one occupies his table.

A buffet has replaced a menu and waiters. He finds it a trial.

Most mornings, he sits a few minutes at his table, gathering his thoughts, gathering strength.

He watches Namhla. There is a brightness about her that pleases him. Her lips are always red and shiny, but the colour on her eyelids and fingernails varies. Her hairstyle changes all the time too; he thinks that sometimes she wears a wig.

It has been years since the hotel put the staff in uniforms: black trousers or skirts and white shirts with a thin black stripe. He would like to see Namhla in her own choice of outfit. He is sure it will complement the boldness of her make-up.

Having sat down, he must now stand up and navigate his way to the buffet. He imagines he hears the creak as he works himself up out of the chair, fearful of angling himself or leaning too far to one side or the other; that is how the sudden back pains come. Walking, he wheezes, and his hands tremble. Some days, he brings his walking stick to breakfast, but on others, he fears it will be a hindrance.

There are people helping themselves to food, their movements quick and decisive. A young woman waiting for her fried egg twitches. They all frighten him.

He has been afraid most of his life, primarily of people, but of other things too, and above all, of himself, of inadvertently doing something that will draw attention.

'What are you going to choose this morning, sir?'

Namhla's colleague has taken over at the dining-room entrance.

It is a ritual they have established whenever she can spare time to join him at the buffet.

'You know me, Namhla,' he says, waiting for a shaven-headed young man to finish filling his bowl with fruit, and beginning to be anxious that there will be no pawpaw or spanspek left. Or papaya and melon as most people seem to call them nowadays.

'No adventure today?' she teases. 'Eggs with bacon and a sausage? A small spoon of baked beans? Gada is a beast and a bully, but he is good at eggs. You would like his omelette, with some chopped pepper, maybe?'

Is it hope that shines in her sparkle-lidded eyes? Her smile rounds her smooth cheeks; she has dusted them with something that shimmers.

Breathing a laugh, he shakes his head.

'My pawpaw and porridge, thank you very much.'

Disappointment closes her lips in a pout. Is it an act? He is sure some of the light goes out of her face.

'One day you will try something different, and make me happy.' Then she glances at Gada, who is sliding a fried egg on to the twitchy woman's plate, and lowers her voice. 'Get your pawpaw. I will bring your porridge.'

She is only supposed to help guests to tea and coffee, but he is always grateful and relieved when she makes this offer, sparing him a second trip from his table to the food, as he cannot manage to carry two bowls at once. He is also touched because he has heard Gada being sharp with her when she assists him.

'Thank you, Namhla,' he says, digging a few pieces of pawpaw out of the bowl of chopped fruit.

Making his careful way back to his table, he is still thinking about Namhla. What makes her kind and interested, when others are impatient? Gada and the other staff, especially the woman who manages the hotel, Mrs P, they all call her, are very impatient. How many times has she spoken about the favour they are doing him, by allowing him to remain a resident? He knows she wants him gone, taken away by non-existent relatives, or any other way.

Namhla is quick to reach the table with his porridge.

'I'll bring your tea now.'

He eats his four pieces of pawpaw slowly, the sweetness a pleasure. He would like to take more, but is afraid of what others would make of his greed. Suppose a guest was to say something?

The other consideration is his stomach, unpredictable these past few years, easily provoked to revolt.

He has the last piece in his mouth when Namhla arrives with the small white teapot and matching jug.

'There you go. Let me take that.'

She moves the empty fruit bowl from the placemat in front of him and replaces it with his porridge.

With his mouth full, he cannot thank her before she swivels and whisks away in response to someone signalling for a coffee refill. He is embarrassed by his failure, because she is good to him.

His hand shakes as he reaches for the teapot. Some days Namhla pours for him. Every time he has to do it for himself, the pot feels heavier. He cannot hold it steady, and some of the stream of hot liquid fills the saucer before he can aim the spout at the cup.

He feels humiliated every time this happens.

'Old age isn't for sissies,' Mrs Cairncross would chirp as if she had just then invented the saying.

Sissies. Sissy. They called him that at his Johannesburg primary school. Pansy. Nancy Boy. The words changed over the decades. By now there are probably new words he doesn't know. He hasn't kept up.

This isn't a memory that has returned with the others. It has never left him. He still hears their voices.

The schools, primary and high, and suburb too, were strangely named for an American president, commemorating his role in *the war*. His mother always gave the words dark emphasis.

The war, during which he was born, his father's leaving present before he left to fight and die in it.

'They have to be nice to you, because your daddy is dead,' his mother said when he fretted about the other children.

She was wrong. They didn't, and they weren't.

Then she got religion, and her words changed: 'Remember that we are made in the image of God. You have to live up to that.'

God wasn't a sissy.

He tried to please: her, his teachers, other adults. There was no possibility of pleasing his peers.

'Try to join in,' his teachers urged. 'Make the effort, and you'll soon fit in.'

*Don't be other,* they meant.

He has lived in fear of being other, in fear too of those who might look and see the truth behind the inoffensiveness he cultivated, identifying him as other, unlike them.

He has lived safe.

In adulthood he acquired friends, never close, ostensibly dull people whose dullness was perhaps a disguise for their own apprehensions, possibly not much different from his.

His timidity kept him from confiding, and in turn the friends revealed little of themselves. There were subjects they never discussed, topics that betrayed or divided: sex, race, politics and religion foremost among them.

His porridge has cooled. He has become a messy eater, not always finding his mouth with the spoon. He imagines anyone glancing his way would look away in disgust, seeing the dirty-white oatmeal dribbling from his mouth.

*T*he church person visits. He has never worked out which day it is that she comes. This could be because he loses track of the days, or because her visits are random. If asked, he would say that she comes once a fortnight, but it would be more of a timorous guess than an opinion.

Sometimes she is accompanied by a young man who is always dressed in the trousers and waistcoat of a three-piece suit, with a toning shirt and tie. He thinks he might be the woman's son. She introduced them the first time she brought the man, but he didn't hear her properly, and was embarrassed to ask.

The young man calls him uncle, but the woman calls him by his first name.

Today she is alone.

He should be grateful, as he receives no other visitors, but he dislikes her. This makes him feel guilty.

Her visits blur into one. They follow a pattern: she arrives in the morning, usually when he is sitting on the terrace to be out of the way of the housekeeping staff cleaning his room. She starts by telling him what a *wonderful* smile he has. He doesn't know why she thinks that. Politeness demands it, but he has to force the smile. The only person left who can make him smile naturally is Namhla.

Next, the woman reads to him from her Bible, verses he

remembers from when his mother sent him to Sunday School. Often he thinks of this woman as some sort of continuation of his mother.

Finally, she reminds him that Jesus is waiting for him.

Once she tried to take his hands in hers as she said goodbye. He flinched so obviously that she has not attempted it since.

She still wants to look into his eyes. He has never been comfortable holding anyone's gaze, but he does his best. It is part of his culture; if you don't meet people's eyes, you are considered furtive, you're hiding something, or you are ashamed.

'Life, what an adventure, hey?' she says, shaking her head in a philosophical way as she gets up to leave. It is clear that she thinks his adventure is coming to an end.

He is relieved to see her go, her good deed done. He has never enquired as to how she heard about him, or why she visits him. He dislikes the thought of being someone's charity, their ticket to heaven.

He would have preferred it if she believed she would benefit materially, but he has never been wealthy. His professional field was too safe and quotidian for the making of fortunes.

He has ceased speculating about the feast and famine that might have marked his life had he dared to attempt the career his secret self had craved.

Adventure. It is strange that the woman should have used the word with which Namhla regularly challenges him.

Does Namhla think him a coward? He shrinks from the possibility.

He is sure she must have many adventures. Her many hairstyles and the colours she uses on her eyes and nails suggest it.

When last did he try something new? Something different? He can't remember.

When did he ever?

Too late now. The phrase *set in his ways* comes to him. Is that him? Or are they his ways simply because they have kept him safe, so not truly his ways?

He wonders which of them will leave the hotel first: him or Namhla. He knows she will move on. If it is her, he doesn't think she will melt into the fuzzy jumble of her predecessors in his memory. He will keep something of her, even if he loses her name.

Here she is now, with his mid-morning cup of tea.

'Sorry it's a bit late. Mrs P had one of her meltdowns.' Her quick smile, and the suggestion of an eye-roll. 'How was your visitor?'

'Holy,' he answers her.

Her laughter is a complex thing, a living tangle of sounds, rising up and down with pauses in the middle.

'My grandmother would like her.'

She frequently mentions members of her family, or her friends, in passing. It could be that she is inviting him to take an interest, but he can't be sure. Alternatively, it could be that she would find any questions about them intrusive.

This is the sort of uncertainty that has always restrained him, restricted him, and still does.

'Enjoy the tea.' She is moving away, but half-turns back to him. 'Guests say the hotel coffee is good?'

'Ah Namhla, still tempting me to live dangerously,' he dares to tease back.

'Or just to live a little?'

He wheezes a laugh. 'With coffee, it would be dangerously.'

He is rewarded with another snatch of her laughter. It is a pleasing substitute for the sweetness of the biscuit that no longer comes with his tea, since Mrs P put a stop to it.

'We're not a nursing home,' she'd said.

Implying that he should be in one.

Now that he has no crumbs to scatter, the birds no longer come to the terrace so frequently. He misses them. They were company, the best sort. He would talk to them, murmuring whatever strayed into his consciousness.

Adventure. The word stays with him all day, and wanders into the confusion of his night-thoughts. Hearing it from two such different people in one day has weighted it with unfathomable importance.

Coincidence. He is firm with himself, in-between reaching for significance. It means nothing. He is a fanciful old fool.

What adventures has he ever had?

*H*e needs his walking stick in the morning, but he will have to leave it at the table when he goes to the buffet. He requires both hands to carry his bowl of pawpaw.

'How are you this morning, sir?' Namhla asks, noting the stick. Her tone is warm, ready to commiserate.

He gives her his daily answer. He is fine.

'Your table is waiting.'

Usually, the repetitiveness of their morning exchange comforts him. Today his mind is still distracted by adventures he has never had. He is not sure why today should be different. Nor is he sure what day it is.

Why should he be thinking about adventure anyway? He can't remember.

The table. His table. The initial sitting down to gather himself. The careful placing of his stick.

Then the effort of rising, and the wavering trip to the buffet.

Namhla is there before him today. She and Gada are exchanging fierce words in their language, but she breaks off when she sees him.

Her smile.

'So are you going to make me happy today, sir?'

Who has he made happy in his life? He has only tried to please.

'Namhla...' Uncertainty makes his voice thready and feeble. He is feeble.

A young hotel guest has lifted the gleaming lid that covers a heap of crisp bacon. As always, the smell tempts him, but when has he yielded to temptation and given himself pleasure?

'What are you going to choose this morning?'

He looks at Namhla. Her vibrancy, her youth.

'Go on, sir,' she urges, full of mischief.

Familiar is unthreatening. Why does he need to be safe? Now? Safe from what?

They stretch on either side of this moment, the nothingness of pleasing people and staying safe, and whatever is left, not very much.

He hesitates.

Then he says, 'Do you know, Namhla, I believe I will try some bacon and eggs today. If Gada will be so kind? Before it is too late.'

Her smile becomes a blazing thing – and he is responsible.

# Shithole

*Michael Yee*

*I*t's as far from the sea as a hotel can be, inland, landlocked, in an African capital more often drought-stricken than not, and yet I swear, it smells like the ocean inside. I've seen how the walls weep, and how, nourished by that salt water, coral reefs flourish on the pillars, the ceilings, the walls. Come evening, the winds roll in and break themselves open inside; come dawn, retreating through the corridors, the ivory tower resounds like a shell, which night after night for eternity trust me, is enough to make anyone want to jump out the window.

The lobby is as neck-achingly high as a cathedral. And as pompous. Two ivory doors shaped like a giant's fingers bar the entrance. To the right is a papal desk of solid gold and chained to it, an overseer's book of slaves. Between its yellowed pages, in quill and ink are names of over one hundred guests named after slurs. They include my friends Sambo, Monkey, Ape, Gorilla, Darkie, Midnight, Fuzzhead, Jemima, and three of our most elderly guests – Boy, Girl and Picaninny. Awful names to be sure, but not new names to be true, which is why everyone's been gossiping about a brand-new guest, named after a brand-new slur for Africa. Today's the day. He's coming.

*D*o I sound excited? As I rise from the bed of my hotel room and take the Bible from the table, I assure you I am not. Every new slur who walks through our doors enters with a Bible like mine. The first page is unique to each of us, bearing each guest's name: the slur, the definition, followed by three hundred pages of the hotel's commandments. I slip on my glasses and read: *Commandment 117: The duty of welcoming new slurs shall belong to the hotel's oldest living guest, now and forever more, or until the day of deliverance. To disobey is to suffer eternity within these walls.* I throw the damned thing out the window, but instead of falling twenty floors to the city below, it explodes in a cloud of dust, and a new one appears in my hand. In God's hotel, a slur wants for nothing. Taps flow with milk and honey. Every night, the dining room hosts banquets fit for royalty, yet should we share even a crumb with the city outside, it spoils in our hands.

I put the book down and collect my daughter's seashell from my bedside drawer. With it safe in my jacket, I leave my room, enter the hallway. The walls have been crying all night, and everything smells of fish. I push the lift button. It's rattling down. At last, the bell chimes, and the doors made of solid gold slide open.

'N,' the lift operator smirks at me. Then, seeing me dressed in my hotel manager's uniform to welcome the new slur, he bows and curtsies.

'C.' I do my best to avoid his eyes. Named after the Portuguese word *barracoos*, a building constructed to hold slaves for sale, this ill-tempered giant of a man, dressed like a colour-blind sapeur, was once my closest friend.

'What floor, Monsieur?'

'To the lobby, please, C.' Long ago, he and I made a pact to call each other only by the initial of the slurs after which we were named.

'So, it is true then,' he scowls. 'We are receiving a new slur!'

I have no time for him today, so of course he goes on. 'In case you have not noticed, the hotel has no room for more slurs.'

'Take it up with God then. What can I do about it?'

'Start giving a shit.'

'What is one more of us in the greater scheme?' I try reasoning with the ox.

'This slur is brand-new.' His voice booms in the golden lift. 'In this day and age how can that be? Tell me, old man, are there so few words to belittle us in the new world they must create some more? There are not. The hotel is full of them, and you do not give a shit.'

'You think I don't care?' I throw my hands to my sides.

'I remember the fire in your belly when you believed one day we'd be free.'

'You think I like having to bring another human being into this prison? You think my heart is not breaking?'

The bell chimes. The golden doors slide open.

'Do not be sad, mon ami.' The scoundrel winks at me. 'We shall continue this discussion on our way up.'

I step out into a wall of humidity.

Salt water has rusted the ceiling fans again, and the air is fish soup. The lobby is filled with over a hundred people from all over Africa. Young and old, tall and short, grandmothers, fathers, sons sweating in the strangling heat, all of them turned to the heavenly doors made of ivory. Many are angry. Of course they are. That is why Jemima is our head of security today, and why our closest friends have been posted as guards, on the watch for troublemakers among the slurs.

Under the enormous diamond chandelier, I see Sambo waving me over with the stub of his cigar. Squeezing through the press of people, I find him standing by the long Chesterfield where Monkey, Picaninny, Boy, Girl and Fuzzhead are seated.

'Ai, ai, ai, old man!' Sambo opens his arms and bellows. 'How unfortunate to see your dinosaur face again so soon!'

'Like looking in a mirror,' I smile as we shake hands. 'Any sign of trouble yet?'

'A few rabble-rousers here and there, nothing we can't handle. You sure we're getting a new slur today?'

I'm about to show him the slip of paper that God slipped under my door a few nights ago, but when I look up, I see that C has followed me here. He swaggers over to Sambo. Both are former wrestlers, seven foot tall, mountains glaring into each other's eyes.

'Who invited you?' Sambo says.

'*Casse-toi*,' C snarls. 'Your wife and your sister.'

He squeezes his giant buttocks onto the Chesterfield between Girl and Boy, sending Monkey spilling over the side.

'Acting like God as usual,' Sambo says, and the others nod and laugh.

'What you say?' C leaps off the sofa and slaps Sambo's cigar from his lips. Before it hits the ground, fists fly.

Eternity: it undoes even the best of us.

Luckily Jemima has rushed over and is pulling them apart.

Tipping my hat to her, I wriggle my way through the guests to the entrance, pick up the chained slave-master's book, and take my seat at the papal desk. I crane my neck at the ivory doors. Twenty feet tall, arched at the ceiling, they are studded with jewels, ablaze in the morning sun. Like my teeth, some have gone missing, but they were quite something that day I arrived.

I was the first slur to enter these doors. C came next. Over the centuries, we witnessed guest after guest arrive, only to be trapped, unable to leave until the day comes when all of God's people stop speaking our names in vain; and so tell me, who am I to judge C for what he has become?

My reverie ends as the ivory doors grind open. A man steps into the hotel wearing a black suit and a red tie dangling past his belt buckle. His face is orange from his forehead to his neck, but not his hands, nor the white circles around his eyes. This is odd enough, but I cannot take my eyes off his hair. What little is left has been combed over like a sandy-blond rooftop. Is it a wig? It never moves.

'Good morning, honoured guest. You are most welcome to our hotel.' I extend my hand to greet him.

'I'm Donald J. Trump.' He peers down his nose at me. 'I'm here to see God.'

This person has clearly come to the wrong hotel, so I ask, 'May I please see your Bible?'

He shoves me aside and takes the three steps down into the lobby. Behind us, the ivory doors grate shut.

Jemima is elbowing her way through the crowd. 'Where is your Bible?' she asks, standing between me and the orange man.

'Over here, sweetcheeks.' He slaps Jemima on the behind and tries to bully past her. I almost feel sorry for him. She grabs him by the wrist, twists it behind his back and yanks his hand up past his shoulder blades. Steering him like a ship's rudder, she frog-marches him to the lift. Fortunately for him, C and Sambo have come to escort us through the furious guests. They stand guard as the doors slide close, and we travel down to the bowels of the hotel.

*J*emima and I have detained the orange man in a windowless room in the basement. The ceiling and walls are covered in algae. Tears drip into buckets spread on the ivory floor. There's a table in the middle, where the orange man sits on a chair. Jemima and I are whispering outside the closed door.

'So, who is he?'

'His story checks out; his name is Donald J. Trump,' she replies.

'How is that a new slur for Africa?'

She hands me his Bible.

As I said, the first page always states the name of the new slur and its definition, but that is not the case with this man. His Bible contains two names. Donald J. Trump. And the name of the new slur: Shithole. I skim through the definition: *Shithole is a slur used to shame developing countries, but African countries in particular. This man created that slur.*

I'm still standing with my jaw hanging when Jemima snatches the Bible from me, and kicks open the door.

'Why are you here to see God?' She slams the book down in front of the orange man.

'Senorita, do you know who I am?' He leans back and clasps his hands behind his head. 'I'm the President of the United States of America. Why wouldn't God want to see me?'

'You invented this new slur?' Jemima sits next to him and prods the first page of the book.

'Oh, I'm the greatest at that! I also created Pocahontas, Horseface—'

Jemima's chair screeches as she leaves the room, then returns with a soda can.

'You must be thirsty.' She sits next to him, opens the soda, then snatches it away when he lunges for it. 'Why you are here to see God?'

'We have an appointment,' he says, licking his lips at the can.

'You and God?'

'Si, senorita.'

'In this hotel?'

'Si,' he starts sliding his hand up and down his red tie. 'Hey, what say we take this interview somewhere private?' He throws a bundle of money on the table, then leers at Jemima.

She pouts at him.

His hand tightens into the head of a snake, then lunges under the table. She shifts back, grabs the predator's hand between her legs, and bends the index finger back until he squeals.

'Where is God?' she growls.

'The rooftop!' His face is turning bright orange.

The Bible forbids any slur from entering the rooftop, which is why Jemima is frowning at me.

'One last question,' she says, still twisting the man's finger. 'Where do you think you are?'

'Mexico City,' he squeaks.

The thick, mouldy carpet squelches under our feet as the three of us leave the interrogation room and march down the fluorescent-lit hall. We reach the lift. Jemima presses the button bringing it rattling down.

The doors slide open, C takes one look at the orange man and thrusts his palm out. 'No.'

'Oh, don't be such an old fart.' Jemima pushes the sapeur aside and drags the man in after her. She whistles at C's swollen eye. 'Sambo took you to school today, huh, big man?'

'Have you seen how I have educated Sambo?' C raises his eyebrow at Jemima, then barks at the orange man. 'What right have you to touch this woman?'

For his own safety, I pull him to the back of the lift and keep Jemima between us.

'Take us to the rooftop, please.' She bats her lashes at C.

'Are you mad? It is forbidden.'

'This one's going to meet God up there.'

'And you believe this asp?'

'Of course not.' Jemima clicks her tongue. 'But consider if it is true. What if God is waiting? What would you not give to spit in his face?'

C thinks on it for a moment, then punches the lift button and roars, 'So be it. If we are going to hell, at least the orange hairball comes with us!'

The lift has been rattling up the shaft for what feels like an age, but now our heads snap back as the compartment is tossed like a bottle on a rough sea. The cables shriek. Explosions pierce the back of my eyes, but under them I hear a voice older than words, *remember*. I remember: my daughter was short like me, but graceful like her mother. I remember after days hunting in the forest, coming back to find our village plundered. I remember running to the coastline, but by then the slavers' ships had stolen my wife. My daughter was left naked in the dunes. The crabs had eaten her eyes. While her body rotted in my arms, I waited in the sea for the waves to devour us. *Come.* Near death, in a fevered dream, that voice called me to the city where God's hotel gleamed. *Come*, that voice is saying now.

We are thrown off our feet as the lift screeches to a halt. The doors slide open.

'*W*hat is this place?' I hear the tremor in Jemima's voice as I shield my eyes from the white-hot sun and peer out across the roof of the hotel, even though to my knowledge the lift shaft does not extend past the top floor. But let me tell you the strangest thing.

Donkeys.

Hundreds strong. Grazing on the weeds pushing through the golden cracks of the rooftop. Old ones, young ones. Grey, black and brown ones. Some sleek with good health, others bearing festering wounds, tormented by flies.

'She's seized.' C's hands are shaking as he unscrews the control panel. Smoke reeking of sulphur pours out of the cavity, stinging my eyes. We're all coughing.

'Well, can you fix it?' I say, trying not to sound alarmed when the smoke finally clears, and I see the thick cord of melted wires in his hand.

'What can I not fix, mon ami?' He winks at me. As the sapeur stretches his great neck from side to side and turns up his sleeves, I catch a glimpse of the person I once knew, who fought and loved with the strength of two men before the waiting pickled his heart.

I put my hand on his shoulder. 'Farewell, old friend.'

'Oui, oui, see you soon.'

He does not see me looking back at him as I step onto the rooftop, into the biting flies looming like a dark cloud over the donkeys.

The air thrums like a power station.

Ahead of me, Jemima and the orange one are battling their way through the herd. I try to make up lost ground, but it is like wading through water up to my stomach while the current keeps changing. The orange one breaks left, away from the herd, and strides to the edge of the rooftop. 'Jesus Christ,' he mutters with disgust as he peers over our city.

I wade past him, press on.

'Jemima!' She is far ahead, but my shout carries.

'Hurry,' she says, but my old legs have had it. I rest my hand on a donkey the size of a horse, and wait to catch my breath.

'C'mon, I'm waiting.' She laughs.

I cannot take my eyes off her as she removes her modest head scarf, wets it in her mouth, then wipes away the discharge gluing shut the eyes of an ancient mare, her legs gnarled with time, her mangy coat bleached white with age. Jemima is humming now. The wind delivers her song to my parched ears. How long have I waited to see her so free?

I see the mare's eyes flick open. Her nostrils flare. Jemima retreats just in time as the mare rears up onto her hind legs and begins striking her hooves on the rooftop. Hundreds of donkeys follow her lead, stomping to a rhythm we have never heard.

The ground trembles as the orange man swaggers towards us,

clicking his fingers, bobbing his head. 'Hey, I know this one,' he starts singing over the thunder of hooves. 'Eenie meenie minie mo. Catch a nigger by the toe. If he hollers let him go. Eenie meenie minie mo.'

He grins at me like he has sung an aria.

Before I can stop her, Jemima shoves him so hard he falls backwards into a mound of donkey droppings. 'Say this man's name again. Say it!' She points at me, tears streaming down her face.

The man gets to his feet, grumbling darkly. While he brushes the dung from his trousers, the ancient mare trots forward and nudges his elbow.

'HELLO, DONALD.'

He peers over her head across the herd, shielding his eyes, searching for the source of the voice. Slowly, he looks down at the mare. 'Donkey?'

'I AM THE LORD THY GOD!' Flames leap from the donkey's eyes. The force of her bellow pushes us into the herd and flips the orange man's hair over like the wing of an airplane. As he turns tail and runs, I see his bald crown, scaly like a frozen river.

'AND WHAT SAY YOU, ANWULICHUKWU, GOD'S JOY?'

I know why Jemima cannot move. The names given by our mothers are spells. They are given to tell others we are somebody. A slur is powerful because they tell others we are nobody. Anwulichukwu is an amulet, making her human. Jemima is a whip, flaying at her singularity.

'Jemima, stand up!' She is kissing the mare's filthy hooves, but long ago we promised never again to kneel before God.

As if hearing my thoughts, the white mare pierces me with her cataract eyes.

'AND THEE, TAU JABARL? WHAT HAST THOU TO SAY TO THY LORD?'

'Art thou truly God?'

'    I                                                    A  M  .  '

'Then release us, Lord.' I bow my head. 'We are weary.'

'IMPOSSIBLE.' The mare swats at the flies with her scabrous tail.

'What is impossible for God?' My voice falters.

'GOD IS BOUND BY THE LAWS GOD CREATED.'

'Recreate them then, set us free.'

'AND INVITE CHAOS? I LOVE THEE, TAU JABARL, BUT I WILL NOT.'

Jemima rises and touches my arm. 'Why hast thou invited the orange one, Lord?'

'TO SEE IF MAN HATH CHANGED.'

'Nothing has changed, Lord,' Jemima says.

The mare scrutinises the man, falling over his feet to get through the herd.

'FORGIVE, TAU JABARL.' God stares into my eyes.

'My Lord, tear down this hotel. Set us free.'

'I MAY NOT.'

'Why bring us here, then?' I cry.

'TO SHELTER THEE, TAU JABARL. FROM HATRED. PAIN.'

I don't know what comes over me, but I kick God on her backside. The mare curls her lips back, exposing diseased teeth and gums, and starts bucking her front and rear legs as if a mad child was pulling her tail.

Jemima takes my hand.

We run.

Fast as we can, expecting the sky to fall, we fight through the herd and collapse near the small ledge on the far side of the rooftop.

We are lying side by side, staring at the stars in the failing light. 'You still alive?' Jemima gropes at my face with her hand and shakes with laughter.

Before I can tell her, C calls to us in the distance.

'Looks like he fixed it. Come on.' She gets up and holds out her hand.

'I am not going back.'

'What do you mean? Of course you are going back.'

'Tell C he will have to welcome the new guests from now on.'

Jemima turns to face the ledge and sweeps her gaze over the city below. The donkeys have fallen asleep on their feet. The flies are elsewhere. She sees me staring at the orange man in the distance, shouting at C to take him back down.

'Is that why you are acting crazy? Because of him?' she asks.

There at the ledge, she lets me hold her hand. Looking over the sprawling city and markets and churches and mosques, I release the words I've been waiting eternity to say: 'In another life I would walk through those dusty streets with you. We would follow the music to a tavern. I would dance with you until dawn.'

'Tau Jabarl.' She says my name for the first time.

'So many things I wanted to tell you, Anwulichukwu.'

'Stay. Tell me.' She squeezes my hand.

'People will be anxious below.' I gaze into her eyes for the last time. 'They will need you now, more than ever.'

Wheeling away, already leaving, she says, 'What do I tell them?'

'Tell them God let me go. Tell them N is a slur no more.'

*D*awn brings the herd out of the darkness, asleep on their feet, their leafy ears twitching at the biting flies. I am east of them, balancing on the small ledge no broader than my arm. But I'm not ready. I sit down and dangle my legs over the ledge. The city in miniature below pulls at my shoes. Hands tingling, I dip into my jacket pocket and take out my daughter's shell. I hold it between my fingers, against the yellow sun, burning in the African sky as morning pools in the hollow, turning the small white cone the colour it was on my daughter's bracelet. All night I have waited to see this. Soon, people will fill the streets and the markets. Soon, trucks and tuk-tuks and morning prayers will rise from the mosques below, but for now the world is silent. For now, I stand on the ledge with the seashell, feeling something higher than fear.

It feels I am falling up, not down. As if it is the hotel, the ground, the sky that is plummeting.

I exist in the eye of the fall.

Tumbling down the side of the hotel, my arms and legs flailing, the windows fly past in a glittering blur. Through the glass I spy the guests still asleep in their rooms. Floor after floor, window after window, I say farewell to my friends.

I am falling past my room now. The orange man is inside, fussing with his hair, so enamoured with his own reflection in the window he does not see me plunging past.

I am done looking at him.

I see the sky.

I see the shell.

I see the earth rushing to meet me.

*A*s night falls, I see the sliver of a moon. I am lying on the cold side of my bed. God spoke the truth: there is no leaving N behind. Salty winds howl through the hotel like the ghosts of blue whales. But the walls have stopped weeping.

# BIOGRAPHIES

HARRIET ANENA is a writer from Uganda. She was the joint winner of the 2018 Wole Soyinka Prize for Literature in Africa for her debut poetry collection, *A Nation in Labour*. Her short stories have been nominated for the Commonwealth Short Story Prize (2018) and published by Short Story Day Africa. Anena's latest works feature in *New Daughters of Africa* (2019), Jalada Africa's *After + Life* issue (2019) and *Adda* (2019).

NKIACHA ATEMNKENG is a retired rapper and aspiring music DJ. His work has been published in the 2015 Caine Prize anthology, *Lusaka Punk and Other Stories*; *Culture Trip*, *The Africa Report*, *Bakwa*, *Saraba* and *Gyara*. He attended the SSDA Migrations workshop in Yaoundé, the Limbe to Lagos exchange programme, and the 2018 Miles Morland workshop, facilitated by Giles Foden. He is a Goethe Institut/ Sylt Foundation writing residency Fellow.

JAYNE BAULING'S short stories and poems have been published in a number of anthologies and literary journals. She is best known for her YA novels, which have won several awards. She lives in Mpumalanga, South Africa.

NOEL CHERUTO is a Kenyan writer whose work has been published in *Kikwetu Journal* and *On The Premises* magazine. She lives in Nairobi.

ANNA DEGENAAR is a short story writer from Cape Town, South Africa. She is currently completing her Masters in Creative Writing and Education at Goldsmiths, University of London, as a Chevening scholar. She did her Honours degree in English Literature at the University of Cape Town, and is interested in the ways that creative writing can positively influence wellbeing.

ADAM EL SHALAKANY lives and works as a lawyer in Cairo, Egypt. He studied political science in Canada, and law at the School for Oriental and African Studies in London. He has loved writing ever since he was as tall as a hookah pipe. This is his first published short story.

DAVINA KUWUMA'S fiction for children and adults, and her poems have appeared in anthologies published by African Writers Trust, Babishai Niwe Poetry Foundation, Uganda Women Writers Association, *New Internationalist,* and *Lawino* magazine. She has received training in the sciences (wildlife ecology) and the arts (education). She's a fan of Adam's apples, bicycles, big cats, carnivorous plants, Monopoly, and strawberry-scented things.

ALINAFE MALONJE is a 23-year-old writer from Malawi. She holds a Bachelor's degree in Economics and International Relations, and owns a small business that provides students with career guidance and assists them with college applications. Stories have played a big role in Alinafe's life: she has spent her whole life escaping into the worlds that others have created. Now, armed with a passion for her culture, her country and change, she writes so that she can one day create a world to which another African child can escape.

WAMUWI MBAO is a literary critic and essayist. He is a lecturer in the English Department of Stellenbosch University and book critic at the *Johannesburg Review of Books*. His short story 'The Bath' was included in the Twenty in 20 project, which identified the best

South African short fiction published in English during the first two decades of democracy.

PAUL MORRIS is a Cape Town-based writer, life and executive coach. His memoir *Back to Angola: A Journey from War to Peace* was longlisted for the Alan Paton Prize for non-fiction. He trained as a psychotherapist at the London Gestalt Centre and has a Master's degree in Gestalt psychotherapy from London Metropolitan University. He is also a travel writer, and is currently writing a novel.

CHIDO MUCHEMWA is from Zimbabwe and has lived in America and Canada. She graduated with an MFA in Creative Writing from the University of Wyoming. Her essays have been published in *Apogee* and *Tincture Journal,* and a short story appeared in *Water: New Short Story Fiction from Africa* by *Short Story Day Africa.*

CHOUROUQ NASRI is a professor at Mohammed Premier University (Oujda), Morocco. Her recent publications include, as co-editor, *North African Women after the Arab Spring: In the Eye of the Storm,* and as editor, the first issue of *Ikhtilaf, Journal of Critical Humanities and*

*Social Studies,* and *Question de genre: Etudes des inégalités Hommes-Femmes au Maroc.*

FRED NNAMDI is a humanist, published short story writer, freelance educational representative, and farmer from Nigeria.

TARIRO NDORO is a Zimbabwean writer and poet. Her stories have appeared on various literary platforms, including *Moving On and Other Zimbabwean Stories, La Shamba, New Contrast* and *Fireside Fiction.* Her debut poetry collection, *Agringada: Like a gringa, like a foreigner,* has recently been published by Modjaji Books. She is currently working on a collection of short stories (or trying to). Links to her work can be found at tarirondoro.wordpress.com.

ADORAH NWORAH is an Igbo storyteller from Anambra in Eastern Nigeria. She earned her Juris Doctorate from Temple Law School, and practices commercial real estate finance law in Philadelphia, USA. Her short story, 'The Bride,' was shortlisted for the 2019 Commonwealth Writers Short Story Prize.

NATASHA OMOKHODION-KALULU BANDA is a UK-born Zambian of Nigerian and Jamaican heritage who lives in Lusaka. Married with three children, she heads a dynamic advertising firm. She is passionate about the growing literary scene in Africa and enjoys the power of story-telling. She has been published in the African Women Writers (Afriwowri) e-publication anthology *Different Shades of a Feminine Mind, The Budding Writer* anthology by Zambia Women Writers' Association (2017), and featured on AfricanWriter.com for her story 'To Hair is Human, To Forgive is Design' (2018).

FAITH ONEYA is a creative writer and journalist who works for Nation Media Group, Kenya. Her writing has appeared in various publications, including *The Standard, African Woman Magazine, the Daily Nation* and *the EastAfrican.* Her short stories were first published in 2012 in the anthology *Fresh Paint.* In 2018, she published her first children's book, *The Girl with a Big Heart,* which is approved for use as a class reader in Kenya. Her short story 'Say You are Not My Son' is featured in *Nairobi Noir,* a forthcoming anthology. She holds a Master's degree in communication from the University of Nairobi. She lives in Nairobi with her daughter, and is working on her first short story collection.

TROY ONYANGO's work has been published in *Wasafiri, Johannesburg Review of Books, AFREADA, the Caine Prize Anthology, Brittle Paper, Kalahari Review* and *Transition,* among others. The winner of the inaugural Nyanza Literary Festival Prize and first runner-up in the Black Letter Media Competition, he was also shortlisted for the *Brittle Paper* Anniversary Award and nominated for the Pushcart Prize. Currently, he is studying towards an MA in Creative Writing at the University of East Anglia, where he is a recipient of the Miles Morland Foundation Scholarship.

BRYONY RHEAM is the author of *This September Sun.* She has also published short stories in a range of anthologies. She is a recipient of the 2018 Miles Morland Writing Scholarship, and is currently writing a book set in Bulawayo in the 1930s. She lives in Bulawayo, Zimbabwe.

LESTER WALBRUGH is from Grabouw in the Western Cape. His work has appeared in the Short.Sharp.Story anthology *Die Laughing,* the Short Story Day Africa anthology *ID,* and *New Contrast.* He has lived in the UK and Japan, and has since returned to his home town to work on a collection of short stories and a novel.

MICHAEL YEE is a South African writer born in Pretoria. His writing has appeared in the Short.Sharp. Stories anthologies and the Short Story Day Africa anthology *ID.*

# EDITORS

AGAZIT ABATE is the daughter of immigrants and storytellers. She was raised in Los Angeles, and writes and lives in Addis Ababa.

OPE ADEDEJI is a Nigerian lawyer, editor and writer. She dreams about bridging the gender equality gap and destroying the patriarchy. Her work has appeared in *Arts and Africa*, *Afreada*, and *Catapult*. She was shortlisted for the 2018 Koffi Addo Prize for Creative Nonfiction, and is an Artist Managers and Literary Activists Fellow. She is an alumni of the 2018 Purple Hibiscus Trust Creative Writing Workshop. She currently works at Ouida Books, where she is the Managing Editor.

ANNE MORAA is a Kenyan feminist and cultural worker, based in Nairobi, who writes, edits and performs. As a member of the LAM Sisterhood, she researched, co-wrote and performed in the sold-out and award-winning documentary theatre show *The Brazen Edition*, which sought to render visible invisibilised women. Her writing can be found in *Catapult*, *The Meridians Journal*, *The Elephant*, *The Wide Margin*, Short Story Day Africa, and *Jalada*, among others. Her performances have taken her from Nairobi to South Korea and Scotland. She is a contributing writer to *Panorama Journal*, develops delectables with the LAM Sisterhood, and works on her debut novel. She balances it all by eating copious amounts of chilli lemon crisps.

KAREN JENNINGS is a South African writer and author now living in Brazil. She edited the first SSDA anthology, *Feast, Famine and Potluck*, which went on to produce two Caine Prize shortlistees, including the ultimate winner. She has edited several award-winning novels for indie South African publishers and imprints. Her debut novel, *Finding Soutbek*, was shortlisted for inaugural Etisalat Prize for African Fiction. In 2014, her short story collection, *Away from the Dead*, was longlisted for the Frank O'Connor International short story competition. Her 2017 memoir, *Travels with my Father*, was longlisted for the Barry Ronge Sunday Times fiction prize, and in 2018 she released her debut poetry collection, *Space Inhabited by Echoes*. Her new novel, *Upturned Earth*, about the mining industry in South African history, will be forthcoming in 2019.

HELEN MOFFETT is an author, editor, academic, and activist. She lives in Cape Town and has published university textbooks, numerous academic pieces, a treasury of landscape writings (*Lovely Beyond Any Singing*), a cricket book (with the late Bob Woolmer and Tim Noakes), the *Girl Walks In* erotica series (with Paige Nick and Sarah Lotz), two poetry collections (*Strange Fruit* and *Prunings*), a history of Rape Crisis, and two books in a green series, *101 Water Wise Ways* and *Wise About Waste: 150+ Ways to Save the Planet*. Her first novel, *Charlotte*, is forthcoming from Bonnier. She has worked as an editor with nearly a hundred authors all over the globe, and believes she has the best job in the world. She is passionate about the Short Story Day Africa project.

# ACKNOWLEDGEMENTS

*A good writer possesses not only his own spirit*
*but also the spirit of his friends.*

– Friedrich Nietzsche

$\mathcal{E}$ very publication is the result of a team effort, and none so more than this. Usually, that team consists of the writer(s), editor and publisher. This project requires the effort of a greater number of people, many of whom are volunteers who get nothing in return beyond a thank-you and the knowledge that they've helped our cause: to give African writing the platform it deserves on the world stage. It falls to me to remember all those who helped SSDA achieve the publication of this anthology, *Hotel Africa*.

*Hotel Africa* is edited by three Fellows as part of the SSDA Editing Mentorship. A special thank you to our editing mentors, Helen Moffett and Karen Jennings, for dedicating their time and skills to the project, and for guiding our 2019 Fellows Agazit Abate, Anne Moraa and Ope Adedeji. The tireless efforts, keen eyes and dedication of this team helped the twenty-one writers featured in *Hotel Africa* improve their stories and their craft. And so the African literary landscape and industry grows, one hand helping another.

Part of the process of editing stories from multiple countries requires checking cultural references – thank you to Yemisi Aribisala and Hawande Golakai for assisting with this. Also to Nerine Dorman who volunteered to spend many hours proofreading these pages.

The gorgeous cover design is by Megan Ross, who also designed the artwork for the 2018 SSDA Prize.

Thanks to Dan Raymond-Barker and New Internationalist, our international publishing partner, for believing in what we're doing and taking our stories to new readers across the globe.

Short Story Day Africa is a project that prides itself on having grown organically in response to the needs of writers on the continent. Over the years, we identified problems with the reading and judging processes that gave an unfair advantage to previously published writers over new talent. As a project that seeks to disrupt preconceived notions of African writing and reclaim a space for African voices to write what they like, it is important to us that raw talent from all over the continent be recognised and nurtured. This is the second year the slush pile was read by a team of volunteers who work in the publishing industry and are accustomed to reading raw work. This year's team consisted of Lizzy Attree, Efemia Chela, Jennifer Malec, Helen Moffett, Catherine Shepherd, Aimee-Claire Smith, Karina Szczurek, Jason Mykl Snyman, Mary Watson, Rahla Xenopolous and myself, who spent months combing through hundreds of stories to compile the longlist.

A new, more democratic approach was taken for the judging process, too. Grateful thanks are due to the Short Story Day Africa Board – which now includes Rehana Rossouw and Kudrat Virk (welcome!) – and *The Johannesburg Review of Books* (with special thanks to *JRB*'s Jennifer Malec). Their careful reading of the stories and the new scoring system gave us a short list of ten exceptional stories – whittling down the list to six, as we've done in the past, proved impossible, and we believe in giving credit where it is due.

Both the reading process and judging, as always, was blind, and stories were judged on merit alone. However, experience has taught us that a meritocracy can only work if the playing field is even. These twenty-one stories were edited before the judging took place, giving emerging writers an opportunity to compete as equals with those who have more publishing experience.

The team at Short Story Day Africa recognises that we have had the privilege of working in a country that has a vibrant publishing industry and literary landscape. The history of the African continent means that not all our compatriots have similar access to spaces where they can develop their craft. With the small resources at our disposal, we work hard to share the skills we have developed. However, without the assistance of organisations with similar aims, our arms would not be as long.

We cannot give enough thanks to the Miles Morland Foundation. Their generous funding assistance allows us to continue our work in developing writers and creating a platform for their voices. Their support has been invaluable in a time when funding for the project is dwindling. Thank you for continuing to believe in us.

Last year, thanks to generous funding from The Beit Trust, and in partnership with the Goethe-Institut, we were able to run twelve Hotel Africa Flow and Editing Workshops across the continent.

The Beit Trust funding took our workshops to writers in Blantyre and Lilongwe in Malawi, Kitwe and Lusaka in Zambia, and Bulawayo and Mutare in Zimbabwe. In most cases, this was the first time we were able to present workshops (not just on writing, but editing) in these cities. We are grateful to all at the Beit Trust for making these workshops possible and allowing us to take SSDA to fresh pastures.

Our continued partnership with the Goethe-Institut helped us reach new voices in Addis Ababa, Cape Town, Kigali, Lagos, Nairobi and Windhoek. Many thanks to the participating Instituts and their liaisons: Stefanie Kastner, Vernon Scholtz, Julia Sattler, Yonas Tarekegn, Yonatan Girma, Katharina Hey, Nina Koopman, Safurat Balogun, Elizabeth Wichenje, Detlef Pfeifer and Paulina Hamukwaya. Thanks especially to Stefanie Kastner, the Goethe-Institut's Head of Library & Information Services, Sub-Saharan Africa, for being so open to our ideas.

Thanks also to the Kigali Public Library, who gave us space to host the Hotel Africa Flow Workshop in their city.

To my co-facilitators, who took the materials Helen and I designed and ran the workshops I could not with superb energy, each bringing their own wisdom and writing experience to the work, I cannot thank you enough: Nebila Abdulmelik, Dami

Ajayi, Efemia Chela, Andrew Dakalira, Donnalee Donaldson, John Eppel, Wesley Macheso, Niq Mhlongo, Blessing Musariri, Sylvia Schlettwein and Zukiswa Wanner.

For an organisation that runs on volunteers and donations, I am eternally grateful to anyone who looks into their wallet and finds any amount of spare cash to assist us in continuing the work. Thank you Nicola Allsop, Iain S Thomas, Karin Van Zwieten, Jennifer Malec, Charles Bukowski, Clare Loveday, Mary Shelley, Jayne Bauling, Lauren Beukes, Jo-Ann Thesen, Abel Vertesy, Jarred Thompson, Bashir Cassimally, Mercy Wambui, Lyle Skains, Caryn Gootkin, Tochukwu Okafor, Rahul Rao and Kari Cousins.

I am grateful to my fellow members of the SSDA Board, who continue to work enthusiastically on all aspects of the project, for nothing more than the love of the African short story and their fellow writers: Helen Moffett, Isla Haddow-Flood, Karina Szczurek, Mary Watson, Jason Mykl Snyman, Lizzy Attree, Catherine Shepherd, Rehana Rossouw, Kudrat Virk and Rahla Xenopoulos. It is thanks to their enthusiasm that the project continues to run in these dire financial times.

The number of people willing to lend a hand grows every year. I am, as always, amazed at the generosity of spirit in the African writing community and those who support it.

If I have left anyone out, I apologise. Finally to all the writers and readers of African fiction: thank you. We do this for, and because of you.

**Rachel Zadok**
SHORT STORY DAY AFRICA

# DONATE TO
# SHORT STORY DAY AFRICA

Please support African writers, editors, and publishers.
Scan this qr code on SnapScan to donate. Every cent counts.

To donate through PayPal, please visit

shortstorydayafrica.org/donate

# Twenty Years of the Caine Prize for African Writing

A jailer's love poems ghost-written by a prisoner... Love blossoming between two girls despite the horror of their community... Street kids stick-fighting or stealing guavas from the rich... A dystopian world where women must go naked until they marry...

Celebrating the twentieth anniversary of the Caine Prize for African Writing – often referred to as the 'African Booker Prize' – this collection showcases all twenty prize-winning short stories, each with its own unique take on modern African life.

Price: UK £11.99, US $19.95
ISBN 978-1-78026-556-8

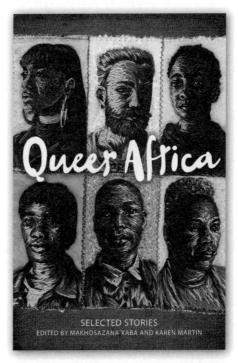

SELECTED STORIES
EDITED BY MAKHOSAZANA XABA AND KAREN MARTIN

In recent years some African governments have attempted to clamp down on sexual diversity. But Queer Africa will not be silenced, as this groundbreaking collection of stories from across the continent makes clear.

'Queer Africans exist in every stratum of society – even if some political leaders say we don't… This sterling collection contains exquisite writing that again and again has the ring of truth. It is a wonderful treat.'                                        **Chiké Frankie Edozien**

'In this timely collection, writers from across the African continent tell their stories of living, loving and longing. Here is fiction that is at times transgressive, at times gentle and tender, at times indignant – but always acknowledging the very human desire to find a place of solace, acceptance and love.'

**Ellah Wakatama Allfrey**

Price: UK £8.99, US $14.95
ISBN 978-1-78026-463-9